Coyote Ugly

and Other Tales

———

Pati Nagle

Evennight Books

Cedar Crest, New Mexico

Coyote Ugly and Other Tales

copyright © 2010 by Pati Nagle.

ISBN: 978-1-61138-211-2

Published by Evennight Books, Cedar Crest, New Mexico.

Illustrations

in loving memory

of

Avery Leeming Nagle

Contents

Acknowledgments...9
Mother Ditch..13
Rescue Work...25
The *Cygnius sedonai* Caper...41
Recipe: New Mexican Cocoa...71
Coyote Ugly...73
On Swan's Wings...91
Stranded...107
The Courtship of Captain Swenk...121
Creed of the Ælven..141
First Love...143
Recipe: Green Chile Roll-ups...165
Dawn's Early Light...167
Kind Hunter..189
Emancipation...203
Rocket Boy on Call...231
Recipe: Cheater's Chicken Chile Soup...235
Arroyo de Oro..237
The Folsom Suit..269
Draw...275
The Cornfield..291
About the Author...311

Acknowledgments

My past editors, especially those who took a chance on a new writer and encouraged me to continue, have helped me immensely. My fellow writers in workshops, especially Plotbusters and the Oregon Writers Network, have given their support, encouragement, and honest critique. My colleauges including the wonderful cooperative Book View Café are a great support network. Patricia Rice in particular helped me bring this book together.

My friends and family, especially my beloved spouse, have championed my work and nurtured my fragile writer's ego. Without them I would have quit long ago.

Heartfelt thanks to all of these folks, and most of all to my readers, without whom there would be no point to the exercise.

Coyote Ugly

and Other Tales

Mother Ditch

Madre slept, dozing in the summer heat as her *contras*, like suckling children, drew her life-giving water out into the fields. To those who treated her with respect, the *acequia madre* was a kind and generous mother. The water coursed through her main channel and out into a network of silvery veins beneath the hot sun, feeding every field and pasture in El Pueblo. Where her waters ran the green grasses sprang up, and tender shoots of wild asparagus bloomed like little ferns, and children played until their own mothers scolded them away from the ditch.

Madre heard them as she drowsed. The people of El Pueblo were her children from planting until harvest, and she rejoiced in bringing them prosperity and happiness. She gave life to their crops, and her power turned their mills to grind the chiles and grain they grew in the fields that she watered.

The people of El Pueblo took their water from her except in late winter and early spring, when her course lay dry and cold. Just as the fields needed to lie fallow sometimes, she needed time to rest, to give the people access to her banks for the annual cleaning. If they did not cut away the weeds and brush each year she would choke and strangle, and their fields would dry to dust.

Madre walked sometimes, at night when El Pueblo was sleeping. She grew herself a shape, a shadow, a whisper of her substance, and walked along her own banks. It amused her to feel how the women walked, or the men, or the children. To look at the world through eyes that were shadows of their own. She never strayed far from her banks, and never showed herself, though now and again someone glimpsed her and made up a story to account for it.

One day, under the baking sun, a funeral was held that made her very sad. Old Juan Delgado, who had been Mayordomo in El Pueblo for years, had passed away. The village mourned, and Madre mourned with them, for the Mayordomo was her caretaker, and Juan had been good to her.

He had seen her once, walking the ditch banks after midnight. Madre walked the banks to explore and to amuse herself, but Juan walked them to see that all was as it should be, that the *compuertas* were open and the water flowing freely, that every field received its rightful share. He had encountered Madre near the *atarque* where the water was taken from the river into the *acequia*, on a night when the air was calm and the sky glimmered with a thousand stars.

Caught outside the shelter of her ditch banks, Madre had stopped short, watching Juan. The shape she had put on was hard to keep still, for by nature she was seldom still. Something like a dress draped around her, but it flowed and wavered softly in the night. Something like hair hung about her shadowed face, but it seemed more alive than hair.

Juan gazed back at her for a very long time, then finally said, "Buenas noches, Madre," and walked on.

Now he was gone. Madre listened to the mass that was said in the little church, and heard the soft crying of the widow. She wept, too, her sadness flowing along in the water.

Now El Pueblo must choose a new Mayordomo. Each year there was an election, though a good Mayordomo like Juan was often reelected every year without question. Now the *Comisión* who set the rules that the Mayordomo enforced summoned all the villagers to the church to cast their votes for Juan's replacement.

Madre listened to them come and go, heard their whispers of sadness and discontent. Soon she heard whispers of anger as well, and she wondered what was wrong.

A day later, she knew. The man elected to be Mayordomo was Esteban de la Plata, a man who swaggered with his barrel chest pushed forward, as if he would like to bump intruders out of his way. He began at once to swagger up and down the *acequia* banks, puffed up with his own importance, carrying the Mayordomo's *tequío*, the stick used to measure the length of ditch each landowner must clear in spring. It was foolish and small of him, but Madre was willing to overlook this if Esteban did a good job as Mayordomo. She watched him, and waited.

He came to the field that belonged to the Benitez family, a long, narrow strip of land with one short end along the acequia, like all the other fields in El Pueblo. Generations of the Benitez family had worked that field. Their houses, three of them, stood on the high ground far at the back of their land, a little cluster standing watch over the crops.

When Esteban reached the *compuerta* that gave water to the Benitez field, he shut it. Madre felt the sudden break in the flow. She was not finished feeding water to the field, she knew the young plants had not drunk enough. So did Manuel Benitez, who looked up from his work, then set aside his hoe and walked up to the ditch bank where Esteban stood.

"Good morning, Esteban. Is there a problem?"

"Yes, there is a problem." Esteban tipped his head forward so that the shade of his hat hid his face as he looked at Manuel. "Your family did not clear all of your *tarea* this spring."

"The work was done."

"Yes, but not by you!"

"The neighbors were glad to help me. My father's foot was broken, and my brother had to take his wife to the city for an operation."

"Your son did not help." Esteban used his *tequío* to point toward the field, where Tomás was bent over, pulling weeds.

"He's only fourteen. He's not allowed."

Esteban puffed out his chest. "You still didn't do your share of the work."

Manuel gazed at him. An angry swallow moved his throat.

"What do you want?"

"You don't appreciate how hard I'm working! All day I walk these ditches looking out for your water!"

"What do you want, Esteban?"

"Maybe it would be easier if I had a woman to cook for me. Maybe your daughter could come—"

"Angelina's engaged." Manuel's eyes were flat and cold.

"Ah, well. I don't know, compadre. I guess I'll have to buy my dinner at the café."

Manuel dug in his pocket and pulled out a handful of change. He looked at it, pushed the silver around with a fingertip, then held it out to Esteban.

"Here. Six dollars and thirty cents. It's all I have."

Esteban took the money, rattling it in his first. He grinned as he opened the compuerta, releasing the water. "Gracias, Manuel."

Madre watched Manuel walk away in silence and go back to working his field. Esteban stood watching, too, for a minute. Then he laughed softly and walked on down the ditch road.

Esteban had never been popular. Madre was surprised the people had chosen him. Now the murmurs she had heard after the election grew and swelled. Each day the level of discontent rose like the river's spring floods, threatening to overflow. There were whispers that the election had been fixed, that Benny Armijo, who counted the votes, was a friend of Esteban's. Benny had been wearing a new hat around, with silver conchos on the band.

"See?" the angry villagers told one another. "That proves it!"

Madre began to pay close attention to everything Esteban did. She heard him threaten old man Sanchez, saying he would turn him in to the Sheriff for drunkenness. She saw him turn off the water to the Lovatos' field when they couldn't pay their *cuota* for the ditch repairs on time. And she watched him count over all the *cuotas* he collected, then put some of the money in a box under his bed before turning it over to the Comisión.

Madre was angry. Esteban was a bad Mayordomo. Surely the people of El Pueblo saw that. Surely they wanted a change.

But they were afraid of Esteban, with his swagger and his stick and his vicious tongue. And until the next election, there was not much to be done. The *Comisión* had the authority to remove him, but that would require a very serious situation indeed. Esteban had not committed any crime, or at least, none that anyone but Madre had seen.

She began to fight back.

One day Esteban turned off the Widow Chaves's water because she refused to pay him a second *cuota* when he claimed she'd never paid the first. Madre had seen him take the money a week before. No one else had been there, and everyone knew Señora Chaves was old and getting forgetful.

Madre broke the *compuerta* late at night and flooded the widow's bean field.

Another day Esteban discovered that a section of one of the *contra* ditches was about to collapse. Instead of hiring workers from El Pueblo to make the repairs, he brought in some friends of his from the city. They slung a few shovelfuls of mud around, then sat on the ditch banks drinking beer half the afternoon.

Madre drew every tiny trickling sound and every watery gurgle in the acequias together, and wove a voice out of them. With it she whispered in the ears of the lazy workers.

"You are a cheating sinner," she said, and to each of them she sounded like his own mother. "Get to work before you loaf your way into Hell!"

The city men jumped up and threw down their beers. Then,

to prove they were not afraid, they talked loudly about how this was a job only for stupid idiots, and how Esteban had lied to them about the hours and the pay (which probably he had). Then they climbed into their cars and drove away. Esteban had to hire workers from the village to finish the repairs.

About a week after that Madre noticed that Esteban had left the *compuerta* to his own field open too long. Now that she could make a voice she whispered to him to close the gate, but he just waved his hand by his ear as if to chase away a fly.

Madre picked up an old sneaker that had fallen into her ditch, and some old rags, and a toy truck that was broken, and half a tire, and jumbled them all together in the compuerta to Esteban's field, making a little dam that stopped the water. When Esteban found it he cursed long and loud, and fished everything out of the water and threw it back in the ditch.

That night Madre made the dam again. This time she added a bunch of weeds that grew in the muddy banks, and an old china dinner plate that was chipped, and every rock and pebble she could roll along. The pile was so big it took Esteban half the next morning to clear it all away. This time he took everything out of the ditch and threw it on the bank.

While he was working, José Mora, one of the men on the *Comisión*, came strolling along the ditch bank. José stopped to watch Esteban, who was up to his waist in water, pulling handfuls of rocks out of the *compuerta*.

"Buenos dias, Esteban," José said after watching a while.

"That's what you think," said Esteban. He pulled the tennis shoe out of the mud and flung it onto a pile with the plate and the toy truck and the rags.

"Cleaning out the ditch a bit? That's good."

"Cleaning out the mess some bastard made of my gate."

Esteban scowled as he reached into the water again. Madre wanted to push something sharp up against his fingers, but he had already taken the chipped plate out of the water.

"That's just trash, Esteban. That just drifted there."

"Yeah? This is the second time in two days I had to clear it out. The same junk. You want to tell me it drifted there twice?"

José raised his bushy gray eyebrows and shook his head, but it was more because he didn't have an explanation. Esteban stared at him with narrowed eyes.

"I know who done it, too," Esteban said. "That lazy Benitez punk, Tomás."

"Eh, how do you know that?"

"I just know."

"Tomás is a good boy."

Esteban didn't say anything, just scooped another handful of pebbles out of the gate. All the rest of Madre's little dam shifted, and it gave way and the water burbled down from the gate toward the field.

Esteban slogged out of the ditch, the mud sucking at his boots. He rolled up onto the bank and lay gasping and frowning in his wet and muddy jeans. José squatted down beside him.

"Listen, Esteban, there been some complaints."

Esteban glared at him. "Complaints?"

Madre felt a wave of hope. She listened to José with all her being.

"It's nothing major," José said. "I know this is your first year, and you don't know all the customs yet. We like to cut people some slack, you know? Don't have to be a hardass about the *cuotas* being on time. We know everybody's going to pay. It's all right if they're a little late."

"Oh, it is, eh? All right with you, maybe. You don't have to hire men to fix the ditch."

"There was enough money for that."

"This time."

"All I'm saying is you should have a little patience, Esteban. Have a little kindness. These are your neighbors, your friends. No one wants to cheat us."

"That's what you think," said Esteban.

That's what you think, thought Madre.

After that, things just got worse. Esteban went right on bullying and lying, cheating the villagers out of their water and their money. Nobody in El Pueblo was rich, but that summer everyone felt more poor than they had ever felt before. People walked around the village with slow steps, unless they saw Esteban coming, when they ran and hid. No one smiled any more. Madre thought the village was dying of a broken heart.

She kept on fighting, but her little tricks and taunts only made Esteban angry. One day after she had broken the latch on the *compuerta* above the Navarros' field (she was getting good at that), Esteban went and found Tomás Benitez and took him into the trees where no one could see and beat him until the blood ran down his face.

"That's for messing with me," Esteban said, breathing hard as he stood over the cringing boy. "Don't you ever mess with me again. Don't you tell nobody neither, or I'll whip you again."

Madre wept for poor Tomás, but there was nothing she could do. He stumbled home, and he wouldn't tell his family what had happened.

That night Madre made a decision. She had to get the village to pay attention. She had to make them see that Esteban was no good. She could only think of one thing to do.

She went up to the *atarque* that guided the river's water into her ditch. It was late in summer and the river was low, so she didn't have much trouble piling rocks up against the *atarque* to shift the flow of water back out to the river. It took her most of the night, tumbling one rock at a time from the riverbanks, but by the morning she was done.

The sun came up over El Pueblo, and the people came out to their fields to work, but they didn't work. They climbed up the ditch banks and stood staring down instead.

The *acequia madre* was dry. Only a little mud in the bottom of the ditch.

A cry went up for the Mayordomo. The villagers hurried to Esteban's house and dragged him out of his bed.

"The *acequia*'s dry!" they said to him.

"What do you mean, dry?"

"It's dry! Go and see!"

Esteban hauled on his clothes and his boots. He grabbed his *tequío* to remind everyone of his authority, and went up to the ditch bank.

The roots that the trees had slipped into the water over the summer dangled out in the air, and the weeds drooped from thirst under the hot sun. An old, flat basketball lay in the middle of the ditch, the mud around its base dark with dampness. Around it the bottom of the ditch was dry and already cracking.

"Sonofabitch!" Esteban said, and his face turned red with rage. "Which one of you *pendejos* did this?"

"Hold on," said José. "No one did this."

"You think it just happened, old man?" Esteban spat at the ground. The little wet spot darkened as it sank into the soil, then began to fade in the heat.

"You got to go find out," said José. "That's your job, Esteban. Find out what happened. If you need help, come and get us."

"Stay away from me," Esteban said, looking from José to Manuel Benitez to Carlos Lovato. "All of you. Stay the hell away!"

Esteban stumbled away up the ditch bank, cussing as he went. The people of El Pueblo watched him go. They were quiet, because they each felt a little guilty. No one really wanted to help Esteban.

It was his responsibility to keep the water flowing. They all hid their secret glee, and stood along the ditch bank talking very solemnly about what could have gone wrong and waiting to see what Esteban would do.

Esteban ran along the bank, all the way up to the river. All the way he cussed. First it was "sonofabitch," then it changed to just "bitch."

"You bitch," he muttered as he ran along the acqeuia, limping a little from a stitch in his side, leaning on his *tequío*. "You stinking bitch."

Madre secretly smiled. At last Esteban was beginning to understand.

He dropped to a walk, and she watched him hobble along the last few yards of the ditch bank. Up here by the river the ditch was deep, the sides steep and wide apart. Esteban stopped beside the *atarque* and stood staring at the pile of rocks filling the head of the acequia.

A tiny trickle of water seeped down the rocks and gathered in a little pool there. Madre waited, watching to see what Esteban would do.

He stood panting for a while until he'd caught his breath. Then he raised his *tequío* and stabbed it down at the rocks.

"Bitch!"

Madre borrowed a little sound from the river and whispered, "Bastard."

Esteban froze. He frowned and his black eyebrows pulled together in the middle of his forehead. He peered at the rocks, then at the muddy sides of the ditch.

Madre drew together all the shape that she could gather, which wasn't very much without her water. All she had was the tiny puddle at the foot of the rocks and the trickle that fed into it. She made herself a shape with it, but she wasn't very tall. No taller than a little girl's doll. She stood in the middle of the puddle and shouted up at Esteban.

"Down here, bastard," she called, and her shout was a whisper, but he heard.

Esteban stared and stared, then he jumped into the ditch for a closer look. The mud made little slurping sounds with each step as he walked up to where she stood.

Madre stared up at him, concentrating on keeping her little doll's body together. She was a muddy little shadow, but he could see her. She could tell by the shock on his face.

"*Madre de dios!*" he muttered.

"Close," she said.

"What the hell are you?"

"I've been wondering that about you," she said in her tiny voice. "You're supposed to be my steward, but you're doing a pretty sorry job."

Esteban's brows drew down in a scowl. "Oh, yeah?"

"Yeah. This is your last warning, Esteban. You better show some respect for your duty and the people of El Pueblo. You're *their* servant, not the other way around."

Esteban snarled. "I'll show you respect!"

He hefted his *tequío* and stabbed it at Madre. It went through her shadow-shape and into the wall of rocks behind her. The rocks trembled, then shifted, then gave. They tumbled forward, the weight of the river behind them.

Esteban tried to jump, but the mud had him in its grip and the rocks rolled over him, pressing him back. The water swept in after, gurgling around the rocks and around his flailing arms until he disappeared beneath the muddy, cool flow.

The water in the ditch ran fast at first, then as the ditch filled, it ran lazily, sleepily through the open gates down into the fields. Madre stretched, rejoicing to feel the life-giving water again flowing uninhibited through her veins.

The people of El Pueblo watched the *acequia madre* fill again and they were happy. They saw the Mayordomo's *tequío* drifting along in the mother ditch and they were curious, but not so curious they went looking for Esteban. They figured he got mad that he'd been caught, and left town after letting the water go.

Manuel Benitez fished the *tequío* out of the ditch. Carlos Lovato joked that it was a sign from heaven, that he was fated to be the next Mayordomo. The people of El Pueblo knew he was joking, but they thought it was a good idea anyway and they elected Manuel to replace "that rat Esteban," as they all took to calling him.

Madre was happy with their choice. She knew Manuel would be fair, and she sighed with contentment as she went back to drowsing in the late summer sun.

Rescue Work

Adele hurried to open the door, hoping it was the newest member of the circle, so they could begin their work. On the honeysuckle-draped porch stood the wide-eyed, dark-haired young woman she was expecting, holding a cellophane-covered plate.

"Clara! I'm so glad you could make it."

Clara smiled, looking little nervous. "I brought some pickle sandwiches."

"That's just lovely, dear. Come on in."

Adele led her guest to the living room, where the others were already chatting away over glasses of sweet tea. They all greeted Clara, who put her plate on the coffee table and unwrapped the cellophane, revealing a heap of little square, crustless sandwiches. Thelma, the eldest in the group, took two right off.

"They're a bit dry," she said.

Adele could feel the younger woman's hurt. She touched Clara's shoulder.

"Come on in the kitchen while I fix you a glass of tea."

Clara followed her away, smoothing her floral print dress. The poor child was still self-conscious.

"Am I late?" Clara said, dark eyes anxious.

Adele filled a glass with ice. "Not a bit. Thelma's in a mood today. Don't you pay her any heed. You want mint?"

"Yes, please."

Adele put a sprig of mint cut fresh from the garden into the glass, and poured tea over it. Clara took a sip and sighed.

"Thank you." She looked up at Adele shyly. "I hope Henry shows up today."

Adele's heart gave a squeeze, because she was hoping so, too. She didn't want Clara to know how much.

"Well, we'll have to see."

They went back to the living room, Adele bringing the tea pitcher with her. The air conditioner was running full blast, and only just enough to take the edge off. Adele sat in her favorite chair by the window, an old-fashioned wing chair, powder blue. Henry had bought it for her years ago.

Thelma leaned forward from the leather recliner to take another sandwich. Donna Sue took one, too, a hand on her big belly, and smiled up at Clara.

"These are my favorite, Clara! I'm so glad you brought them."

Clara smiled back. "Thank you. My, you're getting big already. When are you due?"

"September," Thelma said. "As if anyone could forget."

Adele gave Thelma a sharp glance, then poured more tea into her glass. Clara sat beside Donna Sue on the sofa.

They were all here now, and Adele wanted to start, but she knew they needed to settle down first. She sipped her tea and nibbled a sandwich, listening to them chat, watching Thelma eat a handful of the kettle corn that Emmaline had brought, then another pickle sandwich, then more kettle corn. Why the old girl didn't weigh two hundred pounds, Adele couldn't say.

Emmaline had fallen quiet, like she tended to do, so Adele turned toward her. "How's your Tony?"

Emmaline smiled and peered at her over her glasses. "Ornery as ever. Still can't keep a fishing buddy."

"Don't you like to go fishing?"

"Not with him. Anyway, he don't want a woman in the boat. He sure does miss Henry."

Adele gave a small smile and sipped her tea.

"We all miss Henry," Donna Sue said softly.

"I wish I'd had a chance to meet him," said Clara.

Adele felt a familiar tightening in her gut. She set her glass on the table.

"Shall we begin?"

Thelma grabbed another sandwich and gobbled it. The others shifted, put down their tea, and got ready to work. Emmaline sat up very straight and held out her hands right and left. The circle took hands, and Emmaline led the prayer. It was her task to ground the circle, and she took it seriously, and that helped the others get focused. Time was when Henry had been the ground, but things had changed.

"Dear Lord, thank you for all the blessings you have given us. We are here today to do your work, and ask you to watch over us. In Jesus name, Amen."

The others murmured "Amen."

Adele closed her eyes, and the circle leapt awake in her mind. They all looked so different there—just glowing masses of light—but she still knew who each one was. Beyond them she sensed the second circle, with Mariah, her contact, leading them. Mariah appeared to her as a globe of pinkish-white light.

Greetings, Adele.

Hello, Mariah. What is our task today?

We have a young boy who is lost. He cannot hear us, so we have brought him to you.

"A young boy, lost," Adele said.

Mariah told her the boy's situation, and she passed it along to her circle.

"He was in an accident. A drunk driver crashed an SUV into his family's car. His parents were in the front, and he was in the back. The SUV hit the left side of the car and pushed it into a light pole."

Clara gave a small gasp. "Poor people!"

A shape was coming into focus for Adele: the boy, no more than twelve. He looked around as if trying to understand his surroundings. She could see him almost normally, though a glow of soul-light surrounded him. His wandering gaze came to rest on Emmaline.

Who are you?

"Emmaline, tell him who you are."

"I'm a teacher. I teach seventh grade."

Oh. I start seventh grade this fall. Maybe you'll be my teacher.

"He says maybe you'll be his teacher," Adele said.

"Maybe. Is there someone looking for you?"

No. I'm looking for my mom and dad.

The boy turned, glancing around the room. For a moment Adele was hopeful he'd catch sight of his escort, but instead he focused on Donna Sue. He stared at her a long while, looking at her pregnant belly. His gaze shifted to Clara, beside her.

Do you know my mom?

Adele repeated the question for her. Clara's light flickered with dismay.

"What do I do?"

"Just talk to him," Emmaline said.

Clara turned to face the center of the room and blinked twice. "Um, I don't know if I know your mother. What's her name?"

"Jennifer," Adele repeated after the boy.

"Jennifer. OK. And . . . and what's your name?"

"Good," whispered Donna Sue.

My name is Willie.

"Willie," Adele said.

"Hello, Willie. I'm Clara."

What are you people doing here? Where is this? Where are my parents?

"He's asking about his parents."

"Oh!" Clara said. "I think they're looking for you. Do you see them? Is that them over there?"

A tendril of Clara's light swept out in a gesture. Though Adele knew she couldn't see the other side, she must have had a sense of it, because now Adele could feel two more souls in the direction Clara had indicated.

Where? The boy looked around, then turned back to Clara.

So close.

"Almost," Adele said. "Try again."

"Um, I thought I saw a man," Clara said. "Maybe it was your father. What does he look like?"

He's tall, and he's got brown hair, and he wears glasses. The boy looked around again. I don't see him. Where is he?

"Clara, point that way again."

Clara pointed. The boy turned to stare in the direction of the two souls. Adele felt them reaching toward him, but they weren't strong enough to break through his confusion.

"He can't see them. We'll have to remind him."

Clara's light wavered. "How do I do that?"

"Oh, for pity's sake," said Thelma. "Young man—"

"Willie," murmured Emmaline.

"Willie. When was the last time you saw your parents?"

The boy turned slowly to face Thelma. Waves of dismay ran through his soul-light.

I don't remember.

Adele passed it along. Thelma gave a snort.

"Yes you do, you just don't want to think about it. I don't blame you a bit, but you've got to be brave and face up to it. Now, did you have breakfast with your parents this morning?"

Y-yes, the boy said slowly. Adele nodded.

"What did you do after that?"

We were going to go to the store.

"But you didn't get there, did you?" Thelma said after Adele passed his message. "What happened?"

I ... I want my mommy.

"Keep going, Thelma," Adele whispered as she watched the boy sway from foot to foot.

"You all got in the car, didn't you? You and your folks got in the car to go to the store, only something happened."

Mom! Dad!

The boy's swaying grew more pronounced. The two souls sent tendrils of light toward him, but he did not acknowledge them.

Adele, please have your circle send him pink light. We will do the same.

Thank you, Mariah.

Adele raised her hands to show the circle she had instructions for them. "Pink light," she said, directing her palms toward the boy.

The circle all raised their hands—Adele felt it more than saw it—and began sending light to Willie. Adele focused on this task until she sensed Mariah seeking her attention.

Someone is sending orange rather than pink.

"Everyone please make sure you are sending pink, not orange."

"I was visualizing salmon," Clara said. "Is that not right?"

"Try bubble gum," said Donna Sue.

"Oh! All right."

Adele felt a shift in the light coming from the circle, almost a click as it rose to a greater level of harmony. Willie stopped swaying.

That's better, Mariah told her.

"Good," Adele said. "Keep sending. Thelma, if you'll guide him."

"Willie, your mommy and daddy are looking for you. They're right over there. Can you see them?"

I don't . . .

Adele raised her head, sensing he was close to seeing. She kept sending light to him, and sent some to the two waiting souls also. The boy turned toward them.

Daddy?

With a rush of energy, the two souls reached out and enfolded Willie with light. Adele's perception of him faded to a simple, glowing mass of soul-light. She sighed as the three of them departed.

Well done, Adele. Please thank your circle for us.

"That did it. Mariah says thank you to all of you."

They all exclaimed and stopped sending pink. Adele kept her eyes closed for a moment. A little flutter of hope rose in her stomach.

Thank you, Mariah. Do you have more for us?

Yes, but take a rest first.

Adele was disappointed, but she knew better than to say anything. Mariah was in charge of her side.

She opened her eyes and looked around at the circle. Just a group of ordinary women, drinking tea and eating pickle sandwiches on a hot summer afternoon. She was so proud of them.

Clara noticed her. "So he'll be all right now?"

"Yes. He went off with his parents, quick as a whip."

"Oh, I'm so glad!" Clara looked around the circle. "I'm so honored to be doing this with all y'all."

Emmaline smiled at her indulgently. "It's good work."

"And you're an important part of it, hon," said Donna Sue, picking up the pitcher of tea and pouring for everyone. "He went right to you. You make people comfortable."

"Well, thank you. It just breaks my heart to think of a little boy like that all scared and alone."

Scared and alone. Adele's throat tightened. She stood and took the empty pitcher from Donna Sue, going back to the kitchen to fill it up again. Emmaline followed her.

"Henry going to come today?"

"I don't know."

"It's been quite a while since...."

Adele felt heat rising to her face. She added fresh ice to the pitcher, then pulled the tea jug out of the fridge and poured tea over the ice, listening to it crackle.

"There's always a lot to do," Adele said when she could trust her voice. "Too many lost souls for us to ever take care of them all."

"We aren't the only lighthouse."

"No, but there still aren't enough."

"Mm-hm. Not enough seers like you."

"I'm only part of it. Y'all are just as important."

Adele took the tea back to the living room and topped up everyone's glasses, then sat in her wing chair and indulged in a pickle sandwich. The sweet tang of the bread and butter pickle, the smooth salty butter and cheese, and the soft bread made her think of summers gone by. Summer evenings on the screen porch with Henry, watching the fireflies come out and just talking about anything and everything.

Emmaline poured more kettle corn into the bowl. The sandwiches were disappearing fast. Between Donna Sue and Thelma, the heap had been reduced to a scattering.

Adele took a swallow of tea and closed her eyes, just listening. She could feel the other circle and knew they were talking too, though she couldn't ever hear them except with Mariah's help. They seemed to be excited about something.

Are you ready, Adele?

Just a minute and we will be.

She looked at her circle. "Time to get back to work."

Everyone took a sandwich. There was just one left so Adele claimed it, crunching pickle while the others settled down. They took hands again to center the circle, then Adele told Mariah that they were ready.

Good. This one is a woman, a coast guard officer. She was lost in a storm, trying to rescue a teenager from a wrecked fishing boat.

A twinge of grief; Adele ignored it. All the stories were sad. No one ever needed help from a lighthouse after dying peacefully.

She told the circle about the coast guard officer, then closed her eyes to watch. The woman was young, and she went straight to Donna Sue. Turned out she'd been planning to have a baby, take leave from her job. Donna Sue gently steered her toward moving on, and with a little help from the second circle, they got her to see her grandma who was waiting for her.

Then there was a harder case, a soldier who was still bent on killing some enemy that didn't matter any more. He had a big, loud gun that he'd conjured up for himself, and he kept shooting it off at imaginary adversaries. That didn't bother anyone besides Adele, but it made it hard for her to concentrate, and she wondered how it affected the second circle. Folks on that side were more sensitive to powerful emotions.

The soldier just wasn't going to listen; didn't want to acknowledge what his soul knew somewhere deep inside. All the anger and focus on fighting didn't help. He wasn't ready to pay any notice to his friends who were waiting for him, much less a bunch of women.

"Just like Tony," murmured Emmaline.

Adele continued to describe to the circle what he was doing. Mariah's group kept him from leaving, but they couldn't get his attention either. Better chance of Adele's circle doing that, since he was so focused on earthly energies.

"What else could we say to him?" Adele asked. "He won't look for his friends. He's sure he's surrounded by enemies."

"He still shooting off that dang gun?" Thelma asked.

"Yes."

Thelma stood up. "Hey, you! Jason!"

Adele saw the soldier turn at hearing his name. His eyes narrowed as he faced Thelma. Seeing him point his gun at her raised the hair on the back of Adele's neck.

"He's listening," she whispered.

"Haven't you used up a lot of bullets?"

The soldier blinked. *What?*

Adele nodded vigorously to tell Thelma to keep going.

"That gun of yours seems like it has an endless supply of ammunition. Don't you think that's a bit odd?"

The soldier hesitated, then looked at his gun. Adele sensed his anger dissipating, replaced by confusion. She raised her hands, sending light to him.

Yes, Mariah said.

Adele felt the second circle joining in as everyone raised their hands, except Thelma, who kept talking. The light was so powerful it sent a tingle along Adele's arms.

"You're out of the battle, you know," Thelma said. "You're back on friendly territory. Some of your buddies should be around. Don't you see them?"

All I see is fog.

"He says he just sees fog."

"Well, you see me, don't you? And Donna Sue here, and Clara? Don't you have a pretty girl like her at home?"

Adele winced, because it wasn't safe to make assumptions like that, but getting his mind off the violence was the important thing. The soldier frowned, looking at Clara for a long time, then finally sighed.

Yeah. Michelle.

So he did have a sweetheart. That could be touchy, but it might help.

"His girl is named Michelle," Adele said.

"Don't you think Michelle misses you?" said Thelma at once. "Don't you want to see her?"

Michelle.

His voice sounded like a plea. It made Adele's heart ache for him, poor boy. He was hardly more than a kid. All the anger wasn't natural for him. He had put it on to shield him from worse things, but he didn't need the armor any more.

Adele sensed Mariah's attention. *We are going to try showing him Michelle.*

You can do that while he's here?

In a limited way. Keep sending light to him, please.

Adele focused on the soldier—Jason—and redoubled her efforts. A little tune was running through the back of her mind; she tried to figure it out without letting it distract her. She began to hum it softly, trying to recollect what it was.

"I know that!" said Clara. "My auntie Jo used to sing that to me!"

"Sing it now, please," Adele said, not sure why but knowing she should trust her instincts.

Clara began to sing, her voice shy and sweet. It was a little children's song, a lullaby.

Hush, little baby, don't say a word,
Momma's gonna buy you a mockingbird.
And if that mockingbird don't sing,
Momma's gonna buy you a diamond ring.

Jason turned toward Clara as she sang, and Adele felt the last of all the anger melt out of him. The gun was gone; it had disappeared and he didn't seem to notice. He was listening to the song, looking like his heart ached fit to break.

There wasn't going to be a happy reunion for him, at least not now. Michelle was still on this side, otherwise Mariah's circle would have brought her.

As she thought of Michelle, Adele saw a glow of light rising in one corner of the room, behind Clara's end of the sofa. It was like a little spotlight, shining on a scene where a young woman sat playing cards with some other girls, laughing together.

Michelle!

"She can't hear you," Adele said. "Or see you. I'm sorry."

For a moment she wondered if Jason had heard her, then he turned and looked right at her. His eyes were cold and hard, like they'd been when he had the gun.

What do you mean?

Rescuees rarely heard Adele; she mostly let the others in the circle do the talking, but he had focused on her so it was her task this time. She made her voice as gentle as she could.

"You're in a different place now."

What place?

Adele swallowed. "A place of transition. You have friends waiting to see you."

And family, Mariah added.

"And family. Do you see a light over that way?"

He frowned, looking in the direction she'd indicated, toward where his friends were waiting. There were several souls there. Adele couldn't tell much about them besides their eagerness to make Jason see them.

He took a step toward them. "Poppa?"

One of the souls came forward. The closer he got to the soldier, the more clearly Adele could see him. He looked like Jason, though too young to be his father; hardly older than Jason was now. Of course, on that side they could appear in different ways, depending on how strong and experienced they were. Usually they chose to look like they had when they'd crossed, if they showed a human form at all.

When Jason and his father embraced, Adele let out a sigh of relief. Everyone on both sides rejoiced.

The satisfaction was bittersweet. So many times Henry had led the circle, been the beacon that shone from the lighthouse. Adele had now taken his place, but she never set to work without thinking of him.

Mariah came toward her, taking her human shape: a middle-aged woman with short, dark hair and warm eyes, dressed in old-fashioned clothes. Adele knew that it was an effort for her to do this. Usually it meant she had an important point to make.

You did very well today. Please thank your circle for us.

Adele passed her message along, and answered aloud, "We're all honored to be doing this work."

"That's what Henry used to say," Emmaline murmured. "Every time, after we were done for the day."

Another soul from the second circle moved to join Mariah, slowly drawing into a human shape. Adele's stomach tried to turn over.

Henry?

It was him. Not like he'd been when he passed—so thin and sick—but like when they'd first met, young and handsome, with that unruly blond hair and that big grin.

Hello, Adele. Bet you didn't know I was here all along.

Her throat was so tight she couldn't say a word aloud. She just shook her head.

I've joined Mariah's team now. Took me a while to get up to speed, but here I am.

Yes, Adele thought with tears in her eyes. *Here you are.*

"Adele? You all right?"

She wasn't sure who had spoken—Donna Sue or Clara, probably—a gentle voice. She took a shaky breath and whispered.

"It's Henry."

Everyone started talking at once. Henry laughed and held up his hands.

One at a time!

Adele shushed them all and got them into order, then acted as interpreter. Everyone had something to say to Henry, even Clara, who shyly introduced herself.

Henry nodded. *I've been watching you. You're a great addition to the lighthouse.*

Clara blushed prettily and murmured a thank-you when Adele passed that along. Emmaline said something about Tony, and Adele gave her Henry's answer. She didn't mind letting the others talk to Henry. It was so wonderful just to see him, to watch him smile and nod. She had missed him so!

Even as the thought made her heart swell, Henry turned to look at her with a soft smile.

I've missed you too. It took a while for me to adjust—and there's a lot happening here.

You can tell me about it when we're alone.

Actually, I can't. That's the frustrating thing—I can't make you hear me without the lighthouse. I've tried.

Adele stared at him, understanding slowly sinking in. She felt her throat getting tight again.

That's why I pestered Mariah into letting me join her circle. Usually they only take people who are a lot more experienced—

But you are experienced!

It's different on this side. I've got a lot to learn, Adele.

"Is he still here?" asked Donna Sue.

Adele nodded, keeping her eyes on Henry.

"Henry, I'd like to give my baby your name for a middle name, if you don't mind. It's a boy, and he'll be Joseph after his daddy, but we'd be proud to give him your name too. We'd already planned to. You don't mind, do you?"

Tell her I'd be honored.

She did, then Mariah came forward to stand beside Henry.

It's time for us to go.

Adele drew a deep breath. She wanted to say so much more to Henry. She almost wished she could join him, now that she knew he was with Mariah's circle.

You still have work to do on Earth, Mariah said gently.

And in her heart, Adele knew that was true. She straightened her shoulders and put on a smile.

"We'll see you all next time."

She stood, offering her hands to either side for the closing circle. The others hastened to rise and join hands. Adele closed her eyes.

"Thank you Lord, for being with us today and for allowing us to do this work for you. Please watch over us until we meet again. Amen."

Murmered "Amens" fluttered around her from both circles. She felt the wavering uneasiness that meant Mariah's team was dispersing. She looked toward Henry, saw him smiling at her, even as he faded from her view. The last thing he did was blow her a kiss.

Then he was gone, and she couldn't feel Mariah's team any more. Her own circle said their goodbyes and drifted away. She waved to them from the porch, then went and sat on the swing and breathed in the scent of honeysuckle.

Closing her eyes, she thought of all the times she'd sat there with Henry. She could almost imagine he was beside her.

She smiled, and whispered, "I love you, Henry."

A little breeze brushed against her cheek, like the softest kiss.

The *Cygnius sedonai* Caper

My life may look easy, but it isn't, as anyone on Gamma Station can tell you. I'm no lap cat, despite what half the tourists who come through the station seem to think.

Gamma isn't the roughest assignment around, in fact it's fairly quiet most of the time. You got your fugitives, bail jumpers, your occasional small-time smuggler of cheap knockoff wetware or nanoporn—they're usually easy to sniff out because of the fear sweat—and a whole lot of ordinary tourists who trip up 'cause they just don't know the rules.

I watch and report suspicious behavior to my human teammates. People will do things in front of a cat they would never do in front of other humans, which is what keeps me in kippers. That's why I put up with the petting and cooing, even let the rug rats get away with grabbing occasionally. It's part of my job.

No pulling the tail, though. That's where I draw the line.

It's a tempting tail for the brats, I admit. My genetic ancestors were Maine Coons, and the tail is long and very full because of that.

My coat is a dark blue tabby-stripe, with silvery tufts inside my ears and a silver bib on my chest, which is why some of the bipeds call me Tux even though my name is actually Leon. I suppose I would have been less conspicuous with more average-cat genes, but I wasn't exactly in control of the process.

My breeders were looking for even temperament. In my job, you have to stay cool. Interstellar criminals are no easy cheeses. I've run into a few that would make your average house cat shed a week's worth of dust bunnies in a flat second.

I'm also required to be able to talk with my human colleagues, and my breed happened to have a high adaptability factor in that department. Surprise, surprise—Siamese don't rate so well there. Go figure. Guess there's a difference between conversation and just noise.

The *Cygnius sedonai* caper was a whole different kettle of fish, though. If I hadn't had a good team put together—something Gamma Station Security failed to appreciate at the time—it could have ended very badly indeed.

That morning I did my usual rounds at the market before heading up to watch the first inbound shuttle dump its load. The cleaning crew had just been through, wiping up all the really good, gritty smells and leaving behind their usual chem odor and that fresh-clean slickness to the floors. My claws ticked a little on the polished surface.

Gamma's market is in the central rotunda under the highest ceiling in the station, a full ten meters high with beautiful soaring arches supporting skylights that look out at the stars. The beams are stuffed full of cameras and recorders of every imaginable variety. The theory is that any suspicious characters who come on station will have to come to the market, so the rotunda is the place to get a look at them. That's why all the food and the shops are there. Even the public restrooms are only accessible from the rotunda.

Things can be hidden from cameras, though. Shielded with a turned shoulder or a strategically placed piece of luggage. That's where I come in.

That morning the shops were all open but not doing much business. Everyone was glued to the nearest holopad. That was unusual, so I kept my ears up.

The news feeds were all full of the same story. Someone had broken into the Cygni C IV Global Aviary and stolen a pair of rare *Cygnius sedonai*, a bird native to Cysgee Four and never successfully raised in any other environment. Big news, and since Gamma is the closest station to the Cygni system, definitely worth my attention.

I went on past the game stands and duty-free shops, keeping an eye on the feeds until I got to Ling-Ling's Lightspeed Asian, where I settled down in my usual spot underneath the end of the lunch counter. The place was minuscule, four tables and a half-dozen stools at the counter, all crammed into a kiosk covered in red-and-gold Chinese frou-frou. It had a double advantage, though. Not only did it have a prime view of the inbound tunnel from customs, but Ling-Ling made the best fish dumplings on the station and I had dibs on the day's trimmings every morning.

I had to actually meow before Ling2, Ling-Ling's clone, noticed and gave me my scraps. That's how engrossed everyone was with the news.

No, I don't talk to the cits. Word would get around, and that would blow my cover. Besides, most of them don't have much to say to a cat. Not much that's interesting, anyway.

After a glance around to make sure there was no suspicious activity in view, I settled down with a dish of fish tails and ripe, stinky guts, and turned my attention to the news.

Cygnius sedonai were prized as songsters and for their rare plumage. The feathers were not only a spectacular blend of rust-reds and brilliant, shimmering blue-greens, but had medicinal properties that were just beginning to be explored. The tail-feathers had already been the source of cures for cystic fibrosis and spider-veins.

The stolen pair were the only two *sedonai* that had survived in captivity for a significant length of time. The Executive Director of Cysgee Four's aviary was beside himself with anxiety for their safety. The feeds ran a bite of him: skinny, elderly guy with silver hair that stuck out in odd directions.

"These birds are practically irreplaceable," he said in a mournful voice. "We had hoped that they would be the first *Cygnius sedonai* to breed in captivity."

The feed switched to a rotating full-spectrum still of the two birds, all scarlet and blue with green highlights. I sat up, sniffing to try to catch the olfactory track, but Ling-Ling's holopad was too cheap and I was too far away from it. All I could smell was my breakfast. I lay back down to polish it off.

Who would want, and be able, to steal a couple of highly conspicuous, highly valuable birds? Someone with access to them, and who knew how to exploit them, I figured. Either a contract from the sort of private collector who didn't care about robbing the public, or someone in the med industry who thought they could make a few gigabucks off the plumage.

"Halva, halva, halva!" barked a nasal voice at my shoulder.

I looked up at Ling-Ling's annoying mini-peke, a pampered, papered show-pup. His real name was a mile long and totally unpronounceable. We all—by which I mean all the quadrupeds around the station—called him Hosehead.

"Morning, Hosehead." I spoke amiably, but bent a little closer over my dish.

"Halva bite of that for me?"

He never failed. Despite all the chow he got from Ling-Ling —and by the roundness of him he got a lot, pure caviar for all I knew—he always hit on me for some of my meager handout.

I looked down at my bowl. I was down to the spiny bits anyway, so I stood up and moved aside.

"Sure. Be my guest."

Hosehead dived in. I sat down and started washing my face,

wondering what Ling-Ling saw in such a useless, funny-looking beast.

He had a black, pushed-in schnoz, round brown eyes that watered perpetually, and sandy-colored hair so long it dragged around his paws. A lot of the time it looked like dreadlocks, but he must have been to the groomer's lately, because today it was fairly tangle-free and the stuff on top of his head was caught up into a stupid blue bow. Over the next few days the bow would loosen and finally fall out, but at the moment it was still tight enough that he could probably actually see.

I glanced up at the holopad, where the *sedonai* story had rolled around to the top again. There were no details I hadn't already caught, so I looked back at Hosehead. Might as well see if I could get some useful bit of information in exchange for my breakfast.

"So, Hosehead, buddy. Where's your boss this morning?"

He raised his head, licked the flat place where he ought to have a nose, and sneezed. "Shopping for a big dinner. Fancy catered affair. Important client."

"Anyone I know?"

He swallowed a mouthful of fish bones. "No. Some doc from off-station. One who did her." He nodded his round little head in Ling2's direction.

"Oh."

That made sense. Ling-Ling had probably offered the doc a fancy dinner in exchange for a break on the clone.

"I'll have to go by later to see what she's cooking up."

I had eaten some of the weirdest stuff by the back door of Ling-Ling's big, industrial kitchen, which was out in the business ring of the station. The kiosk had only a tiny prep kitchen to finish cooking food that had been assembled at the main kitchen. All the catering jobs ran out of there as well.

I watched Hosehead finish the last of my fish trimmings. Ling2 came to pick up the empty dish, pushing a strand of black hair behind her ear before bending down. She wore a high-necked, long-sleeved top and trousers made of jade-green silk, and smelled like sandalwood.

Hosehead sniffed eagerly at her hands until he figured out she wasn't carrying anything edible, whereupon he waddled off without so much as a thank-you. Ling2 glanced at me with a rueful smile that told me she knew exactly what had transpired, and reached out to stroke my head.

"Nice kitty Tux."

I gave her a purr. I liked Ling2 better than her boss.

Ling-Ling was too busy for friendly gestures most of the time. She was a tough businesswoman. Not only did she run the most popular food kiosk on station, but she catered out a lot. Anything from kid's birthday parties to elaborate fusion banquets with exotic dishes from all over the galaxy.

That was why she'd had herself cloned. It was too much work for one, and Ling2 was the perfect stand-in when she had to be in two places at once.

I felt sorry for Ling2 sometimes, even though I knew she was as well-paid as anyone in the restaurant biz. Technically she was family, but I'd never seen any sign of affection between her and Ling-Ling. Must be tough to know you were alive only because the boss needed extra help.

Well, that was sort of my situation as well, come to think of it.

I gave Ling2 a big, wide, golden-eyed gosh-you're-swell look and another purr while she scratched my ruff. Then I stood up and stretched, and she turned back to her customers.

Wash your hands, kid, I thought as I stepped out into the rotunda. You don't want to know what I've been rolling in.

✿

I headed across the rotunda for the port. Most people had seen the *sedonai* story by now and were moving on. I threaded my way among the legs of locals hurrying to their jobs.

Just before I reached the tunnel, I heard a "Psst" from between two kiosks. Devin, my human partner, was staring at me from between a rack of leather coats and a shelf of icerock bookends from Ganymede.

He turned away and walked down the service corridor. I rubbed my jaw against the coat rack and glanced around to make sure no one was watching before I casually followed him back to a storeroom full of unopened cargo tubs.

Devin closed the door after I slipped in. He sat on one of the tubs and I jumped up on top of two that were stacked, bringing me eye to eye with him.

"You look like hell," I told him. "Party too hard last night?"

Devin rubbed his unshaven jaw. He was dressed in a null-suit that looked like he'd already worn it a week. I keep telling the guy he needs a wife. At least she could dress him so he resembled a member of the human race.

"No," he said, and coughed to clear his throat. "For your information, you have me to thank that you weren't dragged out of bed four hours ago."

I rolled my ears forward. "Oh-five-hundred? What got you up at that hour?"

"That's when those damn birds got nipped. The boss called us all in the minute the news arrived. I told him you'd had a hard day yesterday with that fish oil incident."

"Oh."

I was touched by his thoughtfulness, and licked my chest a few times to hide my emotion. Devin might look like a deep-sleaze, but he was actually a decent guy. I was lucky to have him for a partner.

"Well, thanks," I said, sitting up straighter and meeting his slightly bloodshot gaze. "So what's the word?"

Devin reached in his pocket and pulled out his hand-held holopad. It wasn't cutting edge, but it was a lot better than the cheap set at Ling-Ling's. He set it in front of me.

"Play file 2birds."

The pad threw up the same image of the *sedonai* that had been on the news, but a much better copy. It must have come straight from the aviary, because it was longer and more detailed than what had been on the news.

I leaned forward, mouth open and inhaling intently, memorizing every detail. The birds' scent was unlike that of any avian I had ever encountered. They smelled delicious, to be blunt about it. Kind of spicy, with tangy overtones.

After one full rotation, the still image broke into motion. I reacted instinctively, putting out a paw to snag the smaller, less flashy female. The ghost feathers brushed under my pads, a silky tease. It was that good a holo.

The two birds flittered around each other and gave a few little mournful "towoos," then the file ended and they vanished. I sat back and gave my chin a lick.

"Central thinks there's a good chance they'll come through here," Devin said. "We're supposed to keep a close watch on all the incoming traffic."

He started to put the holopad back in his pocket, then hesitated. "You got the scent down, Leon? Want another review?"

I shook my head. "No. I'll remember it, unless it's heavily masked."

"There's this, too."

Devin stashed the holopad and pulled out a small, transparent vac pouch. Inside it were a few red and blue feathers. I pricked my ears forward.

"They let those out of their hands? Jeez, aren't they worth a fortune?"

Devin shook his head and scattered the feathers onto his palm, where they lay shimmering. "These are mockups from Cysgee Four's natural history museum. Pretty good, eh?"

I leaned forward, sniffing, then drew back at the stench. "They look great, but they smell like horse glue."

"Yeah, well, usually they're behind plex."

"Can I have one?"

"Sure. Take 'em all, if you want. Everyone else has seen them."

I reached out and gathered the feathers up, careful not to stick a claw into Dev's hand. My thumbs—fully opposable—are another perk of genetic modification, and really, I can't imagine living without them.

I fanned the half-dozen feathers in my paw like a poker

hand, then flicked them shut and stashed them in the pouch I wear under one shoulder like a holster. One of the feather ends poked me in the ribs, and I had to adjust it.

"I'll show them to my buds. Never hurts to have extra eyes watching."

Devin shrugged. He tended to get deaf whenever I brought up the subject of my feline friends.

Teammates, really. They helped me out with certain chores, and I repaid them with choice bits from Ling-Ling's and some of the other goodies that came my way. I'd been trying to talk Devin into getting them official status with Gamma security, but he wasn't interested in non-modified quadrupeds.

He didn't offer to lend me the holopad so I could play the file for my pals, and I didn't bother to ask. It was too big for me to carry comfortably anyway, unless I held it in my mouth, and I hate the taste of plastic.

"Any clues about who we might be looking for?"

Devin shrugged. "Whoever it is had access to the aviary. No forced entry, and no alarms tripped. The dogs came up with zilch, which means the perps covered their scent."

I repressed the urge to sniff. Dogs have their talents—some dogs, not Hosehead—but for anything requiring brain power, they're useless.

"So you might not smell anything," Dev went on, "but keep watch anyway, OK?"

"Roger."

"Time to hit the beat." Devin got up from the storage tub. "Give me a minute to get to Molly's. I'll see you at the customs gate."

"Right."

I jumped down and did a quick inspection of the storeroom's less accessible corners while I waited for Dev to get clear. No mice. Good for Gamma, tough luck for me.

❧

I strolled out and gave the leather kiosk a once-around, rubbing up on all the racks. Along the curve of the rotunda I saw Devin leaning against the counter at Molly's Bar & Grill, talking up the morning girl.

For a smart guy, he showed a pretty undiscriminating taste in females. I flicked my tail in disgust and turned away to head up the tunnel toward customs.

A few doors down was Tammy's Tea Shoppe, a fancy name for one of the lounges where layover passengers could relax for an hour or so. Tammy also ran Steadly's Smoking Room next door, for those customers (usually male) who couldn't face the Victorian bric-a-brac at the tea shoppe. They both served the same basic menu: sturdy sandwiches, meat pies, and soups, plus a selection of frilly pastries over on the ladies' side.

I poked my head into Steadly's looking for Butch, one of my unofficial operatives. He wasn't there, so I figured Tammy had roped him into hanging out in the tea shoppe.

She kept a special stand in the parlor that held a cat bed done up in red velvet cushions. The stand stood about a meter high, had long gold fringe around the edges and a sign that said "Cuddles" in curly script dangling from a little gold chain. Butch hated it.

He was there, though, when I prowled in looking for him. He lay curled up on the red cushions, looking morose. Next to him was an ornate empty bird cage hanging from its own stand of curley-cued wrought iron. Tammy's sick idea of a joke, maybe.

"Psst. Butch."

Butch's head snapped up and he looked at me, then glanced toward the back of the parlor, where three females of different bipedal species, all in snappy travel outfits, were chattering over their tea and scones. Tammy was nowhere in sight.

Butch leaped down from the stand and hurried toward me, a sight that would easily intimidate someone who didn't know him. Butch was a classic orange tabby, your basic alley cat. He looked round and soft at first sight, especially lying curled up on that red velvet stuff, but he was rock solid. His gait might not be graceful, but the power in his forelimbs was obvious.

"Hey, Leon! Any action?" His eyes were bright green with hope.

"Could be. Let's find a quiet place to talk."

"Not in the smoking room. Tammy chased me out of there with a broom earlier."

"Down by the trash chute, then?"

Butch nodded his massive head, and we made for the service corridor where the nearby kiosks disposed of their garbage. Butch sniffed the floor around the hatch to make sure nothing interesting had been dropped, then sat down and invited me to join him.

"I heard about that thing with the birds," he said. "Tammy had the news on in the kitchen."

I nodded. "Good. Did you get a whiff of them?"

"Uh—yeah, sort of."

"Would you remember if you smelled it again?"

Butch licked his paw and thought about it. "Not sure."

"Well, see if you can catch the story again, and pay attention. The boss thinks those birds might come through here."

"No kidding?" Butch licked his chops.

"And they're worth a bundle," I said, frowning, "so whoever recovers them in good condition stands to be amply rewarded."

"Oh, yeah. Right."

I reached into my shoulder pouch and took out the faked-up *sedonai* feathers. Fanning them out, I showed them to Butch.

"This is what the plumage looks like. These are mockups, so the smell is wrong."

"I'll say."

Butch frowned and wrinkled his nose, then batted at my feathers, knocking one out of my paw. He pushed it around, trying to turn it over. I put the others away and flipped it for him, exposing the rusty, coppery top surface. The underside was blue-green.

"Pretty flashy," Butch said.

"Yeah. If you spot the birds, don't try to grab 'em. Just come get me. The boss and I will handle it."

Butch gave a last, wistful bat at the feather. "Okay."

I scooped it up and put it back in my pouch. It wasn't that I didn't trust Butch with it, but he was the sort of tom who might forget and leave it lying around someplace where it might be spotted. I didn't want the perps, if they did come through Gamma, to spot fake *sedonai* feathers on that red velvet stand, say. They'd get suspicious, and I'd get in dutch with Devin.

"Seen Leila this morning?" I asked Butch as we started back.

He gave a snort. "I wish. You know she don't mix with the masses much."

"Yeah, I know. Her human brings her to Tammy's now and then though, doesn't she?"

He shrugged. "It's been a while."

"Well, if you see her, give her the scoop. I want everyone keeping an eye out."

"Okay."

We arrived back in front of Tammy's and Steadly's. Butch cast a wistful glance at the smoking room, where a holographic fire flickered invitingly on the hearth between two leather chairs. Then he turned toward the tea shoppe. I watched him slink back toward the red velvet pillory.

"Take it easy, Butch."

"Sure," he growled over his shoulder.

One powerful thrust of his hindquarters propelled him onto the stand. He turned around a couple of times and settled in for the long haul.

Tammy's honey-coated voice wafted out from the back of the tea shoppe. I didn't want her to invite me to join Butch on display, so I made myself scarce. It was nearly time for the first shuttle anyway.

◈

When I got to the tunnel the yellow light on the gate was flashing, warning of an imminent incoming FTL. Futtle-shuttles, the locals called them. The passengers getting off of them always looked a bit shell-shocked.

I trotted up the ramp and greeted the customs inspectors as I passed through into the waiting area. Huey grinned and beckoned me over with a whistle and a wave of his hand.

Huey was a big, friendly galumph with slick dark hair and a face that was an open book. As a customs inspector he was average, too good-natured to be really tough. Most days he was good for a bite of nutribar or equivalent. I strolled on over to collect.

He tossed me a scrap of bagel. Onion—not my favorite. I was tempted just to lick off the cream cheese, but I believe in oiling the wheels so I gulped it down, gave him a cute look, and rubbed against his leg before moving on.

Beyond the gate the ceiling was low and the walls bland, industrial. Everything port-side was geared toward moving passengers into the station as fast as possible. No distracting artwork or advertising, and the few seats were designed to be uncomfortable.

I eased over to a wall to sniff the floor seam, but the cleaning crew had been here too. No amusing smells.

Disappointed, I chased my tail for a couple of turns, then collapsed to wait for the incoming passengers. It would be a while before they showed up. The gate lights were still flashing yellow—they had to go to orange and then red before the shuttle would spill its load.

I glanced around, wondering if Devin would be here in time or if he'd gotten distracted by the chica at Molly's. No sign of him so far, so I stretched out my forelegs and laid my head on my paws. I was just dozing off when I heard a plaintive mew.

"Leon! Daaarling!"

I raised my head and looked back toward the gate. The last creature I expected to see here was Leila, but there she was, peeking out of a jewel-encrusted tote bag over her human's arm. I got up and ambled back through the gate to talk to her.

Leila's a Burmese, with dark fur and the dainty countenance of the purebred rich. Her human, Elsa Grippe, works high up in station management, and is as sleek as Leila in a blonde, bipedal sort of way.

"What are you two doing here?" I asked.

Leila rolled her large, green-gold eyes. "Mamzelle is meeting a friend coming in from Ross something-or-other."

"154," I supplied.

"I'm sure."

"Do you like riding in that thing? I mean, it looks uncomfortable."

"It is, cher, but it's so chic."

Elsa looked down at me at that point, and gave me a nudge with an alligator-clad toe. "Shoo!"

I flashed her a hurt look and moved around behind her, pretending to shove off. A second later, when Elsa had turned to talk to Huey, I slipped in close again to whisper to Leila.

"Did you see the news this morning? Catch the story about the stolen *Cygnius sedonai* from Cygsee Four?"

Leila nodded, breaking into a purr. "Oh, yes! Such pretty birds!"

"Keep your eye out. Central thinks the thief may try to bring them through here."

She gave a wide-eyed blink. "Ooh!"

Elsa was still chatting with the customs inspector. I glanced around to make sure no one else was watching, then palmed one of the fake feathers from my shoulder pouch and quickly took it in my mouth. It tasted as bad as it smelled.

"Hewe," I said, and reared up to spit the feather into Leila's jeweled carrier. It caught on the fluffy trim around the top of the bag. Leila reached a tentative paw toward it.

"That's just for reference," I told her. "It's not the real thing, but that's what the plumage looks like."

"Pretty! But the birds on the news holo didn't smell like this."

"I know. Like I said, it's a fake. Keep it out of sight, okay?"

Leila tilted her head, blinked at me, then with a swift swipe of her paw knocked the feather into the bag. Elsa looked up and reached around to rub Leila's head, then went back to her conversation.

A loud buzzer went off and the gate lights went from yellow

to orange. I looked up at Leila.

"I've got to get back to work. You let me know if you get a whiff of those birds, all right?"

Leila groomed her left ear. "Yes, yes, cher. I will, assuming I am not still in this bag. It is very hard to climb out when Elsa has the straps over her shoulder."

I gave her a deadpan look. "The birds are extremely valuable. There could be a substantial reward involved."

Leila edged one ear further forward. "How lovely. I will keep watch for them."

I couldn't tell if she was being serious or sarcastic. It wasn't as though Elsa didn't have enough money to keep Leila in obscene luxury. On the other hand, most of the people I know who can't seem to get enough money are the ones who already have too much.

"Gotta go," I said. "I'll bring something by for you later."

"Thank you, cher," Leila purred as I headed for the gate.

I had thought more than once about making a play for Leila, though Elsa would be an obstacle. Nothing but the best purebreds for her little Leila-kins.

I had a pedigree, but it was—shall we say—unusual. Even if it hadn't been, I doubt Elsa would have let me near her darling. A Burmese/Maine Coon cross was a bit of a frightening thought.

I slipped through Huey's gate again as the lights went from orange to red. The shuttle had landed, and in a minute the gate would become a zoo. I went back to my spot by the wall and lay down to watch.

Devin slouched up to Elsa and weaseled his way into her conversation with Huey. I hoped he was just doing it for the sake of work, cause I didn't think much more of Elsa than I did of the bar girl at Molly's. Too polished, too cold. Devin needed a nice girl with warm, gentle hands who cooked great fish dinners and always had leftovers.

The first incoming passengers started to arrive, looking tired, clumping their way down the long, sterile tunnel. I sat up, sniffing for a whiff of that exotic tangy-spicy scent.

Anyone with a hand-carry deserved special attention. The

regular luggage all got scanned and would be picked up on the other side of the gate. It was the people wanting exception to the scan procedure who were most likely to be trying to sneak something through.

Trouble was, the *sedonai* were small, about the size of a terran robin. One would fit easily into a decent-sized pocket. I watched for people with loose clothing—unusual on an interstellar flight because of its awkwardness in zero G—and people with packages that they were handling as if the contents were fragile.

A father in a business-casual nullsuit walked up to one inspector, leading his little girl by the hand. The father's briefcase interested me less than the girl's doll—one of those pucker-faced things that didn't move or do anything interesting. It was wearing a dress that was even frillier than the girl's.

I prowled through the legs of the crowd to get closer to her. The doll was just barely big enough to hide a bird inside. If it was there, though, where was the other? On the father? With another passenger?

Just as I was getting near enough to try to sniff out the evidence, the girl got impatient waiting for Dad's briefcase to be searched. She took her dolly by the legs and slammed its head against the floor three times.

"Dad! Dad! Dad!"

So much for that. Any bird inside that dolly was now dead, dead, dead.

I dodged away, my pulse jumping at how close I had come to being in range of that weapon. I continued to prowl through the crowd, trying to look nonchalant while I settled my ruffled fur.

Would the thief care if the bird was dead? I had been assuming the *sedonai* would be more valuable if they were still alive, but it depended on their ultimate destination. I'd have to think about that.

My eye was caught by a solitary female carrying a bright red leather case. She had the fluid swagger of someone who's spent a lot of time driving heavy waldos, but it looked okay on her. So did her nice silver-blue clingsuit, presently set on medium. She'd probably relaxed it after getting off the flight, and it had probably looked damn stunning set on tight.

I glanced in Devin's direction, wondering if he'd seen her and come to the same conclusion. Couldn't see him for the crowd, so I wove my way in close to try to get a sniff at her bag.

Boy, was that a mistake. I nearly choked on the perfume. Three or four different kinds, from the smell of it. I fell in behind her and let my mouth hang open despite the caustic fumes, hoping for a whiff of the *sedonai* scent.

Nothing. She walked into a customs line and cheerfully opened her case for the inspector, who flinched despite his dull bipedal sense of smell. I turned back to the crowd, scanning for the unusual or the slightly out of place, counting on my eyes and ears until my olfactory recovered from the perfume.

The mass of passengers was beginning to thin out a bit, and I started to think this batch might be a wash. I noticed Ling-Ling in Huey's line, waiting behind a tall, orange-skinned biped that wore what looked like a portable oxygen tent on its head. Ling-Ling was dressed in close-fitting black flowered silk, and carried a small cooler in one hand and Hosehead in the other.

Surprised to see her, I started edging her way. I glanced at the counter where the fem in the blue clingsuit had just passed inspection. She dashed out to the station and into Elsa Grippe's arms, making delighted squealy noises.

Dismissing her, I made my way to Huey's counter and watched Ling-Ling. I couldn't figure out why she would be coming in from off-station, until she put her cooler on the counter for Huey to inspect. Then I remembered she was throwing a big do for the clone-doc. She must have gone to the intersystem market at Eps Indi to pick up something exotic to dish up.

A slug of fear hit me. What if she was cooking up *Cygnius sedonai*?

But, no—she opened the cooler and stood calmly petting Hosehead while Huey took out every piece of meat—including some gigantic green eggs with purplish spots—and even turned the thing upside down to look for hidden compartments.

I kept watching, troubled by my suspicions. Ling-Ling didn't notice me. Neither did Hosehead, but that was not surprising. He wasn't exactly the brightest bulb in the chandelier to begin with, and with his hair down in his eyes it was no wonder his gaze slid right over me.

"Hey, Leon!" said Devin behind me. "How're you doin', buddy?" He squatted down and scratched my ears. "Anything?" he said softly.

I shook my head like a wet dog, my signal for "no" when we were out in public.

"Well, keep looking. I'm heading back to the market."

I gave him a yowl intended to express my hope that he wasn't going to waste any more time at Molly's, then pretended to chase an invisible rat over to the wall. When I looked up again, Devin was gone and Ling-Ling was closing her cooler. Huey grinned at her and patted Hosehead, who continued to pant like an idiot as Ling-Ling stepped into the station.

I resurrected the invisible rat and used it to get close to the remaining passengers, chasing it all around their legs and sniffing like mad for the birds. My nose was still a bit numb from Elsa's friend's perfume, but I was pretty sure the *sedonai* weren't on any of the last dozen or so to go through customs. When they were all through the gate I went back to the rotunda and resumed prowling my beat.

I was frustrated. Of course, it was possible that the birds hadn't come to Gamma. Something told me they had, though, and we had missed them.

I passed Tammy's, where Elsa and her friend were guzzling tea while Leila sat at their feet in the jeweled carry-bag, looking bored. Butch was up on the cat stand, watching Leila and thumping his tail against the red cushions. I gave them both a nod but continued on my way.

What if the birds were dead? I mused as I passed the leather kiosk. I gave the nearest rack of sheepskin coats a half-hearted rub, then moved on past the ice-rocks and the taco place, the duty-free pharmacopeia and the instant credit booth. I paused to spray on the latter. Just a personal statement.

Dead birds would be easier to hide, I thought as I moved on, and still valuable for some things, if not for breeding. Could use the feathers for drugs, though you'd get a finite yield.

A collector might want the birds, but they'd bring a lot more alive than stuffed. A really sick collector might even want to eat them.

An image flashed through my mind, of Ling-Ling serving up a dish of *sedonai* in plum sauce to her doctor client.

Her clone doctor client.

Holy crap.

I cut off my beat, making a beeline across the rotunda for Ling-Ling's.

Dead *Cygnius sedonai* would be just as useful as live birds to a clone artist. If it weren't for the purists' disdain for clones, those damn birds could be as common as puke in Molly's restrooms on a Saturday night. Cloned *sedonai* feathers, however, would presumably be as good as originals to the drug industry.

♠

I dashed into Ling-Ling's kiosk and jumped up on the counter, ignoring a dirty look from a gate guard having lunch in the nearest seat. Ling2 was still playing hostess.

I sniffed open-mouthed at the smells wafting out of the kitchen, but they were only ginger and peanut oil, soy-beef and shrimp that made my mouth water. I was willing to bet that the birds were not back there. That was something of a relief, but where had she taken them? And how had she got them past us? And was this really a lead, or was I full of it?

Ling2 turned around with a tea carafe in her hand and saw me. "Oh, no kitty! Get down!"

Not wanting to get her in trouble, I hopped down. I had seen what I could from there, anyway. She refilled the guard's teacup, then brought me a couple of fried shrimp tails. I sat crunching one, debating whether to try to sneak into the kitchen.

Hosehead wandered out of the back, saw me and came over. I hastily snapped up the second shrimp tail.

"You here mooching again?" he said, and sat down to scratch his head with his hind foot. When he straightened up, the stupid blue bow was dangling to the left.

The stupid blue bow. He had not been wearing it at the customs gate. Holy, holy crap!

I swallowed the half-chewed shrimp tail, which went down rough and scratched my throat. "Hosehead, where's Ling-Ling?"

"I dunno. Went shopping, but she's back now. Probably over at the big kitchen."

"Right. Thanks."

"Why?" he asked, blinking his watery eyes at me, but I was already on the move.

He was even more clueless than I'd thought. That's why he hadn't noticed me at the customs gate. Whatever dog that was—if it was a dog at all—wasn't Hosehead.

❧

I ran toward Molly's, looking for Devin. No sign of him, so I headed for one of the corridors out to the exterior of the station, where the locals lived and conducted any business that was not aimed at travelers.

Passing Tammy's, I saw Butch still up on the stand. I paused and thought, what the hell.

"Butch!" I called, trotting into the tea shoppe.

A familiar gagging blend of perfume assailed my nostrils. Elsa and her pal were at the front desk, paying for their tea. Tammy frowned at me over her filigreed glasses. I ignored her, turning back toward the rotunda and calling over my shoulder.

"Come on, Butch! Got a hot lead, and I want your help."

He needed no further encouragement. He took off from the stand and landed with a meaty thump on the carpet not a meter from where I stood.

"Cuddles! Come back here," cried Tammy, but we were already out the door.

We both broke into a run. I ducked into the corridor and Butch took the corner right behind me, paws scrambling for traction on the slick surface. I slowed to a trot again, trying to plan the next move.

"I think I've sussed out the birds, but I've got to prove it," I told him.

Butch panted a little as he kept up with my longer stride. "Where are they?"

"Not sure, but I think I know who's got them. I only hope we're not too late."

"May I be of help, cher?" purred a voice to my right.

I glanced down at Leila, serenely trotting beside me. She had her eyes partly lidded and was looking smug.

"Sweetheart! How'd you get loose?"

"Mamzelle was distracted by some shouting. Very wrong for a tea shoppe. The proprietress was in great distress over something, I can't imagine what."

Butch laughed. "She'll live."

"OK, hang on," I said, stopping just around the corner from Ling-Ling's main kitchen.

I had a half-baked plan for catching Ling-Ling red-handed. It sucked, pretty much, but it was better than no plan.

"Leila. You move pretty smoothly. Slide in there and help me find Hosehead. I mean—not Hosehead, but something that looks like Hosehead. Might be another dog, but I'm thinking it's an animatron. I think Ling-Ling used it to sneak the birds past Huey."

Leila gave one forepaw a dainty lick. "Cherchez le chien. I understand." She stood up, walked to the corner, then with a coy over-the-shoulder look at me and Butch she sidled around the wall out of sight.

"Butch." I dug one of the mocked-up feathers out of my shoulder pouch. "Find Devin and show him this. He should get the message and follow you back here."

"Got it." Butch took the feather in his mouth. "God, it tasses tewwible!"

"I know. Go."

I watched him head back toward the rotunda, then took a deep breath. Hoping that Devin would come soon, I went around the corner at a casual prowl.

◈

The kitchen was huge, probably four times the size of Ling-Ling's Lightspeed kiosk, all shiny steel. It was full of exotic, enticing smells, heaps of colorful vegetables and fruits and containers of who knows what waiting to be made edible. Full of cooks, too, all chopping and stirring away.

I saw the tip of a dark tail curving out of sight beneath a work table. I was too big to go under there, so I slunk around the edge of the kitchen, smelling every cupboard and shelf I passed. I came across a basket of the gigantic purple-spotted eggs Ling-Ling had brought through customs, but no sign of the *sedonai*.

Leila emerged again at the far end of the work table. She glanced over her shoulder and caught my eye, then gave a little shrug and moved on to the next table. I had to admire the way she slunk between the legs of the cooks. A little sable Burmese shadow.

I heard a brisk, high-heel-clicking footstep behind me. Ling-Ling, coming to check on her crew.

I grabbed a cupboard handle, yanked it open, and dove in, hoping she hadn't seen me. I pulled the door almost closed and peered out through the crack.

Ling-Ling started giving rapid-fire orders in Chinese. Leila emerged again, and I felt my neck fur start to stand up as I watched Leila hop from floor to counter right behind Ling-Ling.

She leapt from counter to shelf, then shelf to top of the upper cupboards without a sound. None of the cooks saw her, or if they did they ignored her.

I held my breath as she began slinking around up there, sniffing at boxes and crates. She stopped at a huge, blue and white ginger jar, the lid of which was ajar.

I nearly yowled as Leila put her forepaws on the neck of the jar and sniffed intently at whatever was inside it. She nudged the lid, and it slid off. It missed landing on the cupboard top, falling all the way to the floor where it shattered with an ear-splitting crash.

Ling-Ling stopped talking and whirled, staring up at Leila who sat frozen, wide-eyed, with her paws still on the edge of the jar. Ling-Ling's eyes went wide, too.

"Get that cat!" she shouted.

Leila dropped to all fours, started to jump down, then thought better of it and ran along the cupboard top, dodging between boxes and baskets. Ling-Ling and all the cooks went after her. Food went flying.

I knew they had her trapped, and I did the only thing I could think of. I pulled the fake *sedonai* feathers out of my shoulder pouch and stuffed their ends in my mouth.

Never have I had such a wretched taste in my mouth, and I have eaten some pretty weird things. Those feathers might smell like horse glue, but they tasted more like horse piss. I prayed for Devin to show up soon as I shouldered open the door of my sanctuary.

Ling-Ling was standing on a box, climbing onto the counter. I trotted up and planted myself in front of her, feathers dangling artfully from my jaws, and said, "Mrow?"

She stared down at me for a full second, then let out a shriek worthy of your worst nightmare. Raised my fur, let me tell you.

She made a grab for me but I managed to evade her and ran down the far side of the kitchen away from Leila. The cooks were still doing their circus act on the counter. Ling-Ling shouted at them to catch me, and the place turned chaotic as pots and pans and bowls of stuff I don't want to mention hit the floor.

A foot-long butcher knife buried itself in a cupboard door a split second after I'd passed it. Ling-Ling was right behind me with murder in her eyes. I put on speed.

I risked a glance up at the cupboard top, but Leila was

nowhere in sight. Everyone who'd been chasing her was now after me, and I decided to lead them away from the hot spot.

I dashed out into the corridor and put on full speed for the rotunda. Where the hell was Devin? If he didn't show soon I'd wind up on the menu at Ling-Ling's fancy do.

I could hear her behind me, cussing in Chinese, or so I assumed. I dodged a clot of cits coming home with full shopping bags, and prayed that they would slow Ling-Ling down. Beyond them, a familiar orange shape was speeding toward me.

Butch! I could have cried with relief, except my mouth was full of feathers.

"Whewe's Devin?" I yowled.

"Right behind me," Butch called back, panting.

So he was, stretching out those lanky legs in a run. He saw me and started to slow down. I howled at him, not wanting to risk speech but trying to communicate that I would like him to please rescue me from the homicidal restaurateur behind me.

His gaze rose. "Ling-Ling," he said, sounding surprised. "What's the problem?"

"That cat! Get that cat!" she screeched.

Devin swivelled his head to look at me. "That cat?"

I paused, wishing I could get Devin alone for just ten seconds to explain what was going on. He raised an eyebrow at me, then said, "C'mere, kitty."

I growled, which between him and me means "Fuck, no."

Ling-Ling lunged for me and I ducked. Her fingertips caught at my fur.

"Hang on, take it easy," Devin said. "What did the cat do?"

Ling-Ling crossed her arms, looking pissed as hell. "He ate . . ."

Devin looked at her. "Yes?"

"Something extremely valuable."

"Ah—looks to me like he ate a bird."

"Never mind, I just . . . never mind!"

She turned abruptly and stalked back toward her kitchen, heels clicking sharply on the floor. I caught Devin's eye, then dashed past Ling-Ling, back toward the kitchen.

I had to get there before Ling-Ling did. If we were very, very lucky, the birds were in that ginger jar and still alive.

"There he goes!" yelled Devin. "I'll get him for you!"

On this clever excuse he ran after me, and Butch came along. When we got to the kitchen I turned and spat out the disgusting feathers.

"Close the door, Dev!"

He punched the control. I glanced around belatedly to see if any other humans were in there. Fortunately not.

Butch started investigating the many items of interest that had hit the deck in our earlier adventure. I headed up toward the top of the cupboards, calling to Leila.

"Leila? You all right? Answer me baby—"

"Hey, Leon, what gives?" Devin called from the floor. "Where are the *sedonai*?"

"Up here, I think," I told him. "Don't let anyone in."

"OK."

Devin pulled out his security card and started tinkering with the locks, while I leapt up top of the cupboards and made my way toward the ginger jar. Halfway there I found Leila crouched behind an industrial-sized tea caddy. Her eyes were very wide and she was breathing shallowly, staring at the kitchen floor as if expecting a broom to come out of nowhere.

"You all right?" I asked her.

She focused on me finally, blinked, then sat up and started to groom. "Leon."

"The birds—are they still in the jar?"

"I don't know. I never saw them, though I smelled them."

She looked like she needed a minute to compose herself, so I slid past her toward the ginger jar. With the lid gone, the birds might well be gone, too. I hoped they had been frightened enough to stay inside.

A pounding commenced on the outer door. I glanced down at Devin.

"Better check for other entrances," I called.

"I sure as hell hope you know what you're doing," he said,

starting through the kitchen. "Jesus, what happened in here?"

Not bothering to answer, I climbed over a fifty-kilo sack of rice and reached the ginger jar. I sniffed at it and caught a definite whiff of *sedonai*. My heart started racing.

I crept up to the jar, slowly, silently. Flattening my ears so they wouldn't be a tipoff, I cautiously looked over the edge and saw two large black eyes staring back at me.

"Crap!" I shouted, jumping away.

"What?" yelled Devin.

"It isn't the birds. It's—oh."

I realized that the eyes I'd seen were Hosehead's. I took another look in the jar.

Sure enough, the little creep was in there, or rather his bowless double was. I watched for a few seconds. The thing wasn't breathing.

"Dev. Come and get this jar down."

He worked his way toward me, cussing as he slipped on spilled wontons. The pounding on the door, which had continued all the while, stopped briefly and a string of vehement Chinese took its place. Then it started up again, louder. It sounded like all Ling-Ling's cooks were taking turns hurling themselves against the door.

Devin hauled a chair over and stood on it to get to the counter. He stepped between a basket of bok choy and a bamboo steamer full of spring rolls, and reached for the ginger jar.

"Careful," I said. "If I'm right, the birds are in there."

He looked in, and nearly fell backward. I made a grab for the jar in case he dropped it, but he got his balance back and threw me a dirty look.

"This is a dog."

"No, it isn't," I said, hopping down to the counter. "It's an animatron, I think. Take it out of there."

He stepped down and put the jar on the counter, then reached in and removed the Hosehead double. I sniffed at it.

"This thing reeks of *Cygnius sedonai*. They must be inside it. Look for a switch."

Devin turned it over, turned it every which way. Butch wandered over and jumped on the counter to sit beside me, watching with ears pricked forward.

Finally Devin fiddled with a spot behind the dog's ear. Its chest popped open, and the two birds fluttered out.

Butch and I pounced on them, even as I yelled, "No claws!"

"Right, boss," Butch said, and held his bird down with a gentleness at odds with his massive frame. "It sure smells good, though."

"I'll take that," Devin said, reaching for Butch's bird.

Butch released the tiny thing, which fluttered and twittered, its feathers shimmering. Devin looked around helplessly with the bird in his hand and the dog in the other.

"I guess a bird in the hand is worth two in the shaggy dog," I said.

He turned a look on me that would wither a cat tree.

"Just kidding," I told him. "Open the dog up and stash that one, then I'll give you this one."

He did, and added the second bird before shutting the hatch again. I admit, I had trouble giving it up. Butch was right, they smelled delicious.

The pounding on the door stopped. Devin looked at me and I knew what he was thinking—Ling-Ling had figured it out and was on the run.

Devin whipped out his com and connected to central security. Luckily, they shut down all access to the port before Ling-Ling could skip the station. They caught her in her quarters, stuffing cash into her cooler.

Clever distraction, that cooler, and poor Huey had fallen for it. All the while the real contraband had been inside the fake Hosehead.

❧

Devin and I discussed it later, after everything had been settled. We sat in his place, Dev having a beer and me digging into a ginger calamari appetizer from Ling-Ling's, part of an unofficial thank-you from Ling2, who would inherit the business once Ling-Ling was put away.

"What I don't understand," I said to Dev, "is how Ling-Ling got hold of the birds. I mean, she had to be working with somebody inside the aviary. No forced entry, right?"

Devin paused to pull at his beer. "Right. Did you notice those green eggs with the purple spots in the kitchen?"

"Yeah. The ones she brought through customs."

"She got them through the aviary's exotics marketing program. Ordered them for her catering business. Perfectly legit, but it was just her cover for getting in to pick up the *sedonai*. She bribed some poor schmoe to kipe the birds for her."

"Schmoe is going down, yes?"

Devin nodded. "Deep down."

I licked the last of the calamari crumbs off my plate and sat up to wash my face. "Well, Dev, I gotta shove off. I'm escorting a lady to dinner."

His eyebrows went up. "Anyone I know?"

"Deputy-Agent Leila, since you ask."

Leila and Butch had finally been given official status with Gamma Station Security as a result of the *Cygnius sedonai* Caper. I was proud of them, and had already celebrated with Butch, spending an evening going through the trash bin back of Molly's. Thumbs are a wonderful thing, yes indeedy.

Tonight, though, was going to be something else. Leila was a class act, and I'd arranged a very special entertainment for her. I waited to see if Devin was going to comment, but he just sat watching me, swigging on his beer. I headed for the door and reached up to press the switch.

"Good luck, tiger," I heard Devin say softly as I left.

Leila was waiting for me in the corridor outside Elsa's place. I didn't ask how she'd gotten out, and she didn't offer to enlighten me. For a cat with ordinary thumbs, she was pretty damn clever.

"You look beautiful," I said, admiring her glossy coat.

"Thank you, cher," she purred as we started toward the rotunda. "And I owe you thanks as well for taking the heat off me in that horrid kitchen. That was a gentlemanly thing to do."

I could have told her I'd done it for the birds, but I didn't. It wasn't entirely true.

"So, Leon, cher. Where are we going?"

"I have a place in mind if it's all right with you. You like Chinese?"

For a second she froze, and her tail twitched once, sharply. Then she relaxed.

"Of course, cher. I trust you. You have excellent taste."

I smiled, and rubbed against her slightly as we strolled through the rotunda filled with soft, evening lighting. I knew this would be the start of a beautiful friendship.

Recipe: New Mexican Cocoa

This variation on Mexican style cocoa will warm you up on a cold night. The anise seed evokes biscochitos, a favorite New Mexican cookie (our official State Cookie, in fact).

Ingredients (per serving):
  1-1/4 c milk
  2 T cocoa powder
  2 T brown sugar (or agave syrup or honey)
  1/2 t cinammon
  1/4 t red chile powder
  1/8 t hand ground anise seed (optional)
  dash salt
  1/4 t vanilla

Preparation:
In saucepan over medium heat, scald milk (heat until just below boiling). While milk is heating, measure remaining ingredients into a small bowl, adding vanilla last. Stir with fork until well blended. Whisk into milk, simmer and stir for three minutes. Serve.

Coyote Ugly

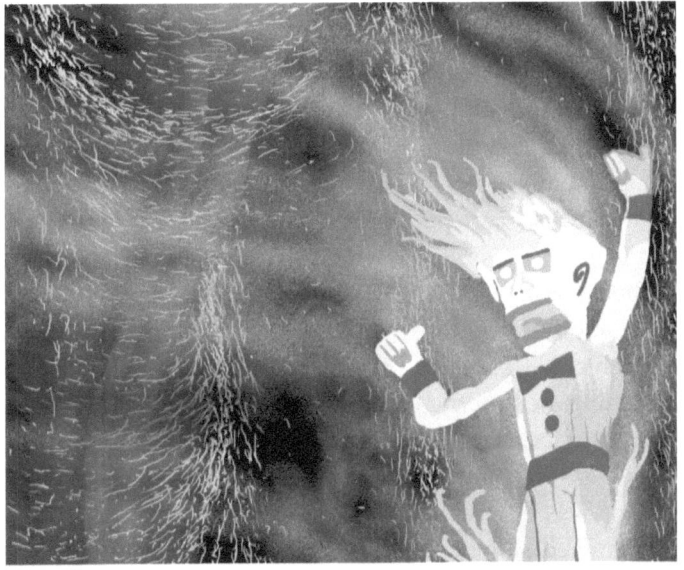

Eva scuffed her feet on the polished brick of Lincoln Avenue as she crossed the plaza. She walked ungracefully, stumping along, her new carving tucked carefully in her arms. She passed the galleries and boutiques without glancing in the windows. Their contents—designer fashions, bizarre "art," and the inescapable coyotes; bandana-adorned caricatures in pastel blues, pinks, and greens—were no part of her Santa Fe.

She paused to watch the workers setting up a bandstand for tomorrow night. It sent her back to Fiestas years ago; driving out from the pueblo to picnic on the hood of the pickup in Fort Marcy Park, with mariachis playing and kids and dogs rolling in the dirt. She remembered playing with the wind when her mother wasn't looking, weaving twists of air into dust devils—miniature cyclones of stinging sand. Sometimes, when her older brother Joe had been pushing her, she would send a dust devil to plague him. She would laugh while he spat dust and rubbed his eyes, and Grandfather would laugh with her. Grandfather was the only one who didn't scold her for her wind tricks. Mother, if she noticed, would silence them both with a fierce glare. But on that one night of the year, even Mother could not frighten Eva.

Fiesta marked the end of summer and always began with the burning of Zozobra—Old Man Gloom—a puppet effigy, everyone's symbol for their worst troubles. When the flames rose around his giant paper head and his eyes began to glow with green fire, everyone felt the magic of that purge. Eva remembered softly chanting, "No more trouble, no more fear, no more for another year," while Grandfather's warm arms and an old wool blanket kept out the sharp wind. She wouldn't dream of imagining her mother as Zozobra, but she let the hurt of being scolded burn away in the fireworks.

That was a long time ago. Fiesta was different now; everything was different.

Eva walked slowly past the Palace of the Governors, where she'd sat under the portico helping Grandfather sell his carvings on many a lazy, dusty afternoon. Kachinas, carved the old Hopi way (the Hopi were Grandfather's people) from a single cottonwood root, and painted in the summer colors or the winter colors by Grandfather with Eva helping. Now the kachinas were intricate meaningless sculptures that sold for thousands of dollars in hushed carpeted galleries.

Eva stopped at the corner where Grandfather had liked to sit, back in the shade behind the half-wall at the eastern end of the portico. Back then the plaza smelled of sunshine on dry dirt, cottonwood breezes, and the warm leather whiff of La Fonda on the corner, where Eva would run to fetch a lemonade with the shiny nickel Grandfather gave her. Now it was all expensive restaurants and the fancy perfumes of rich patrons and sightseers. You even had to have a permit, certifying you were a

"Native American," to sell under the portico.

She turned her eyes away from the silent hawk-faces of the traders in the shadows and clutched her little package tighter, walking head down, away from the plaza. The *turistas* in their bright holiday clothes gave her a wide berth. Indians were for staring at, not for talking to. No one wanted to say hello to an ugly Tewa girl walking down Palace Avenue.

She wound her way through the streets to an old adobe house, trim newly painted bright turquoise, that bore a copper plaque inscribed "Alamosa Gallery." Eva stepped inside and stood blinking after the bright sunlight.

A young woman looked up from the antique desk. Pretty, blonde, slim. She could be a model. She could be on TV. Eva clutched her package tighter. Inside it was the only beauty she had.

One bag ugly—you go to bed, you put a bag over her head.

"Can I help you?"

Eva stepped forward. "I'm here to see Mrs. Rougier." Her tongue stumbled over the foreign word.

"Do you have an appointment?"

"She knows I'm coming, " said Eva, fighting the cringe inside her. "I said I would come today."

"I see. Well, let me tell her you're here. What's your name?"

"Eva Trujillo," said Eva, struggling to keep her voice above a whisper.

The pretty girl's heels rapped hollowly on the wooden floor as she left the room. Eva was alone again, staring at sculpture and paintings illuminated by track lighting hung from the ceiling's ancient *vigas*.

She wandered down the room, gazing briefly at pieces that stirred nothing in her. Cowboy bronzes, static pot-and-squash still-lifes, views of Chimayo in every kind of weather. Time-worn images that were sure to please the tourists, interspersed with cactus collages in neon hues and other new "Southwestern" art.

Even the Gorman, occupying a place of honor above the mantel, held little meaning for her. The shapeless woman, huddled in her blanket, only reminded Eva of how the world saw her. She shivered.

Two bag ugly—you put a bag over her head and one over yours in case hers slips.

"Here she is!"

Eva turned as she heard the footsteps coming down the hall. Mrs. Rougier, holding out a perfectly manicured hand. "I'm so glad you came in today! This is Ms. Messersmith, one of our best customers."

"Hello," said Eva, shaking Ms. Messersmith's hand in her own cold one.

The woman wore a heavy squash-blossom necklace over her black silk blouse. Her face was sharp and she didn't smile. She avoided looking at Eva after the first glance, turning back to Mrs. Rougier.

"Eva is a very promising new artist," smiled Mrs. Rougier. Large silver earrings flashed out through her auburn hair. "Let's see what you've brought, shall we?" She led them over to the desk, where Eva unwrapped her carving.

It was a fawn. A beautiful baby, lifting innocent eyes to a new world. Eva had let the wood's own dappling form its markings, brought the whorls to life in shaping muscle. She smiled softly at it, looking up from its nest of paper.

"Very pretty." Ms. Messersmith sounded bored.

"Why, yes, Eva, it's lovely," said Mrs. Rougier.

Eva looked from one woman to the other, her heart sinking. "You don't like it."

"No, it's very good," said Mrs. Rougier, with a glance at her client. "It's just not the style Ms. Messersmith is looking for. We'll show it, of course. Heather, make out a consignment slip for it."

The pretty girl nodded and placed a form in her typewriter. Eva resisted the impulse to snatch up the carving again.

"Ms. Messersmith is looking for a piece for her foyer—"

"Something that reflects the desert—savage, stark. My home is designed to capture that feeling."

Eva nodded. She could imagine Ms. Messersmith's home;

had seen pictures of such homes in magazines. All angles and skylights, with freestanding adobe walls inside, built only to display expensive interpretations of the desert's starkness.

"Perhaps you're working on something along that line? We could stop by your studio and see?" said Mrs. Rougier.

A glimmer of interest appeared in Ms. Messersmith's eyes. Eva opened her mouth to refuse, but Mrs. Rougier interrupted.

"Yes, why don't we, it would be lovely! Eva has a delightful little studio—in the older part of town."

In the poorer part of town, thought Eva, why don't you just say it. Aloud, she said, "I don't have guests come there. I can bring a new carving here."

"Oh, no, I wouldn't dream of troubling you to walk so far again, Eva. We'll just drop by tomorrow, say four-ish? We won't be in your way, I promise. Don't you think, Frances?"

Ms. Messersmith nodded. "Charming."

"Thank you so much, Eva. We'll see you tomorrow."

Dismissed, Eva had nothing to do but trudge slowly home.

◈

Joe was there. She could tell by the smell of the room—a hint of tobacco and beer. She glanced at the stove and saw he'd been into the stew she'd left simmering.

She put the receipt for her carving on the work table and walked over to the kitchenette, began to clean up the mess he'd left, wondering why she put up with it. To get away from her family's demands and criticisms, wasn't that why she'd left the pueblo? If she were a white woman, she could have just thrown her brother out.

"Hey, Eva." Slam of the bathroom door.

She turned on the water in the sink. Hot bubbles foamed over her hands. "You sell?"

Eva shook her head.

"Shit. Give me twenty, then."

She fought the rising fear and anger. "I don't have it."

"Well, you better get it."

"Go away, Joe."

He muscled up beside her as he'd done when they were kids, thrusting his barrel chest forward from skinny hips. Eva turned her head and stared hard into his eyes, the way she'd defended herself all the years. Her look said, don't push me, or I'll set the wind on you. She held it, praying he wouldn't hear her heart pounding.

He backed down, eyes growing shifty and nervous; he shuffled away. Eva breathed again, rinsed a dish and set it in the rack.

"I gotta pay somebody," Joe said, whiny now.

"I can't help you."

"Shit."

He pulled a beer out of the refrigerator and popped it open. Eva dried her hands and went to her work table, taking out a new piece of cottonwood. It was silky smooth under the bark, soft and pale. Two little knots right together reminded her of eyes—an owl?

She stroked it, and sighed. An owl was not Southwestern enough. People carved owls back east.

She set the wood back on the shelf and took up another piece. This one was twisted, deformed. Like Santa Fe.

Joe belched.

"Go away, Joe. I can't concentrate."

"Listen to the big artist."

Eyes flared. "Shut up!"

"You haven't sold nothing since the Market."

"That's more than you've done. If you want any money you'd better leave me alone to do my work."

"You should go back to the pueblo and get married."

"I mean it, Joe."

"'Cept nobody'd take you. You coyote ugly."

"Get out!"

The shifty look came back, and his eyes slid away from hers. He got up and pitched his empty in the sink. Grabbed his denim jacket from a chair back, and headed for the door with a parting shot.

"Women aren't supposed to work wood. Grandfather was crazy to teach you. A woman should get married, have kids. That's what you're good for."

He dodged out as a whirlwind of pencils, dust, and small objects blasted across the room and into the door behind him. Eva's anger drained and she blinked stupidly at the mess. Then she got up to fetch the broom.

❧

Coyote ugly—you chew your arm off to get away the next morning rather than wake her up.

Eva rubbed her temples, then her eyes. The tiny light on her work table cast a golden pool of brightness in the dim room. In the pool lay the twisted stick she'd been trying to coax into life. It had a rattlesnake's head—sharp fang danger—and the beginnings of rattles, but in between it was just a stick, stripped of bark and with a few scales carved in.

Sighing, Eva got up and went to the kitchenette, lit the stove and put the kettle on. Then she walked over to the metal shelves where she kept her tools and her few books.

On the top shelf lived Coyote, little eyes shining black up by the cracked plaster ceiling. Gently Eva lifted him down.

Grandfather had carved him while Eva watched, and given him to her before he died. She remembered receiving Coyote from trembling, blotched hands. Now she set him in the pool of light on her table. He stood half crouched, gazing intently, poised to fight or to flee. Warm memories washed over Eva as she looked at him.

Every curve, every line, every hair lovingly carved was a lesson. Grandfather had talked as he worked the wood, telling her stories, how Coyote had tricked, stolen, cheated, and been tricked and cheated in return. Yet there was always another layer of meaning, peeled back like bark from satiny wood.

Coyote never lost his innocent wonder at life. Coyote learned his lessons the hard way and in this he was a teacher. He did what he had to, he survived, on his own.

"Coyote is like you, Eva," Grandfather had said. "He frightens silly humans with his mischief." And Eva had shrunk against the tree-roots.

"Coyote is like me, too," said Grandfather, as little curls of wood fluttered off his fingers onto his faded dungarees. "He has no friend but himself. He licks when he can lick, he bites when he must bite. He's free."

"But you have me, Grandfather. I'm your friend."

"You are? Are you sure I won't ... bite you!" He caught her up, tickling, and Eva's shrieks filled the summer sky.

The kettle screamed; Eva hurried to turn it off. She made coffee and carried her cup back to the table. Set Coyote back from the light, where he watched while she picked up the snake-stick.

Tiny flakes of wood fell from her hands to the table. Every couple of minutes Eva sent a twist of air across to carry the debris into the wastebasket at one side.

Each puff of air was an act of defiance. At home, her mother would have punished her for it. "You want people to think you're a witch?"

Eva remembered the beating she'd received one winter during the Turtle dance, the year her mother had caught her using wind to sweep the house instead of a broom. She'd been terrified just at the sight of the *Tsave Yoh*, with their masks and their Spanish whips, and after they beat her they told her mother to tap on the chimney if Eva was bad again, and they'd come and take her away to their labyrinths under the hills.

"And if we find you are a witch, we will eat you," they'd told her.

That night, as she lay shivering in her bed, trying to weep as quietly as she could, Grandfather had laid a hand over her mouth, and silently placed Coyote under her arm. She had never slept so well.

Eva looked up from the stick in her hands to Coyote watching warily from the shadows. Smiling, she reached out to stroke his back.

"You are my only friend," she whispered.

Coyote just kept watching.

☾

At four the next day Eva sat at her table, nervously listening as she whittled her stick. It still wasn't a snake. Maybe it would never be one.

She held it at arm's length. It looked like a stick. She put it down and pushed away from the table.

Eva went to the stove and put on the kettle. it was still hot from the last time she'd boiled it, but she put it on anyway. She wiped the spotless counter and looked around the room. It was tidy and comfortless. It needed painting. Eva sighed and sat down again, picking up her carving.

The long, straight section was the least snake-like. Maybe a slight twist would bring it to life. She picked up her knife and gently scraped at the carved scales, finding smoothness beneath, her mind already picturing the arc of scales up the side of the wood. Yes, much better. She glanced up at Coyote, still watching from the back of the table. He seemed to approve.

A sharp knock at the door made her start. Eva rose and smoothed her skirt as she went forward. The door creaked as she pulled it open.

"Hello, Eva," said Mrs. Rougier, stepping inside. "Didn't you hear the bell?"

"It doesn't work," said Eva, closing the door behind Ms. Messersmith.

"Oh, yes," laughed Mrs. Rougier. "I forgot."

She was wearing a skirt painted with Hopi designs in pink and purple, a pink woolen shawl, pink suede boots. She unwrapped the shawl from her shoulders and dropped it on Eva's chair. Ms. Messersmith wore black, and a sour look. She stood just inside the door, gazing around the room.

"Would you like some coffee?"

"That would be lovely, thank you, Eva. Oh, is this your latest piece?"

Eva glanced to where Mrs. Rougier stood by the work table,

nodded. She put a filter and coffee in the top of her old battered pot, poured hot water over. It spattered in the bottom half, and a warm smell arose.

"You see, Frances? A snake! Isn't it lovely?"

Eva carried cups of hot coffee to the ladies. Mrs. Rougier had the carving in her hands, turning it around.

"See how she's done the tail? Look at these rattles. Eva, isn't there something about the rattles?"

"They grow a new one every year."

"So this snake would be one, two -"

"What's that, some kind of fox?"

Eva looked up, saw Ms. Messersmith pointing at Coyote. Mrs. Rougier stopped counting. Eva stepped around the table and picked him up.

"No," she said. "He's a coyote."

"Oh, let me see," cried Mrs. Rougier, taking Coyote from Eva's hands. "Oh, how beautiful it is! Frances, look!"

"I never saw a coyote that wasn't howling at the moon," said Ms. Messersmith.

"That's wolves," said Eva, fighting anger. "Wolves howl at the moon. Coyotes sing to each other."

"Oh, it's lovely, Eva! Why haven't you brought it to the gallery?"

"I didn't carve him." Eva reached for Coyote, but Mrs. Rougier turned away to her client.

"Look at his eyes, they almost look alive! Did you paint them, Eva?"

"They're beads."

"Very good," nodded Ms. Messersmith, running her hand along Coyote's back. Eva clenched her fists at her sides.

"How much?" asked Ms. Messersmith.

"He's not for sale."

"Oh, Eva, you must sell it! Such a beautiful piece! It should be on display where it can be admired."

Eva could hear the front door opening. She felt panic rising, stepped forward and took Coyote back. "My grandfather made him. He's not for sale." She hurried to the shelves against the back wall.

"I want him," said Ms. Messersmith. "Just name your price."

Eva stretched to place Coyote back up in his corner. "Not for sale," she repeated.

She turned back to the room. Ms. Messersmith looked offended, Mrs. Rougier disappointed. Behind them Joe stood in the doorway. With a tiny jerk of her head she told him to leave. She was not sure whether to be glad when he obediently closed the door.

Ms. Messersmith's coffee cup clacked hard on the work table. "I've seen enough."

"Oh, Eva, I hope you'll reconsider. It doesn't matter if you didn't carve the piece...." Mrs. Rougier faltered under Eva's silent gaze. "Or maybe you could carve another one? Yes, your *own* work! That would be lovely, don't you think, Frances?"

"Mm," grunted Ms. Messersmith.

Mrs. Rougier's smile fluttered hesitantly around her face. "Well, I think we should go now. We don't want to keep Eva from her work." She retrieved her shawl and hurried to the door where Ms. Messersmith waited. "Thank you so much, Eva. Be sure to bring the snake by when it's finished."

Eva watched from the door as they went down the uneven stone steps to where a silver Mercedes was parked. Hurrying away from her because she wasn't what they wanted her to be. It made her angry.

She had tried—she'd spent hours on the snake. Instead they wanted Coyote, whom they could never, never understand.

The air was sharply cool already, hinting of fall. Eva shivered and closed the door.

She sat down at her work table, but did not pick up her knife. Instead she stared up at Coyote, crouching in his corner.

The door creaked open; Joe.

"Who were they?"

Eva's gaze dropped to her hands clasped in her lap. "Mrs. Rougier owns the gallery. She brought a customer over."

"They buy?"

"Maybe a commission."

Joe grunted and headed for the fridge. Eva watched him fix a sandwich. He took the sandwich and a beer and plopped down on her bed, turning on the TV.

She frowned, wishing he would go away. It was hard to concentrate when he was around. Sighing, she got up and poured herself a cup of coffee, brought it back and sat down to work. The TV blared.

Slowly, patiently, she began to coax the snake out of its stick. The twist she'd added lent just the right movement to the form. Eva sighed, anger fading, and bent closer, beginning to enjoy this new carving. She deepened the scale cuts, added more detail to the rattles, feeling the snake's emotion begin to emerge. Forgetting the TV, forgetting demands from Mrs. Rougier and Joe, she lost herself in the work and felt free; only her hands and the knife, and the beauty she was creating, existed.

After a while she stretched and looked around, noticing the room beyond her work light was dim. The *Sangre de Cristos* glowed pink outside her window; sunset. She flipped on the light switch on her way to the bathroom.

As she washed her hands, she looked up at herself in the mirror and smiled. Set in her flat face her eyes glowed with warm excitement; triumph of creation. Times like this were good, she thought, drying her hands.

The front door creaked, then shut.

"Joe?"

No answer, TV still blaring. She went over and turned it off, picked up Joe's dirty plate and beer can, put them on the counter and returned to her table. As she sat she glanced up with a smile at Coyote.

He was gone.

With an anguished cry she jumped up, knocking over her chair as she ran for the door. Yanking it open, she saw Joe halfway up the street, Coyote tucked under his arm. He turned, saw her, ran.

"Joe!" she screamed.

For a moment she stared in disbelief, then she snatched her keys from the nail behind the door and slammed it behind her as she flew down the steps and into the street. Joe was rounding the corner, heading for Agua Fria Street. Eva tore after him as fast as she could.

She reached the corner just in time to see him turning east. The chill evening air burned her lungs as she gasped it in. She followed.

As she started across the street a turning car shrieked its brakes at her. Eva screamed back at it, then kept running, the driver's curses fading behind her and her heart pounding.

Joe was leading her toward the plaza. The closer she got, the more people and the fewer cars she met.

Fiesta was beginning, and soon the plaza would be swarming with pedestrians. The streets were already blockaded. Eva dreaded the crowd where she might easily lose Joe. One dark head in a denim jacket looked much like another.

She reached the southwest corner of the plaza and stood gasping, eyes searching the crowd. At the far corner she spotted Joe, and forced her aching legs to run again. He struck north, and Eva knew a moment's dread—he was heading for the gallery, and would reach it before her.

Then joy burst into her mind. The gallery was closed, Mrs. Rougier was treating her best customers to a gourmet picnic in Fort Marcy Park, to watch Zozobra. Eva would catch up with Joe at the gallery, and take Coyote back.

Brushing past tourists in festive colors and locals in their own fashion statements she hurried uphill. The light was fading fast and Eva could hear the dull roar of many voices and a distant throb of mariachi music.

She slipped onto the twisted street that led to Alamosa Gallery and the crowd thinned suddenly. She ran on.

Slowing to a walk as the gallery came into view, Eva saw Joe staring at its locked door. She closed her parched mouth and breathed the crisp air through flaring nostrils. Joe turned and saw her.

"They're gone," she called, and in the same moment Joe sprang from porch and dashed up the street.

With a cry Eva followed, slowing by the gallery door just

long enough to recognize Mrs. Rougier's handwriting on the note taped to it. Joe turned north again between two buildings, making for Fort Marcy.

Breathing hurt now. Eva focused on continuing to move.

She crossed streets choked with people and got soft dirt in her shoes in rough alleyways. Occasionally she remembered to look for Joe. She spotted him twice; they were moving across the tide of people heading for the park's gates.

Across the arroyo, uphill skirting a gently eroding bank, and suddenly Eva was above the park and Zozobra loomed before her, the huge white-robed figure with its black bow tie and buttons, dwarfing the nearby buildings, standing still in the darkness like an actor waiting for his cue while tiny mariachis warbled at his feet. Beneath him the park teemed with people— no lazy picnics now. People crammed through the gates, shouldering each other for a view.

Eva stopped, panting. Her head throbbed and her legs were shaking. She looked around for Joe. The mariachis flourished to an end and the sea of people below her applauded, yelling and whistling over the unintelligible announcer's voice that boomed through speakers and echoed off the hillside.

From her vantage point Eva could see tiny figures moving forward to positions behind Zozobra, ready to work the cables that moved his arms and head. She searched for her brother among them. Then she spotted a pale gleam against denim; Coyote's head peeking from beneath Joe's arm.

Joe was scanning the crowd below, searching the picnic cloths which were the only spaces not totally covered with bodies. Eva began to work her way toward him.

Small white-sheeted torch bearers filed across the platform and down the steps, performing their traditional opening dance. A part of Eva responded, remembered excitement and anticipation awakened as the drums began their slow heavy pounding and Zozobra uttered his first low moan.

She dragged her mind back to her brother and hurried forward. Joe had climbed down the hillside heading for the park. Eva scrambled after him, puffs of dust kicked up from soft caliche.

She kept his bobbing head in sight; the only face not turned toward Zozobra. He had reached the fence and was starting to climb it.

Eva began to run, but stopped as a policeman accosted Joe from the other side of the fence. Joe dropped to the ground, started back up the hill at an angle. Eva scrambled after.

A flash of light and a roaring cheer announced the entrance of the Fire Dancer. From the corner of her eye Eva glimpsed silver and red flying ribbons, but she kept her attention on Joe and caught up with him halfway up the hill. She grabbed his arm.

"Get off!" he yelled, still climbing up the hill, dragging her with him.

"Coyote's mine, Joe! Give him back!"

"You can carve another, big shot artist." He tried to wrench his arm away. "Let go, bruja!"

"Give him back! She won't buy from you anyway."

"Yes she will. You watch."

"No!"

Eva grabbed for Coyote. The back of Joe's hand slammed into her face and she fell, white lights flashing in her head.

Zozobra's outraged howl penetrated the ringing in her ear, and softer voices nearer asking, "You all right?"

Eva struggled to her feet, brushing off dust and helping hands, and ploughed her way backup the embankment. Joe was running north; he would skirt behind Zozobra's puppeteers to the west, to sneak through the clubhouse and into the park.

Eva tried to run but every step brought pain; she stood with tears streaming down her face, watching the dark form slide through shadows along the back of the hill, while Zozobra flailed his giant arms at the fire dancer's threat and the crowd chanted, "Burn him, burn him!"

Twin waterfalls of fireworks flared to life on either side of Zozobra, illuminating Joe's denim back, and a sudden breeze lifted the failing sparks. Without thought Eva caught the breeze and fed it, pouring anger into it and wrenching it into a screw.

The crowd gasped as the vortex caught dust and sparks and swelled suddenly. Eva's scream of anger joined Zozobra's roar and the dust devil leapt taller than the puppet, sucking the fireworks into itself and spitting sparks in all directions. She pushed it toward Joe.

He was still running but the devil caught him and he stood struggling for balance, buffeted, dust and sparks flying about his head. Zozobra was burning a few yards away, fire glowing inside his howling mouth; Eva caught a strand of flame and wove it into her whirlwind.

The fire was hers now, and into it she put not only Joe but Mrs. Rougier, Ms. Messersmith, her mother. All the people who pushed her; she gave them all to the flames, the purging fire of Zozobra, flames and the white heat of her rage blotting out everything else.

Vaguely she heard screaming; the crowd was frightened by the fire. Silly people, she thought. The fire's good. Let it burn away your troubles.

The flaming whirlwind stood like a torch against the night, dwarfing Zozobra. Someone near her cried, "It's beautiful!" and Eva smiled.

Joe's jacket was on fire. He flung his arms up over his head and fell to his knees, flames dancing over his back. Coyote dropped to the ground.

Shrieks filled the air; the crowd's hysteria obliterated the drums and Zozobra's amplified howls. Dark shapes were swarming up the hillside like cockroaches. Joe disappeared behind the tide but the whipping flames kept the rescuers at bay.

The wind had quickened the fire and Zozobra ceased to thrash, abandoned by his manipulators, his eyes glowing green in his burning head and bits of flame already falling to the ground from limp skeletal arms. The recorded drums continued but Zozobra was silent. Shocked chatter ran through the crowd, someone nearby whimpered.

Enough. Eva sighed and let go of the flames. The dust devil sailed gently overhead, whispering now as its power dissipated.

Pandemonium erupted in the park. Eva ignored the frightened, excited voices; she slowly climbed the steep embankment and drank in the deep, cool night.

A mass of firemen and policemen were swarming like ants around where Joe had fallen. An ambulance that had been standing by drove up, and she glimpsed Joe standing, arguing, then being strapped onto a stretcher.

A pang of sadness was gone in an instant; Joe had earned his punishment. All their lives he had pushed her, now Eva had finally pushed back. She knew he wouldn't bother her again.

Looking at Zozobra, now engulfed in flame but forgotten by his audience, she thought of the old tradition; burn your troubles for a year. Eva smiled. She was free.

And she was beautiful. You didn't have to have a pretty face to be beautiful, you didn't have to be what other people wanted. You just had to make your work—carving or fire—the best it could be. She knew that now.

She looked up at the stars, hundreds of them piercing the black night. Grandfather's voice echoed in her mind, telling of Coyote, who set out to help place the stars in patterns but then scattered them over the sky because it was too much work. It made the others angry, but Coyote said, "It's better that way," and he was right.

Something soft and warm touched her leg. Eva looked down into Coyote's glowing eyes.

Beautiful Coyote. Yes, she was like him. She didn't need anyone else to say so. No one else could ever understand her own particular beauty.

She picked Coyote up, cradling him to her, and padded through the back streets toward home, attended by summer's last sweet breeze.

On Swan's Wings

A shorter version of this story appeared in Cricket *magazine.*

Valentina Alberti leaned out of the window of her bedchamber to see how close the sun might be to setting. Tonight was the last night of Carnival, and she and her family had been bidden to a masked ball at the Palazzo Medici.

Golden light slanted through Florence's streets, lighting the ornate walls of the villas and warming the stone paving. It was not warm enough to chase the February chill from the air. Soon the sun would set and night would throw its cold blanket over the city.

Valentina shivered. In the street below, her neighbors were already celebrating the last, frantic night of excess before the beginning of Lent. The laughing cries of young men—half-earnest, half-mocking—rose to her.

"Valentina! Valentina, will you be mine?"

She ignored them, the sons of neighbors, merchants and citizens of Florence. She was no longer permitted to play with them. She was a lady now, and if her father had his way, she would marry a Medici.

By happenstance, today was also her sixteenth birthday, the day of the saint whose name her father had made her burden. Valentine, friend of lovers, martyred for marrying Roman couples in defiance of Emperor Claudius's ban many hundreds of years ago. Married men made bad soldiers, so the emperor had decreed none should marry. Valentine had married them in secret.

"Valentina! My heart is yours, *cara mia!*"

She pulled the mullioned window closed. Those boys had taunted her thus ever since they were all children, playing in the street together, blissfully unaware of future responsibilities. Every year on her birthday they had teased her. *Be mine, Valentina! Marry me, Valentina*—to Beatrice Rossi!

Once she had even pretended to conduct a secret marriage, like her namesake. When her mother had found out, Valentina had been scolded for mocking the holy rites and punished with confinement to her room.

She turned away from the window and looked at her gown for the evening, lying on her bed ready for her to don. A new gown, commissioned by her father especially for the masquerade this evening.

The Medicis' ball would be more controlled than the Carnival festivities that were already spilling into the city's streets. Her family would never permit her to attend such wild celebrations as those, though she might watch them from the safety of her chamber window.

She swallowed a sigh, reminding herself that it was a great honor to be considered worthy of marriage to a Medici. The Medicis ruled Florence, and only took their wives from the very best of its families.

She touched the gown, certainly the richest she had ever worn. It was of velvet, deep red with narrow stripes of gold, soft as a kitten's fur against her fingers. The sleeves were slashed so that the white silk lining could be pulled through. The overdress, which was long and full, cape-like in back, was of heavy ivory brocade in a large floral design, so rich with gilt thread that it almost looked like cloth of gold. It was bound below the bosom with a belt embroidered with roses and adorned with pearls.

A lady's dress, designed to proclaim her family's wealth. A dress that offered its wearer's riches to the highest bidder.

Her chamber door opened and her mother came in, carrying with her something large bundled in cotton cloth. She was already dressed for the ball, in a gown of green floral brocade. Her hair was taped to her head in a coronet bound with green and gold ribbons, and she wore a slightly worried smile.

"Valentina! You have not begun to dress yet! It is high time, child. Come and see what your father has bought for you to wear."

With these words her mother laid the bundle on Valentina's bed. Carefully she unwrapped the cloth, revealing a magnificent mask, or rather a headdress, for the mask was but the smallest part of it.

It was a swan, brilliant white, with sapphire eyes and elegant, swooping feathers. Valentina had never seen its like. So beautiful and fragile! She felt a little flutter in her heart as her mother lifted it and placed it on her head.

"Bring the mirror, Giada," said her mother.

Her mother's maid brought forward a large hand mirror and held it up so that Valentina could see herself. The white swan was brilliant, its feathers softly draping behind her head, its neck a graceful curve rising from her brow. Her dark eyes peeped shyly through the jeweled mask as her hand crept up to brush against a soft feather.

That was not her standing there, not Valentina. It was someone else, a beautiful, alluring maiden who was brave instead of shy, confident in anonymity. That lady had no need for modesty—she stood under the protection of the swan's white wings. She was a lady whose heart was free, destined for love.

"You will shine tonight, my daughter," said her mother, squeezing Valentina's shoulders. "You will win the heart of your future husband."

Valentina turned. "Who is he, Madre? Has my father made an agreement?"

A slight crease formed on her mother's brow. She took away the swan mask and set it carefully back into its nest of cloth.

"Nothing is certain yet. You are not to trouble yourself about it. Just enjoy yourself at the ball, and leave such concerns to your father."

Valentina asked no more questions, but silently obeyed as her mother and Giada dressed her in the white silk underdress, then the velvet gown, then the brocade overdress. While Giada pulled the linings of her sleeves into tiny puffs through each little slash, Valentina thought about her future husband.

It could not be Lorenzo, the old Capo's elder son, for he was married. The younger, Giuliano, was fifteen, and already had a mistress according to Giada, who always knew the city's gossip. It would be the duty of his wife, whenever he chose to wed, to disregard the mistress.

Could Valentina's father have arranged for her to wed Giuliano? If so, she would be the envy of every young lady in Florence. She would live in a grand palazzo, with rich furnishings and many servants. She would give her husband sons and stay home to care for them while he cavorted with his mistresses.

Valentina stifled a sigh, knowing her mother would reprove her if she sighed aloud. She sat at her dressing table while Giada brushed out her hair and bound it back from her brow with a wide ribbon tight across the back of her head, but let it fall in loose waves behind. A maiden's hair was worn loose. A matron's was reserved to her husband's private enjoyment.

How strange to think that she might soon have a husband. Valentina had not met Giuliano de'Medici, though she had sometimes seen him in church. She tried to imagine herself as his bride, and could not.

Of course, her future husband might be someone else. There were many lesser branches of the Medici clan, many cousins and kinsmen. Valentina knew, though, that her father would strive to make the most advantageous match possible.

At last her mother picked up the swan mask once more and carefully set it on Valentina's head. She felt again the secret flutter of boldness, hidden behind the swan's wings.

Her mother donned her own mask, a simple green domino, then hurried Valentina downstairs. Giada followed, bringing both their cloaks.

Valentina's father waited in the atrium. Signore Alberti was handsome, and kind enough, though his business kept him from spending much time with his family. Tonight he wore his best tunic of black velvet trimmed with gold and silver, a matching hat with a dagged-edged drape, and a bright red mask with a long nose like Pantalone.

"Ah, Valentina! Let me look at you."

She stood still while he slowly walked around her. At last he stopped before her again and nodded.

"You look very well, Valentina. Remember that your behavior tonight will reflect on all your family."

"Yes, Padre. Thank you for the beautiful gown, and the swan."

"You are a good girl. Come, give me a kiss."

Valentina stepped forward and placed a dutiful kiss on his cheek. He then ushered her toward the door.

Giada bundled Valentina's cloak about her and helped her step into the pattens that would protect her red velvet slippers from the dirt of the street. They were awkward to walk in, but necessary in the streets of Florence, particularly tonight.

Servants waited outside the house, bearing torches to light their way. The men surrounded the Signeur Alberti and his family, forming a circle of golden torchlight around them. Outside the circle, Carnival raged in all its wild abandon.

The sun had now set, though the sky was light enough yet to see. A blue twilight cast its coldness over the city, pushed back here and there by golden candlelit windows, and by the torches surrounding the little party as they walked. The Palazzo Medici was a blaze of light that could be seen all the way from the foot of the Via Larga.

Valentina had never been to the Medicis' palazzo before, though she had seen it from afar. Torches illuminated the rustic stone arches of the entrance, and every window above was alight. A few were cracked open to let the heat of so many candles and torches escape. Valentina heard strains of lute music drifting down, and the high piercing tones of recorders.

Servants in Medici livery greeted them, leading them into the palazzo and taking away their cloaks and pattens. One of them guided the Albertis up a broad staircase. Music and laughter could be heard from above.

They entered a long chamber filled with people chattering, laughing, drinking wine, all wearing masks and costumes that ranged from the ordinary to the outlandish. A trio of musicians were tucked into a corner nearby, playing a lively tune.

A long table, draped in red cloth, ran the whole length of the room beneath the windows. It was covered with platters of roasted meats, cheeses, figs, nuts, and cakes. Candles crowded the table amidst the food, and torches burned in sconces between the windows and on the opposite wall, which bore a vivid fresco of the lush Tuscan countryside.

Valentina stood blinking at the dizzying noise and color of the assembly. Never had she seen so many people all in one room, except in church. Her father, whose eyes had been searching the crowd, now hastened his wife and daughter across the room.

At the far end of the room the old Capo sat in a massive chair, surrounded by his family. Though he was masked, old

Piero's gray curls betrayed him. He was dressed as a Roman emperor, in white robes and crowned with a golden laurel wreath. From an archway to his left, even more music, light, and laughter were pouring.

Lorenzo stood beside him, smiling and chatting with some of the guests. He was also dressed as an ancient Roman, as was the pretty lady standing with him who must be his wife. On the Capo's other side stood a young man dressed as a centurion, with a scarlet silk tunic showing beneath his gilt armor, a real gladius hanging at his hip, his sandals laced all the way up to his knees. Valentina could only see his eyes through the gilt helmet he wore, but she was sure he was Guiliano.

Her father waited for the guests ahead of them to finish speaking with their hosts. When they at last moved on, he took Valentina's hand and drew her forward.

"Greetings, friend," said Piero. He did not rise, and Valentina remembered hearing that he was troubled by gout.

"Thank you for welcoming my family, Signore," said Valentina's father, bowing low. "Allow me to present my only child."

No names were given. This was a masked ball, and the conceit was that everyone was a stranger until midnight, when they would all unmask. It was all feigned, for the better families in the city—and no one else would be invited to a party at the Palazzo Medici—all knew one another. Yet Valentina had not recognized anyone so far, except for the Capo and his family.

Valentina curtseyed before the head of the most powerful family in Florence. She held her head high, though she kept her eyes modestly lowered. She knew that not only Piero but all his kindred were watching her closely, looking for any excuse to declare her unfit to join their family.

"What a pretty little swan," Piero said. "We must see how well she flies. Signor Centurion, please escort her into the dance."

Piero nodded toward the archway at his left. The centurion bowed briefly to the emperor, then approached Valentina and bowed again, displaying a shapely leg.

"Will you dance, Lady Swan?"

She gazed into the black eyes behind the mask. She was even more certain now that this was Giuliano. She laid her hand across the arm he offered.

"Thank you, yes."

Valentina cast a glance over her shoulder at her mother as the centurion led her toward the archway. Her mother's hands were clasped tightly together before her.

The chamber into which the centurion led Valentina was as broad as the first, but much longer. It was filled with light from sconces along both walls. Many people stood talking and watching the dancers who crowded the center of the room. At the far end a half dozen musicians provided the music, lutes and flutes striving to drown out the laughter of the revelers, who only talked louder the louder the musicians played.

Giuliano drew Valentina into the dance. She recognized the music as that for Amoroso, for her mother and Giada had spent hours teaching her the steps of all the current *balli*. She stood beside Giuliano and watched him perform each figure of the dance, then repeated it herself.

Valentina realized her heart was beating very fast, not only because of the exercise. Dancing was a little like the street games she had played as a child. It made her giddy, and the shelter of the mask, even though Giuliano must know who she was, made her feel slightly bold.

Others present were taking advantage of their false shelter to behave more freely than they ordinarily would. Many were flirting together, and Valentina wondered whether she should be flirting with Giuliano. She glanced at him, thinking it should be he who began flirting, not herself, but he showed no sign of doing so.

Valentina looked away from him, watching the other dancers and seeing their enjoyment. This might be her last chance to play. She was determined to make the most of it. She had until midnight to laugh, and it was her birthday after all. She would fly free until she had to give up the swan mask.

With a start, she realized Giuliano was speaking to her as

she danced. She turned her head toward him.

"What?"

"I said you dance prettily, Lady Swan." He shouted over the chatter and the music. His voice sounded wearied, as if he found her tiresome.

"Thank you, Lord Centurion."

The music ended before she could think of a compliment in return. Guiliano took her hand and made as if to lead her to the wall, where she saw her mother standing. Before they reached it, a man somewhat taller than Giuliano stepped before them.

He was young, though older than Giuliano, she thought. Closer to Lorenzo's age, or even a little older. He wore a doublet of red velvet the exact shade and pattern of Valentina's gown. It was a new fabric, she knew, and quite costly. He must be from a family of considerable means.

His mask was formed like a long-nosed fox's face, with shiny black whiskers and rusty-red fur. Valentina glimpsed green eyes through the fox mask, and felt her heart jump.

"The next dance is Belfiore," the fox said in a voice that was smooth and seemed quiet, even in the noise of the hall. "May I have the honor of dancing it with you?"

He bowed, and his green eyes held Valentina's. She could not move or speak, she was so struck by his gentle grace. It was Giuliano who answered.

"Very well, Lord Fox, but you had better not bite my pretty swan, ha, ha."

Valentina thought his laughter a little forced. She gave her free hand to the fox, whose hand was warm and gentle as it clasped hers. The three of them returned to the dance floor as the musicians struck up a new tune.

Belfiore was a dance for two men and a lady. Valentina had practiced it with her mother and Giada, but though her feet knew the steps, this felt very, very different. Her heart was aflutter with the attention of the two strong men beside her. She tried to share her smiles equally between both her partners, but found her gaze drawn more often to the green-eyed fox.

He danced gracefully, fluidly, and seemed more elegant than

Giuliano. Perhaps that was the fault of the gaudy centurion's garb, or perhaps his quiet manner appealed more to Valentina than a Medici's arrogance. She began one step on the wrong foot, and the fox gently corrected her, while the centurion huffed with impatience.

The dance ended far too soon for her liking. As the musicians played their final flourish and the room was filled with applause, Valentina glanced at the fox and saw him watching her.

"Lord Fox," said Giuliano somewhat haughtily, "do me the kind favor of returning Lady Swan to the lady in green over there. Lady Swan, I beg you to excuse me."

Giuliano did not wait for an answer, but bowed curtly and turned away, leaving Valentina's side so abruptly that she felt her cheeks color with embarrassment. If her father had arranged for her marriage to Giuliano, he showed no sign of being pleased.

"Will you walk with me, Lady Swan?" said a gentle voice beside her.

She turned, and smiled gratefully. "Thank you, Lord Fox."

He led her toward her mother as the musicians began another dance. The center of the hall was instantly crowded again. Valentina wished the fox would ask her to dance, but he merely guided her around the other dancers and off the floor.

"That was the first time I danced Belfiore," she said, a little nervously.

"I would never have known it. You danced it perfectly."

"You are very gracious, and also very kind," she said, stealing a glance at the fox's profile. "If I danced perfectly it is because you helped me."

He smiled, but made no answer. They had reached Valentina's mother, and the fox bowed low to her, making a very handsome leg.

"Madame, I return your swan to you."

Her mother made a small courtesy. "Thank you, kind sir."

Valentina added her own thanks, and the fox turned and made another bow to her. She returned a courtesy, and shyly smiled at him. He smiled back, then stepped away and strode toward the archway at the bottom of the hall.

Valentina saw Giuliano standing there, talking and laughing with a group of young men and women. His smile flashed as he leaned toward a pretty blonde lady dressed as a shepherdess.

He had not smiled so at Valentina. She began to fear that she had failed her family.

"What did you think of him?" her mother asked.

Startled, Valentina looked up to find her mother eagerly watching her. She swallowed, and stood up a little straighter.

"Oh—he is a very good dancer."

"Is that all?"

Valentina caught her breath, and lowered her gaze. She had seen the fox join the centurion and the shepherdess.

"It was kind of him to dance with me."

"Yes, he is a kind man, or so I have heard. He will make a good husband."

Valentina looked swiftly up at her mother, who was smiling at her. Her mother nodded, taking her hand and squeezing it.

"Your father has made an agreement with him. He wanted to see you tonight before concluding the bargain. I think he is pleased with you."

Valentina's mother turned her head to look toward Guiliano, who was now listening to something the fox was saying. Valentina saw Guiliano nod, then laugh. Her heart went cold.

If Giuliano was to be her husband, she would have no joy in marriage. She would be lonely while he busied himself with city affairs, or amused himself with shepherdesses.

She bowed her head, blushing at the ingratitude of her thoughts. If she married a Medici she would never want for anything. She would be respected throughout Florence, throughout Tuscany, even throughout all Italy. Her joy would come from her children, and from upholding the family's honor.

Yet she longed for more than that. She longed for a husband who was kind and understanding. Who cared for her, as her own father cared for her mother in his quiet way.

"Come, child. You look a little warm. Let us find you a cool drink."

Her mother led her down the hall, past the dancers, past the corner where Giuliano was holding court. Valentina glanced up at the little group, and her gaze met the fox's. She felt a jolt of pain in her heart, almost as if she had been stabbed.

Who was he? Even as she wondered, she realized she might never know. She might never meet him again. Most likely she would not, unless he were a close friend of Giuliano's.

That thought gave her no pleasure, for it would be no pleasure to welcome green-eyed Lord Fox to her husband's home. She liked him far better than she would ever like Giuliano.

She followed her mother out into the first chamber, which seemed cool and dark by contrast with the hall where she had been dancing. Piero had left, but Lorenzo and his lady still stood talking with the guests who came and went.

Valentina followed her mother to the long table and accepted a goblet of cool, sweet wine. She sipped it, but her stomach twisted. Suddenly she wished she were home.

She no longer wanted to play. What good would it do her to dance until midnight? She would only meet more people she liked better than the man her parents had chosen for her husband.

Her father joined them, his face lit with a happy smile beneath the ridiculous long nose of his red mask. "My daughter, there is a noble gentleman here who wishes to make your acquaintance!"

Valentina's heart jumped with dismay. "Should we not wait until midnight?" she said, hoping to delay her doom a little longer.

Her father shook his head, and held out his hand, commanding her to attend him. "He is impatient to be presented to you, my child. Come, he is waiting in the loggia."

Impatient. Yes, that sounded like Giuliano. He did not seem to like waiting for anyone.

Valentina felt her mother's hands on her shoulders, gently urging her forward. Her father beckoned her toward the entryway. She set her wine down on the table and followed her father out, her mother keeping close behind.

She thought wildly of escaping, of running away. Perhaps she could find the fox, and they could have a secret wedding, a Valentine wedding, and be happy together.

Foolish thoughts, she knew. The fox would probably be appalled at such an idea. Certainly her parents would never forgive her.

They went up a flight of stairs to the palazzo's third story, a broad loggia that was open to the chilly night air. It was quiet here, and dark. They had left the light and laughter of the masked ball below.

Valentina looked down into the palazzo's central courtyard, where she saw statues, including one of a winged angel. How she wished she had wings, like the swan she had pretended to be. She could fly away from all her troubles.

Or she could fly without the wings, she thought bitterly, looking at the hard stone of the courtyard below. Her heart jumped sharply at the thought. Which would be worse, to throw herself to the wind, or to be bound to Giuliano de Medici?

"Signore," her father said beside her, "I have brought my daughter to meet you."

Valentina glimpsed a man standing in the darkness nearby. She lowered her gaze to the stone floor, unwilling to meet Giuliano's cold eyes. She heard his footsteps as he approached. She clasped her hands together, wishing they were not so cold.

"We are most grateful to your cousin for bringing her to your notice," her mother said brightly.

"As am I," said a quiet, gentle voice.

Valentina's gaze flew up. In the darkness she could not really see the features of the man before her, but the starlight was just enough to show her the stripes on the doublet he wore. Gold stripes on red velvet, like her gown.

"Valentina Alberti," said her father formally, "I present to you Signore Prospero de'Medici."

Prospero. She had heard the name, some cousin of Piero's, she thought. The gentleman bowed, and Valentina saw in his hand a mask, shaped like a fox's face. At that same moment she felt her mother lift the swan from her head.

She curtseyed slowly, never taking her eyes from the man before her, feeling warmth steal into her cheeks as her heart beat with excitement. The gentleman straightened, and starlight lit a glint of green in his eyes.

"I am honored to make Signorina Alberti's acquaintance," he said softly.

Valentina found her voice. "The honor is mine, signore."

She reached out her hand, and Signore de'Medici caught it in his warm clasp and bowed over it. She felt his lips brush her skin, and a tingle went all through her as her heart took flight on swan's wings.

Stranded

"You scared the piss out of me."

She dug in her purse for her cigarettes. One left. She pulled it out, crumpled the pack and tossed it into the road. It glinted, reflecting the flame of her lighter, then winked out.

She took a long drag, let it out slowly, and said "Shit."

She was perched on her suitcase on the side of the road in the middle of godforsaken nowhere. Her boyfriend was nearby, muttering obscenities as he inspected the damage to his Mustang convertible. The pickup that had forced them off the road had continued blithely on into the night, and they were alone.

"It won't start. I can't figure out the problem," he called to her, up to his elbows in the guts of the engine.

"Must've died of fright," she yelled back.

"Ah, fuck it!"

He came over, flashlight in hand and looking as pissed as she felt. He reached for her cigarette.

"Uh-uh," she said, holding it away. "It's my last one."

"Shit." He picked up her purse and began to rummage.

"Hey—"

"Last one?" He held up an unopened pack, dropping the purse back to the ground beside her. "Thanks a bunch, sugar."

"I didn't know that was in there," she protested, but held strolled away, lighting a smoke and sticking the pack in his shirt pocket.

She could just see his silhouette, head tilted up to look at the moon. The air was still and misty, making the moonlight soft, fairy-like. She hadn't noticed the fog coming in. It had been clear when they'd crashed.

Thinking of it made her shudder. Lucky they hadn't been hurt, in an open car like that. Memory replayed the bouncing, the lurching, the sick fear.

To get away from it she stood, and as she did something flickered on the outskirts of her vision. She turned, but whatever it was had gone. Vanished into the mist. She shivered.

"Wait up," she called, hurrying after him.

Her spiked heels were awkward on the rough pavement. Fuck the stockings, she thought, and kicked off the shoes, stooping to pick them up. She took a last pull on the cig—almost down to the filter—and stubbed it out on the road, then straightened, ears straining toward a faint echo.

"Was that you?"

"Was what me?" came his voice from down the road.

"I thought I heard something."

"I didn't say anything."

"Oh," she said, casting a glance around. "Wait up."

"Well, come on then."

She hobbled toward him, sharp asphalt hurting her feet through the stockings. His shape loomed out of the mist, standing in the middle of the two-lane highway, looking back the way they'd come.

"When did we pass Kingman?" he asked.

"About an hour ago, I think." She stood next to him and peered into the white blankness. "How far are we from Vegas?"

"Over thirty miles," he said, dropping the butt of his cigarette and stepping on it. "Got a long walk ahead of us—"

"Not me, not in these!" she waved the heels.

He sighed. "You can wait here, then."

"Alone? No thanks!"

"We can't just sit here. You got a better idea?"

She turned away, angry. She wanted her coat, not because she felt cold, but because she felt vulnerable in the slinky outfit she'd worn. If they were going to have to hitch a ride with some trucker, she didn't want to be ogled.

There were some new designer jeans in her suitcase; maybe she'd slip into them. Too bad she hadn't packed sneakers. But you don't wear sneakers on a romantic weekend getaway.

God, what a disaster.

She walked gingerly back to the car, rough pavement biting at the soles of her feet. Sat on the suitcase again, setting the heels down beside it, and checked her stockings for snags. Couldn't tell in the moonlight. She reached down for her purse and automatically rummaged it, then remembered about the cigarettes.

"Shit."

He had them. She didn't want to go back down the road to ask for one. Maybe she had some gum. She dug around in the purse some more. Her hand closed on a package and she pulled it out. Cigarettes.

A creepy feeling crawled across the back of her shoulders, making her shiver. She looked up sharply, looked all around. No one in sight.

She must have forgotten and bought an extra pack. She had to have. There was no one around to sneak cigarettes—her brand, no less—into her purse.

She lit up, hands shaking a little as she cupped the flame.

Stop it, she thought. You'll just make yourself nuts.

She glanced back at the car with its nose in the ditch, tangled in the barbed wire fence. Past the fence was a figure, some local ranch hand, maybe. It was hard to see. She jumped up and called "Hey!" and it faded into the mist.

"What?" shouted her boyfriend from down the road. She turned and saw him hurrying back.

"I thought I saw someone," she said. "Over by the car."

She waited for him, not wanting to investigate by herself. He walked up to the car.

"Hello," he called out. "Could you help us? Hello?" He turned back to her. "There's no one here."

"I just saw him! Behind the fence!"

He shrugged. "Not here now. If he wanted to help, he'd have stuck around." He leaned over the engine again. "Could you hold the flashlight?"

"You already said you can't fix it," she groused, limping up to the car. She peered into her seat. "Is my coat in the trunk?"

"You weren't wearing it."

"But I just had it—" she stopped. She'd just had it cleaned, specially for this trip. And she'd forgotten to pick it up from the cleaners.

"Damn it! Give me yours then."

"It's in the back seat. Or it was. Could be anywhere now, the way we bounced around."

Don't say anything, she thought. Don't start a fight. You've got to get home. Then you can chew him out for speeding around a blind curve.

She leaned over the side of the car and felt around in the back seat for his leather jacket. Instead her hands closed on wool —very familiar wool. She froze for a second, then slowly drew her floor-length, silk-lined, lightweight wool coat from under the passenger seat. She stood there holding it like it would bite her if she didn't keep an eye on it.

"Could you *please* come hold the flashlight?"

She walked to the front of the car, stopping short of the barbed wire mess. "Something very strange is going on."

He looked up from the engine. "Come around this side, there's more room."

"Did you hear what I said?"

"Baby, if we're gonna get out of here—"

"Look." She held up the coat.

"You found it. Great. Now could you—"

"Why didn't you tell me you picked it up for me?" she demanded.

"Huh? I didn't."

"You must have. I forgot to."

"No head trips, baby. Not now. If you're not going to help —"

"I'll help."

She tossed the end of her cigarette onto the road and walked around behind the car, feeling the coat all the way. It was clean, pockets empty, no tag from the cleaners. She shrugged into it, took the flashlight and pointed it where he indicated.

"It doesn't look like there's anything wrong," he said.

"Then why won't it start?"

"If I knew that—"

"Yeah, yeah."

She didn't want to get into the sort of inane conversation where they both knew they were telling each other things they'd said before. She was feeling edgy and grouchy and didn't want to talk. Instead she stared over the fence at white nothingness, thinking about the weekend she'd looked forward to, the condo they'd reserved, the show they were missing.

There was movement out in the fog. Definitely. Looked like someone walking.

"Look, there he is again!"

"Where?"

She pointed and he looked, but the mist had obscured the figure. He shook his head. "I don't see anything."

"I'm getting my jeans," she said, shoving the flashlight at him.

She hobbled back around the car and headed for her suitcase. She crouched, opened it and pulled out her jeans. A pair of sneakers—her favorite black ones—lay in the case beneath them.

"Shit!" she cried, truly frightened. She fell back, sitting down hard and nearly tumbling over backward on the sloping verge.

"What is it?" He came running up, flashlight bobbing in the mist.

"I didn't pack them," she said, shaking her head and clutching the jeans to her chest. "I know I didn't pack them."

"What are you talking about? Are you OK?"

"I didn't pack my sneakers."

He knelt beside her, gathering her into his arms. "It's OK, baby, you don't need them. It's all right."

"I'm scared."

"Shh."

She buried her face in his shirt. He held her close, rocking gently back and forth to calm her down.

She squeezed her eyes shut. Maybe she'd imagined it. Had she hit her head in the crash? Was she hallucinating? She didn't feel dizzy, but when she looked again the sneakers were still there.

"Can you see them?" she asked.

"See who?"

She pointed toward the suitcase. He glanced at it, looked back at her, frowning. "You just said you didn't pack your sneakers."

She sighed, comforted by the fact they were *both* crazy. "I didn't."

"Don't," he said. "This is not the time for this kind of game."

"I'm not playing games. I really didn't pack them."

He picked up the sneakers. "Then would you care to explain this?"

"I'd love to, but I don't have a clue."

He frowned, looking concerned now. "You should lie down. There's a blanket in the trunk—" He started to get up.

"I'm OK," she said.

"I think you're in shock, a little. You should rest."

"I'm fine."

She stood up and stared out over the barbed wire, but saw only mist. She took off her coat and tossed it in the car, then unzipped her leather miniskirt and quickly took it off, stepping into her jeans and pulling them up while he watched. Behind the appreciation in his eyes was a shadow of uneasiness. She sat down on the pavement and pulled on her sneakers, extracted a sweater from her suitcase and shrugged it on over her tube top.

"Come on, let's get out of here."

"I don't think you should be walking around," he said.

"I'm all right," she said, her voice taking on an edge.

"This place gives me the creeps. Let's go."

"We shouldn't try to walk out," he said. "I just realized we don't have any water."

With a sick certainty, she went to the car, knowing and not wanting to know that she'd find water if she looked for it. He followed her and watched as she reached into the back seat and felt around until she found a plastic bottle. It sloshed as she hefted it and handed it to him without a word.

"That's weird—"

"—you don't keep water in the car," she finished for him.

"Did you bring it?"

"No."

He frowned. "It isn't funny."

"No, it isn't." They stared at each other. "Got any cigarettes in your glove compartment?" she asked.

He pulled the pack out of his pocket and offered it. "No, in your *glove compartment*."

"No."

"Open it," she said.

He set the water bottle on the seat, opened the glove compartment, reached in and came up with something. He shone the flashlight on a pack of cigarettes. His brand.

"Cut it out," he said sharply.

"I'm not doing it!"

He gave her an angry look and stalked back toward the engine. She called after him. "What did you leave at home that you wish you had now?"

"My socket wrenches," he snapped.

"You're sure they're at home?"

"Yes."

She reached into the glove compartment and found a smooth metal case. She carried it around to the front of the car and held it out to him. He looked at her like she'd offered him a scorpion.

"In the glove compartment," she explained.

"Shit!" He took the box, opened it, picked up a socket. It gleamed softly in the moonlight. "Shit!"

She leaned against the car, staring out into the mist, and started to giggle. "Why don't you just wish the car back to life?"

"It's got a loose connection somewhere," he said.

"Oh, well no wonder. If you gave it a loose connection, no wonder it doesn't work."

He gave her a dirty look, then bent over the engine. The

socket wrench made a rachetty noise.

"Why don't you wish for a taxi?" she said. "Or a helicopter?"

"Baby, please go lie down. You're making me crazy."

She giggled again, hysteria creeping into the laughter. She couldn't stop, kept giggling and giggling until suddenly he took her by the shoulders and shook her roughly.

"Stop it!" he yelled into her face.

She gasped, hiccupped, and was quiet. She clung to him, shaking a little. "I want to get out of here," she said.

"We will, as soon as I get this fixed. Go sit down, baby. Please."

Reluctantly she moved away from him and walked back to her suitcase. She stuffed the heels and her skirt into it and closed it, carried it back to the car and set it down.

A whisper of sound reached her ears, like a far away voice, saying ".... all right.... safe now...."

"What did you say?" she asked, knowing he hadn't spoken.

"I found it! I found the connection!" He ran around to the driver's seat, turned the ignition. Nothing happened. "Aw, shit! There must be another one."

"If you say so," she said in a numb voice.

This could go on indefinitely, she realized. Despair crept over her and she glanced around at the fog. A patch of it parted and a taxicab appeared, driving toward them from the empty desert beyond the fence. She yelped, running back to her lover, and the taxi faded.

"Come on, let's get out of here!" she cried, grasping his arm.

"Let me finish," he grumped.

"You'll never finish! As long as you keep looking you'll keep finding loose wires—OHMYGOD!"

He flinched as she shouted and his head bashed into the car hood. "Ow!"

"Get down!" she yelled, dragging at his arm as she crouched beside the car.

A helicopter with blue-white running lights swooped toward them. He ducked. The chopper vanished into the mist.

All was still again.

"Sonofabitch!" he hissed, rubbing his head.

"I'm sorry," she said as they got back to their feet.

"What the hell's going on?" he demanded.

"I wish I knew! Just be careful what you think about."

"Huh?"

"Whatever we think about's turning real," she said, trying to keep the tremor out of her voice.

"Oh," he said. "Oh!!"

A shimmer disturbed the fog past the fence and she whimpered, shrinking behind him. Again she thought she heard the whisper of a voice, but couldn't make out the words.

"Did you hear that? Did you see—"

"Yes, yes," he said, shushing her. "I'm thinking."

"I want to go home," she mumbled into his shoulder blade.

"This must be some kind of weird dream," he said.

"Oh, right! We're both having the same dream?"

"Well of course not," he said, looking uncertain. "Can you feel this?" He reached out to pinch her.

"OW! Dammit!" She punched him in the ribs, then rubbed her arm where he'd pinched.

"It's not like my usual kind of dream," he admitted.

A glow of light nearby caught her attention. She gasped and grabbed his arm.

"Look," she said, pointing.

Just off the edge of the road her apartment living room had appeared. Sunlight was pouring through the windows onto her Chinese carpet. She took a couple of steps toward the vision, then looked back uncertainly.

"Don't go in," he said.

She turned back, staring at her apartment. It looked real. There was only one way to find out.

She took a deep breath, then stepped off the highway onto the plush carpet. The living room was warm and bright, and silent. She went to the sofa, picked up a cushion. It was real. It was her apartment, everything was right except—it was too clean. All the ashtrays were sparkling, and it smelled of fresh country air, not the city smog she was used to.

She walked to the window, saw empty green fields where there should have been a street filled with noisy traffic. A shiver ran down her spine and she looked back the way she'd come. The front wall was still open to the night and the deserted desert highway. Her lover stood by the wrecked car, watching her.

"It's not the same," she said. "I mean—it's the same, but it's different."

"Come out," he said, looking nervous.

She glanced around the living room again. "Yeah. Yeah, OK."

She started back, but then on impulse stepped into the kitchen and pulled two beers out of the refrigerator. She looked at the oven. What the hell, she thought. She opened it and pulled out a boxed pizza, fresh hot.

"Here," she said, handing him the beers.

"Are you sure we should eat this stuff?"

"We've been smoking the damn cigarettes!" she snapped. "I'm hungry."

She balanced the pizza box on the edge of the car and opened it. Pepperoni and mushroom; the warm smell rose enticingly. She picked up a piece, accepted the beer bottle her lover had opened for her.

"It's disappearing," he said, pointing back toward her apartment.

She bit into her pizza, holding down the panic. "I guess I can get it back if I want."

He took a swig of his beer, looked at the label and nodded.

"Where do you think we are?" he asked.

A weird keening sound rose all around them and she jumped. The air seemed to quiver like heat convection waves.

The noise faded in and out, like a bad radio signal, and a tinny-sounding voice came through it: ".... home .... you've...." Then it faded into silence.

They stared at each other.

"All right," he said, "we've got to figure this out. What started it?"

"The cigarettes," she answered. "I was out, and you found more in my purse."

"That was the first thing?"

"Yeah."

"OK. Why cigarettes?"

She shrugged.

"It doesn't make sense."

"You just noticed?" she said, and took a gulp of beer. Fizzy-cool, delicious.

"Why cigarettes," he repeated, starting to pace in a little circle beside the car. "Why—"

"I don't think it's the cigarettes," she said impatiently. "That's just where it started."

"Maybe there's something in them!"

"Oh, for crying out loud—"

"Where did you buy them?"

"I *didn't* buy them! Mary Poppins put a whammy on my purse, and they just showed up!"

"*Before* that—where did you buy the ones before—"

"I bought them at the gas station, and I've been smoking them all day. And you haven't," she added, "not until after the wreck."

He glanced up at her, stopped pacing. "After the wreck. This all started after the wreck."

The shivery feeling started creeping up her spine again. She tossed the crust of her pizza to the side of the road and shook another cigarette out of her pack. "So?"

"Do you think we're...."

"No!" she shouted.

The word echoed hollowly and hung in the air between them. She lit the cig, the scrape of the lighter echoing strangely. She took a long drag and just stared at him. He stared back. The sinking feeling in her stomach matched the dismay in his face. Then his eyes flicked to the car behind her and got big.

"Look out!" he said.

She glanced at the car. It was shimmering, quavering like it had been hit by a sci-fi disintegrator beam.

"Shit!"

She jumped away from it, went over to stand beside him. He put an arm around her shoulders and they watched the car evaporate into nothingness.

"Hi, folks."

They turned their heads toward the fence. The mangled barbed wire was gone and a guy in t-shirt and jeans was smiling at them from the edge of the field.

"Glad I finally got your attention," said the guy in jeans, still smiling. "I'm kind of new at this myself. You ready to come along?"

"W-where?" she asked, clinging to her lover.

"Well—home," said the newcomer. He gestured toward the field, where light spilled out of a causeway she hadn't seen before.

She glanced up at her lover, eyes full of questions, and saw them reflected in his. He looked back at the guy in jeans.

"I, um."

She felt him shift beside her, and clung tighter, glancing up at him. He looked uncertain and embarrassed.

"I thought there were supposed to be—you know, angels and stuff."

The guy shrugged. "You can have that if you want. We figured since neither of you is that religious we could just skip it." He looked from one to the other of them. "Should I—"

"No," she said hastily. "No, don't. It's fine."

She looked back at the causeway. The light was brighter than anything she'd ever seen, brighter than the desert sun, but it didn't hurt her eyes. It had a smell, too, and a flavor. It tasted of home.

"Shall we go?" said the newcomer. "You've got friends waiting."

She found her lover's hand and squeezed it hard, looked up at him and nodded. They started toward the light.

"Oh, wait."

She paused to take a last drag on her cigarette, then dropped it on the road and stamped it out. She glanced up at her lover with a sheepish grin.

"I thought they tasted kinda light."

The Courtship of Captain Swenk

"Where d'you suppose General Lee might be going?" asked Buck McAlexander of his two companions as they strode through a thicket of cedar.

"Idiot," said Henry Ball, pushing a branch out of his way. "That's what we're supposed to find out. Didn't you hear a word the judge said?"

"Course I did, and I ain't an idiot, thank you very much," Buck replied, tossing a shank of black hair out of his eyes. "If we don't try to guess where he's going, how're we going to know where to look?"

"Got you there, Henry," said Nathaniel Swenk, their companion and fellow scout.

Apparently considering this statement the end of the discussion, Swenk returned to chewing on a blade of barley-grass and gazing over at the column on the pike in a contemplative way. Mr. Ball observed this bovine activity with an expression of distaste.

Captain Swenk, recently returned to town after receiving honorable discharge from the United States Army, was understood to be courting, and was consequently considered not quite in his right mind by his acquaintances. If there had been surprise at the captain's failure to re-enlist after his two-year term of service had concluded, it had been abated by his popularity among his townfellows, and by curiosity (extending, in some reprehensible cases, to the placing of bets) as to which of the eligible ladies in the vicinity he would select for his bride.

He was fairly new in Chambersburg, having moved to town early in 1861 with the announced desire of settling permanently there and starting a family. The commencement of hostilities had preempted this amiable scheme, but since his discharge it had apparently been foremost in his mind, and the little task of ascertaining General Lee's movements seemed not to be interfering overmuch with his prosecution of it.

"And anyway, these fellers aren't with General Lee. They're under D.H. Hill," Buck declared.

"Rodes," said Ball, shaking his head. "Hill has a beard."

"Well, and so he did have a beard when he rode by."

"No, he had a mustache, but no beard."

"It was trimmed close—"

"Hold up, boys," Swenk interrupted.

They came to a stop just inside the end of the grove. Before them was an open oat field, recently relieved of its crop. A short distance to the east lay the turnpike out of Chambersburg, Pennsylvania, full of Confederate soldiers marching north and stirring up a good deal of dust as they went.

They gazed at the marching Rebels. Buck shifted from foot to foot.

"Over to the creek," Swenk said softly, and struck west toward the Conococheague. The trees growing along the watercourse would afford them cover until another wood could be reached.

The three of them—Swenk, Ball, and McAlexander—had been charged with their important task by Judge Lemmik who, since the 22nd of June, had sent messages by secret means to General Couch about the activities of the Confederate forces occupying Chambersburg. Getting this information past the net of Confederate pickets surrounding the town was impressive in itself, though Buck, being merely nineteen, had expressed the opinion that the secrecy of Lemmik's operations robbed them of all glory.

Kept from enlisting by the earnest entreaties of his mother, whose husband had been visiting relatives in Tennessee when the war broke out and had not been heard from since, Buck had been overjoyed to receive the judge's invitation to act as an observer, gathering Important Information to send on to the Union army's headquarters. It had sounded more glorious than it had so far turned out.

"We must've walked every danged road in the county," Buck complained. "We know General Lee ain't here. We should be looking out south of town."

"The judge said all enemy movements are important," said Ball.

Buck let out a guffaw. "Only enemy movement worth seeing was that crack-fine fiddle dance Jenkins's cavalry gave last night in your barn, Henry."

Ball's expression grew yet more sour. Captain Swenk, failing to notice, said, "That was a mighty fine dance, indeed. I was surprised at how many of our ladies attended. Miss Kindle is a delightful dancer, don't you think?"

"She wouldn't dance with me," Buck said. "Only had eyes for you, Cap'n."

"And General Jenkins's staff were generous hosts," added Swenk.

"Generous with my beer," Ball replied.

"Didn't they pay you for it?"

"In Confederate scrip. Same worthless stuff they're giving all the merchants in town."

"At least they didn't just break into the shops and help themselves," Swenk remarked.

"Yet," said Ball darkly, and kicked a rock off the bank into the creek.

The pike was now obscured from view, but the cloud of dust was plainly visible. They were approaching the neighborhood of Ball's house and farm, which he had only recently purchased, being like Swenk a newcomer to Chambersburg. The annoyance he demonstrated at the recent infestation of Confederates was understandable to his companions. His wheat and his animals had been confiscated, Rebel pickets lived in his cornfield, and his house had been taken over by General Jenkins's staff. Mr. Ball had consequently spent a good deal of time in town, of late, and was often to be found at Judge Lemmik's when he was not tramping the roads and byways of Franklin County.

The day—a Thursday afternoon late in June—was warm,

and birds peeped in desultory tones as the three men walked northward. Captain Swenk was the only one of the trio who seemed at ease with the world. He smiled placidly as they reached a footbridge across the creek just short of where the waterway bent northeastward.

The land was a blend of cultivated fields and wild, wooded areas. Mr. Ball's farm occupied the far side of a hill across the creek; the near side was owned by a Mrs. Bannister, a widow, who was one of the ladies Captain Swenk had been courting. Her house, neatly painted white, lay just beneath the crest of the hill and was shaded by a great, ancient live oak.

"I think," Swenk said to his companions, "I shall stop at Widow Bannister's a while. You go on ahead and I'll catch up."

Buck and Ball exchanged a glance of knowing disapproval. "We are to share the task of counting the Rebels, are we not?" Ball said in a stiff voice. "How are we to divide the work without your presence?"

"You two make your best count, and I'll verify it," Swenk replied. "That way we'll know our information's good." He tipped his hat to them, smiling, and strode off across the bridge toward Bannister's Farm.

"We won't see him for an hour or more," grumbled Ball.

"Hopeless," Buck agreed.

"How such a great stupid ox of a fellow ever got anywhere in the army is beyond me!"

"Come on," Buck said, nodding his head eastward. "Let's go count Rebs."

⚜

"Good day to you, Mrs. Bannister," called Captain Swenk, bowing as he removed his hat, his face slightly reddened by the exertion of climbing the hill to the farmhouse.

The widow, not a handsome woman, stood on the step of her tidy home dressed in a gray gown, modest cap and stiffly starched apron, and bestowed a smile of more politeness than warmth upon her visitor. "You did not come to feed this morning," she said.

"I beg your pardon," the captain said humbly. "I was unavoidably detained. I hope you sent Will to do it."

"I do not like sending him into the cellar with the animals. One of them might kick, and injure him," the widow said, a slight frown creasing her brow.

"He knows better than to expose himself to harm," Swenk replied, smiling.

"I am still not convinced this is the wisest course," the widow complained.

"But, ma'am, do you not wish to keep your horse and cow out of the Confederates' hands? I assure you, they've snabbled up everything on four legs in the county."

"I do not like keeping Dobbin and Daisy underground, and in such close quarters with your mare," she said.

"They will neither of them suffer for it," he assured her. "Have you—"

"Captain Swenk!" cried the big live oak tree that shaded the house and yard.

"Willie! Come down from there this instant!" the widow called to the tree. A rustling of leaves preceded the arrival upon the ground of a grubby ten-year-old boy who immediately flung himself upon Captain Swenk, soiling the sleeve of that gentleman's coat.

"Hello, Will!" the captain said, beaming upon his youthful admirer.

"General Jenkins went out riding this morning!"

"Oh, he did?"

"How could you know that?" demanded the widow.

Will glanced at the captain, then said, "I can see Mr. Ball's place from up there," and pointed to the oak. "The General had a big black hat with a feather in it, and a big long beard."

"Don't point, Willie. It's rude," said his mother in an irritable tone. "I wish you will not climb that tree."

"Oh, it's a fine old tree," said Captain Swenk. "Must be one of the oldest in the county. How could he not climb it?"

"His sister has begun to copy him," the widow complained.

"I live in fear of her falling and breaking her head."

"Where is little Katie?" asked the captain, smiling as he produced a small box from the depths of his coat pocket. "I've brought her some crayons."

The widow's face relaxed somewhat, and she said, "That was kind of you. I suppose you want some coffee? Well, come inside."

A smile curved up one corner of the captain's mouth, which gave him a somewhat foolish appearance. He looked down at Will and winked, then ruffled his hair, and the two of them followed Widow Bannister into the house.

⚬

Judge Lemmik always poured the best beer in Chambersburg, and Buck always strove to do it justice. Henry Ball sat next to him at Lemmik's parlor table with a half-empty tankard before him and a slight frown creasing his brow. The judge, an energetic man who seemed unencumbered by his three-score years, set a full crockery pitcher in the center of the table, closed the parlor door against unwanted intrusion, and seated himself.

"I have some bad news, gentlemen," he said, graciously including Buck in the description.

"Withers was caught?" asked Ball.

The judge nodded. "I've just heard General Jenkins has a new prisoner at his headquarters. I must assume it is he."

Ball grimaced. "I suppose you want me to go home and learn what I can?"

"No, I doubt you'd find out anything more, and we don't want to draw their attention." The judge took off his spectacles and began to polish them. "That makes three couriers captured since Wednesday. Either the Confederate pickets have suddenly become much more efficient—"

"No sign of that," Buck offered, refreshing his tankard from the pitcher.

"Or we're being spied upon," Ball concluded.

"I'm afraid so," the judge said.

Buck looked around at the door, which was shut, and the windows, which looked out onto the judge's peaceful garden, where the last sun was gilding the leaves of the rosebushes. Having concluded this survey without discovering any spies, he returned his attention to the beer.

"Shall I try to get through?" Ball offered.

"No," the judge said. "The news Withers was carrying is stale now. The Rebels are preparing to move, from the looks of it. We'll wait until we have something decisive to send." He poured beer into a small horn cup and took a sip. "What did you learn today?"

"That column kept marching north on the Harrisburg pike," Ball said. "They had artillery, but we don't know how many guns. If Swenk had been with us we might have done more—"

"He went off a-courting again," Buck supplied, swirling his beer around. "Danged if I know what he sees in that Widow Bannister. Got a face like a mule."

"It is admirable in Captain Swenk to pay attention to a widow with children," the judge said kindly. "Not every man would consider courting such."

"Not any man, other'n Swenk," said Buck.

Henry Ball shifted in his seat. "Should we not be discussing our plans?"

"We should indeed," said the judge. "This infantry column —were you able to identify the units?"

"Alabama, we think," said Ball.

"Saw D.H. Hill riding with them," said Buck, setting his tankard down and wiping his mouth on his sleeve.

"It was General Rodes, not Hill," Ball said in an annoyed tone.

"I'm pretty sure it was Hill—"

"And how far did they go?" the judge asked.

Buck looked at his partner and shrugged.

"Green Village," Ball said. "Maybe as far as Shippensburg."

Sounds of an arrival in the house penetrated the door, precipitating a pause in the discussion. Buck set down the pitcher and put a hand to the butt of his pistol. All three men tensed as the parlor door opened.

Captain Swenk strolled in, smiling benignly. The housekeeper, Mrs. Ellis, cast the judge a wry look behind the captain's back and came in to set about lighting the fire.

"Afternoon, Judge. Afternoon, boys," said Swenk. "Say, I never could find you again."

Judge Lemmik got up to fetch the captain a tankard. Swenk made himself comfortable in the judge's armchair by the fireplace, and accepted the beer with a nod of thanks. He stretched out his feet to the blaze Mrs. Ellis had struck, and gave her a kindly smile as she arose from the hearth. She sniffed, and took herself off, closing the door.

"We weren't hard to find," Ball said dryly. "Your afternoon must have been taken up with other business."

"Well, that's true enough, I suppose," said the captain, grinning. He pulled at his beer, set it carefully on the slate hearth, and withdrew a sheet of notepaper from his breast pocket. "Here you are, Judge," he said.

Judge Lemmik perused the page with interest. "Twenty-four regiments under Rodes and Johnson—3rd Alabama, 6th Alabama, 12th Alabama—you're sure this is accurate?"

"Should be."

The judge sat down at the table, one finger tapping its polished surface as he read through the notes. "Very good, very good," he murmured.

"Did the Widow Bannister tell you that?" demanded Ball.

"No," said Swenk with a pleasant smile. "She doesn't care for armies. Thinks they're a nuisance."

The judge folded the page. "You've done very well, Captain, but I think we shall wait to see what tomorrow brings. Most of Lee's army is still to the south of us. Perhaps tomorrow we'll learn whether they are headed towards Harrisburg or York."

"The units that passed today went toward Harrisburg," Ball pointed out.

"But they went into bivouac," said Swenk. "They could turn right around tomorrow and head for Gettysburg."

"We must learn where the bulk of the army will go," said

the judge. "If it's Harrisburg, we know they'll attack Philadelphia. If Gettysburg, they're after Baltimore and the capital. As soon as we know which, we must get word to Couch's headquarters, and quickly. Tomorrow or the next day should tell."

Swenk finished his beer, and stood up. "I'll be going along, then, if you don't need me. I have an invitation to supper."

"We'll meet again in the morning," the judge agreed, shaking the captain's hand. "I'll see you out."

The door closed behind them. Ball stared at it, frowning thoughtfully.

"It was Hill," said Buck, reaching for the beer.

❦

Friday dawned cloudy and quiet. There were few soldiers to be seen in the town, so the three observers struck southward to a hilltop overlooking the road to Greencastle.

Captain Swenk had brought a pair of field glasses, which he and Mr. Ball passed back and forth like drunkards sharing a flask. Buck sat with his back against an oak, alternately watching his companions and the glowering clouds.

"Could be Heth," Swenk said, handing off the glasses. "We could tell for sure if we got a bit closer."

"Too risky," said Ball. "They're coming this way anyway, might as well wait."

"That's right," Buck said, stifling a yawn. "Judge told us not to take chances, on account of too many men have been caught. He thinks there's a Reb spy in Chambersburg."

Ball shot him a withering glance. "We've had hundreds of Rebels through Chambersburg. A spy would be rather superfluous."

"But he said—"

"It's getting on," Swenk said, putting the glasses away. "I think we've learned what we can for now."

"Good," said Buck, getting to his feet. "I'm ready for breakfast."

They turned their steps northward, back toward town, descending the hill to the road through a meadow of daisies. Captain Swenk delayed them for five minutes while he collected a couple dozen of the bright-eyed flowers, to the disgust of his companions.

"The Reb spy could be setting our men up," Buck told Ball while they watched Swenk's operations. "First they caught Barnes, and then Byrd, and then Withers—"

"Withers went up the railroad tracks," Ball said. "He was caught because he was plain stupid."

"Judge is right to be careful," Buck insisted. "Could be all of us are in terrible danger. Spy could be fixing to capture us all!" His eyes glowed at this thought.

Ball didn't appear to share his enthusiasm. He leaned in to Buck and said in a fierce whisper, "That spy may be closer than you think!" He jerked his head toward Swenk—who strode unconcerned through the daisies—and frowned his young companion into silence.

Buck fixed his gaze on the captain with a look of new appreciation. He whispered back, "Swenk's a spy, and hoodwinked us all? Well, what a stunner!"

Ball put a cautionary finger to his lips. Captain Swenk appeared not to have heard.

"I don't know," Buck added, still whispering. "Fellow who walks about picking daisies with a big, silly smirk on his face— just don't seem right for a spy."

"Won't they be pretty, bound up in a blue ribbon?" Swenk asked, displaying the bouquet as he returned.

"Quite," said Ball in a sour tone. "Shall we go? It's beginning to rain."

He strode off without waiting for an answer. Buck looked at the captain, who was watching Ball's departure with a bemused expression. With a shrug, Buck fell in with his comrade as they hurried back to town.

◈

By Saturday morning, Chambersburg was swarming with Rebels. Captain Swenk and the Widow Bannister stood together atop the courthouse steps among the crowd of citizens who had come out to watch the Rebel army pass.

Below them a column of Confederate infantry poured into town from the south, passing through the Diamond at the center of town in a continuous stream. Now and then they raised a cheer of "Hurrah for the Southern Confederacy." The townspeople made no answer, merely watching, exchanging words of apprehension in lowered tones.

"Mrs. McAlexander entertained four of their officers to dinner last night," said Mrs. Bannister, disapproval in her voice.

"She may be trying to ensure her family's safety," said the Reverend Biggs, who stood nearby. "After all, her husband is not at home."

"If she thinks harboring the enemy will ensure her protection she is sadly mistaken," pronounced Mrs. Bannister.

"It is better than being robbed," said the captain with a shrug.

"We will all be robbed sooner or later," complained Dr. Lengham. "They've taken all the sheets from the hotels for their wounded. No doubt they'll want ours next."

Miss Katie Bannister, who had reached all the dignity of six years, tugged at Captain Swenk's trousers. He picked her up, cradling her in powerful arms.

"I drew you another picture," she said, proffering a slightly crumpled page.

Swenk took it, balancing the child on one hip while he admired her artwork. "That's beautiful, Katie. What a pretty flag."

"That one was the prettiest," Katie agreed. "I saw a man with a peg-leg," she added.

"A peg-leg? Was he a pirate?"

Miss Bannister gravely shook her head. "He was a 'federate."

"Katie Bannister!" cried her mother, becoming aware of her presence. "Where is your brother?"

"Up there," Katie said, looking up toward the cupola atop the courthouse. The widow, the minister, and Captain Swenk all followed her gaze. Mrs. Bannister emitted a muffled cry of dismay.

"I'll fetch him down, shall I?" the captain offered. He kissed Katie's cheek, gently set her on her feet, and strode into the building.

"A kind and considerate man, Captain Swenk," said the minister, nodding approval.

"He talks too much," the widow told him, "but he is well enough, I suppose. Katie, your apron is smudged."

⌂

Buck leaned against the wall of Hoke's store, not quite succeeding at appearing nonchalant. Henry Ball stood nearby with his hands buried deep in his pockets, watching the sea of Rebels continue to wash through the Diamond.

Officers on horseback, leading columns of weary infantry, were beginning to give way to artillery and wagons full of supplies. It was not as colorful as the annual 4th of July parade —which would take place next week and in which Buck, wearing Parson Biggs' second-best wig, was to portray George Washington—but it was much, much bigger.

"Is that General Lee?" Buck whispered in a tone of awe.

Ball looked up at the mounted officer entering the Diamond, a man of erect carriage and silvered beard, wearing a black felt hat and a heavy caped overcoat, and riding a gray horse. "Has to be," he admitted.

The column behind General Lee halted right on the pike while the general moved forward to consult with one of his subordinates. This man, also mounted, had a long, reddish beard and made a crisp salute.

"Who's that he's talking with? Longstreet?" asked Buck.

"I think it's A. P. Hill," said Ball.

"Isn't Hill shorter than that?"

"He's on horseback, it's hard to tell."

The two generals withdrew a bit from the throng. Ball restrained his young friend from trying to get close enough to hear their discussion.

"They'll clap you in irons, you fool!" Ball hissed.

"We mustn't have that," Judge Lemmik remarked, joining his volunteers by Hoke's store. "I believe I'll need you to run that errand today, Buck."

"Right now?" Buck asked, his eyes a-glitter with excitement.

"Possibly. Let's see which way the wind blows."

They all looked toward the two Confederate generals. As they watched, a third general joined them, tall in the saddle.

"*That's* Longstreet," said Buck and Ball together.

The judge nodded, and softly said, "Don't appear too interested, boys." He ambled a few steps away to talk with some of the other citizens who were out to watch the show.

Ball turned his back to the Confederates, shot Buck a glance full of warning, and proceeded to examine the goods in Hoke's window. Buck took some dice from his pocket and squatted to toss them, but he didn't take his eyes off the Rebel generals.

◈

"Will, your mother doesn't like you being up here," Captain Swenk said from the top step of the stairs. Young Mr. Bannister knelt on the floor of the cupola, peeping over the rail at the crowded town below.

"She wouldn't mind if she came up here and saw it," Will said. "I counted thirty-six flags so far."

"That's excellent," the captain said, placing a hand on Will's shoulder as he joined him to peer down at the Rebels. "But you ought to come down now."

Will looked up at the captain, who wore a slightly strained expression. The boy made no protest, but quietly gathered up his pencils and notebook. Captain Swenk, however, made no move to go.

Below, in the Diamond, the conference of generals had broken up. General Lee rode forward, the column falling in behind him. In the center of the Diamond, the general pulled on his right rein, and his horse turned eastward.

"Gettysburg," the captain murmured.

A frown creased his brow. Below, Buck McAlexander slipped behind Hoke's store and started off swiftly through the alleys, heading north. Henry Ball paused to speak to Judge Lemmik, then followed. The captain's frown deepened.

"Come on, William," he said. "Let's go."

◊

"We should go across country," Ball said, dabbing at his brow with his handkerchief as he strode along the railroad beside Buck.

Insects buzzed in the grasses and the tracks glowed dully under a sun dimmed by thin clouds. A haze hung over the valley ahead.

"This way's faster," Buck said. "Judge said get there as fast as possible."

"Withers was caught on this road."

"We'll slip off if we see any pickets."

"If we see them it'll be too late," Ball said crossly.

"You don't have to come." Buck waved his arm westward. "There's your farm over yonder. Don't you want to see what the Rebs left?"

Ball was silent for a moment, then said, "Wouldn't your mother be alarmed if she knew what you were doing?"

Buck merely grinned. "She knows it's for a good cause."

No more conversation passed between them for some minutes. Mr. Ball glanced from time to time at his house and fields, but did not stray from Buck's side. They walked quickly, and Ball was perspiring quite strongly by the time they reached the shade of an apple grove growing close to the tracks. The rail fence that had once bordered it had been torn apart and used for firewood by the Rebels who had camped in the neighborhood.

"Want to rest?" Buck asked.

"I thought you were anxious to go on," said Ball with

asperity.

"Don't want to wear you out," Buck replied kindly. "You set a spell, I'll climb up and look for the enemy."

"Get down!" Ball said, but Buck was already into the branches of an apple tree.

From the south a tall figure was approaching, loping up the tracks. Ball redoubled his entreaties, but Buck refused to budge. Ball turned to face the new arrival, and his expression of displeasure deepened as he recognized Captain Swenk.

"I'm glad I caught up to you boys!" called the captain, huffing cheerily. "You certainly made good time. Come on down, Buck."

"I'm looking for Rebels," Buck announced.

"Well, you won't find any up there," Swenk said. "Come along, I'm going with you."

"Won't three men be rather conspicuous?" said Ball.

"More so than two? I doubt it," said Swenk. He glanced ahead to where the railroad crossed the Conococheague. "There was a picket at that bridge two days ago. We'll be much better off away from the railroad."

"Mighty thoughtful of you to come and warn us," Ball said, still frowning. "Those aren't ripe," he added as Swenk pulled an apple from the tree.

The captain glanced at it, said, "You're right," and tossed it aside.

A rustling and scraping issued from the tree, followed by Buck's emergence. He landed in the road so close to Ball it made him jump. In his hand was his Colt revolver.

"Put that away, you fool, before you hurt yourself," said Ball.

"No, I don't think so," Buck replied, aiming the gun at Swenk.

The captain slowly put his hands in the air. Ball looked from him to Buck with an expression of fury.

"What do you think you're doing?"

"I believe he thinks he's capturing us for the Confederates," said Swenk calmly.

Buck grinned. "You're sharper than you look, Captain. That's exactly right. I'll have your pistol, the one you keep in your pocket. Nice and easy."

Swenk handed over the weapon. Buck relieved Mr. Ball of his own defense—a wicked little knife—then smiled at them both in a friendly way.

"Now you two walk on up to the bridge there where my friends are waiting. I'll be right behind you, so no tricks. Ain't fired this gun in weeks, and I wouldn't mind some target practice."

Captain Swenk looked at Ball, whose fury had turned his face purple. With a shrug, Swenk obeyed and started toward the bridge, a good quarter-mile away. Ball walked beside him, frowning intently at the ground.

Buck started whistling, which seemed only to increase Ball's rage. Captain Swenk managed after some moments' effort to catch Ball's eye.

"On three," Swenk whispered.

Suddenly alert, Ball faced forward and gave a short nod. A step, another, then he and Swenk turned as one and grappled with Buck, who yelled in surprise.

The pistol fired into the air, Swenk having made it his business to grab Buck's arm and direct it skyward. The three of them tumbled to the ground, Buck kicking and squirming.

At last Swenk wrested the pistol away and placed the barrel against the traitor's chest, at which Buck lay still. Ball, pinning his legs, looked up at the captain.

"How did you know?" he asked, out of breath.

"I only suspected," Swenk said. "I didn't know until he tried making a present of us to the Rebel pickets."

Buck's eyes narrowed, but then he smiled wickedly. "Tried and succeeded," he said, nodding down the valley.

A half-dozen pickets were running toward them from the bridge. The captain frowned, then looked back at Buck.

"Sorry for this," he said, and fired.

Ball flinched at the sound, then gaped at the awful mess the pistol had made of McAlexander's chest. The youth's eyes went blank, and a haze seemed to film them over.

Ball worked his jaws, but only managed to say, "Wh-wh-"

"No time," said Swenk, quickly retrieving his gun and Ball's knife from the spy's pockets. He handed the knife to its owner and dropped the gory pistol by Buck's corpse, pocketing his own gun.

"Come on," he said, and with a glance toward the shouting pickets, took off running down the tracks.

They sped along the cinders to the bottom of the hill, then Swenk left the tracks and climbed in loping strides up through the trampled fields of Ball's farm. Ball kept up as best he could, the shouts of the pickets behind them and the occasional *whiz* of a musket ball serving to speed him.

"Not my house," he shouted to Swenk, gasping for breath.

"I know," called the captain over his shoulder. "The wood."

Ball followed him into a stand of oak that grew uphill of the house. The captain dropped speed, trotting through the wood, still angling uphill. The oaks climbed over the hilltop, affording some cover at least to their flight. Shouts came from behind and beside them now; the pickets were splitting up.

At last they reached the crest of the hill and the tall, old oak. Both men picked up speed, the captain running, Ball stumbling downhill toward Mrs. Bannister's house. The captain ran to the cellar doors at the side of the house and flung them open, leaping in. Ball, a hand pressed to his side, halted in the opening, gasping as he peered into the darkness.

"Come on, hurry," the captain's voice called.

Ball took a step down the sloping, earthen ramp. A jingling sound made him pause, then hurry forward.

"Your mare's been here all along?" he cried. "I thought the Rebels had taken her!"

"Here," the captain said, thrusting a bridle into his hands. "That's Dobbin's. I'll get the saddle."

Ball moved to the plow horse's head and coaxed him to take the bit. "Was it necessary—" he began.

"Yes," Swenk replied, tugging at the girth. "If I'd let him go he'd have betrayed Judge Lemmik and the others, not just you and me."

Ball swallowed, and nodded, passing the reins over Dobbin's head. "Captain Swenk," he said, and paused to clear his throat. "I've been mistaken in you. I've not given you the credit you deserve."

"I thank you, Henry," said Swenk, his grin a pale glow in the darkness. "But we'll sort that out later. You must get to Lemmik's and warn him. Wait two minutes while I lead the pickets off."

"General Couch—" Ball began.

"I'll take care of it," Swenk said, mounting the mare.

He had to crouch low in the dark cellar. Clicking his tongue, he eased her toward the light of the open doors. A figure appeared to bar his way, silhouetted by sun.

"Get inside, Will!" the captain called harshly. "Remember what I told you to say if the Rebels come around."

"Yes, sir! I'll close the door for you first," said the boy.

Swenk didn't answer, but urged his mare up the slope. By the time Ball had followed, blinking in the daylight, the captain was galloping over the hilltop.

Dobbin heaved a sigh and began cropping the grass at his feet. Will Bannister stared at the horse and its rider for a moment, then grinned and tossed Mr. Ball a salute before shutting the cellar doors and running for the farmhouse door.

Gunfire sounded from beyond the hilltop. Sparing a glance for the house, where the widow's face peered indignantly from one of the windows, Ball urged his mount forward, riding for Chambersburg.

◈

Two weeks later, on July 10th, the only Rebels remaining in town were either residents of the hospital that had been set up in the schoolhouse or prisoners. News of the mighty battle at Gettysburg, a glorious victory for the Union, had set all the bells in town to ringing, and a huge crowd had gathered to watch the 4th of July parade despite its having been delayed a week on account of the Rebel occupation.

Nearly every person in town was present to view the spectacle. Among the few absent was the grieving Mrs. McAlexander, who remained at home, packing for a visit to her cousin in Clarksville.

Henry Ball sat watching the parade from a place of honor on the reviewing stand in front of the town hall. Beside him sat Judge Lemmik on the one hand and Widow Bannister on the other.

Mrs. Bannister, upon receiving Mr. Ball's abject apology for the peremptory borrowing of her horse, had graciously bestowed her favor on him, expressing the belief that, short of losing her children or her home, she could bear any suffering in the cause of the Union. If thoughts of the convenience of joining his farm to the widow's—they were adjacent, after all—had occurred to Mr. Ball, he was gallant enough not to voice them.

"Here they come," he murmured to Mrs. Bannister, who gave him a fleeting smile in return before shifting her gaze to the parade.

The grand finale, a hay cart decorated to resemble a row boat, with men pulling oars through imaginary waters as it passed majestically through the Diamond, boasted the proudly waving figure of Captain Swenk, dashing in the parson's wig and a fancy coat covered in braid. If Washington had not crossed the Delaware in company with two small children—one a young scamp tootling on a fife and wearing a gory bandage about his brow, the other a pretty child in her best Sunday dress —none of the observers seemed to mind. Cheer after cheer rained upon the captain and his two recruits as they were carried through the Diamond.

"He makes a fine George Washington," Henry Ball remarked to the widow.

"He is too broad-shouldered, I believe," said the widow, but she deigned to smile on him nonetheless.

Creed of the Ælven

Walk many paths, leaving no mark behind but of beauty.
Honor the ældar and spirits who watch over all.
Serve in good faith, with true heart, those who share the
*   bright journey.*
Live in the world, giving thanks, speaking truth, harming
*   none.*

—*Creed of the Ælven, first stave*

First Love

Eliani stared at the bard Ishanen, drinking in every nuance of his expression, every tone of his voice. One was allowed to stare when a bard was performing.

At table it was discourteous. She had managed to be a little more discreet during the feast her father, the governor, had arranged to welcome the visiting bard, though not enough for her cousin, Luruthin, who had more than once nudged her beneath the table.

Luruthin sat beside her now, eating pine nuts, cracking the shells with his teeth while the bard sang. Eliani shot him a glare but knew it would do little good, so she chose to ignore him and returned her attention to Ishanen.

He was tall and lithe, with a voice like honey. He sat with his back to the great hearth at one end of the feast hall, pale hair glinting gold in the fire's flickering light. He had his instruments around him—harp, drum, flutes, and the lute in his lap—and his audience, the most honored folk of Highstone and nearby Clerestone, surrounded him in a larger half-circle.

Eliani had seen very few Southfælders in her short lifetime. All of them had fair hair and rich, brown eyes. Their exotic looks intrigued her, and in Ishanen they were combined with grace and talent. In the space of an afternoon she had gone from being intrigued to being half in love with him.

He was a member of the Bards' Guild in Glenhallow, the largest city in Southfæld and the second largest in any ælven realm. Eliani had never visited Glenhallow, or indeed any part of Southfæld save for the Midrange Valley, where her father had once ridden with her when he was teaching her about the Midrange War. Midrange was within a day's ride of Highstone and only just within Southfæld's northern border, so Eliani felt it did not count as a visit to the realm.

She dreamed now of going to Glenhallow with Ishanen when he returned to his home. Unlikely, her more cynical self concluded. She was only twenty-nine come Evennight, and her father would not approve her leaving home so young. He would want her to stay in Highstone until she reached her majority, at fifty.

She would die if she had to wait that long for love.

As Ishanen sang, she yearned for him to hold her, to teach her the ways of love. A bard must know a great deal about love, for it was the subject and the inspiration of so much great music. She wished she could sing, so that she might join Ishanen, her voice blending with his even as their souls met in an understanding of their shared destiny.

But alas, she had no musical ability to speak of. Her singing was more enthusiastic than precise, and though as a rule she ignored Luruthin's protests whenever she was inspired to warble out a tune, she knew instinctively that she had nothing like Ishanen's gift, and had best not demonstrate that lack to him.

Ishanen concluded his song, and nodded and smiled in response to the gathering's applause. He set down the lute and took up his harp, a beautiful instrument carved of whitewood, with vines twining up its curved front. Ishanen strummed a chord and Eliani shivered with delight.

Luruthin turned his head toward her, then laughed under his breath. "This is sudden."

Eliani glanced at him and whispered back. "What?"

"Your interest in music this evening."

Eliani glared at him. "My father is partial to music."

"But usually you are less so. Perhaps it is more the musician than the music that appeals to you."

"Shh!"

Ishanen had raised his hands to the strings. As he began to play, Eliani breathed a soft sigh.

His hands danced in the air, pulling rippling waves of sound from the harp. His face, deeply shadowed by the firelight behind him, took on an air of tragedy as he sang of a maiden whose lover went away to war, leaving her to weave a silken robe while she waited for his return. The robe became two robes, then five, then ten, and the warrior lover still did not come home.

Eliani felt tears rising as Ishanen sang of the weaver's despair, though she knew the story. When the maiden had woven ten robes, she carried them to the battlefield and learned that her lover had died in the war, whereupon she shredded the robes into ribbons and tied them around the conce that had been placed in his memory.

A sharp *crack* to her right made her glance at Luruthin. He looked back, apologizing with his eyes as he removed a pine nut shell from his mouth, then offered her the bowl of nuts. She frowned and turned her gaze back to Ishanen.

He sang with such beauty, such passion. Eliani's breath caught in her throat and she brushed away the wetness from her eye as he concluded the final verse. She burst into applause the moment the last chord faded away.

Luruthin tossed a handful of shells into the fire, set the bowl in his lap, and brushed his hands, which might be seen as applauding. Eliani ignored him; likely he was trying to goad her. He had always teased her, ever since they were both children, and showed no sign of stopping even though he was now past his majority.

One would think a member of Alpinon's Guard would have more dignity, more gravity. One might wish it, indeed.

Ishanen put down the harp and picked up his drum. Standing, he began to play a lively rhythm, recognizable as a popular dance. Folk jumped up from their seats and formed a circle out in the hall, clapping along with the drum. Ishanen's voice rang out, clear and true, cutting through all the noise to sing the dance's melody.

Luruthin grinned and stood up, setting the bowl of nuts on his chair. He held out a hand to Eliani.

"Come and dance."

She shook her head, watching Ishanen.

"But you love to dance!"

"Not tonight."

Luruthin was silent for a moment, then muttered something she did not catch as he strode off to join the growing circle of dancers. She glanced after him, momentarily regretful. She *did* love dancing, but Ishanen would only be here for a few days. She did not wish to miss a moment of his performance.

She moved to a chair closer to the bard, now that nearly half the company had gone away to dance. Ishanen did not see her; his eyes were closed as he held the drum high and played it while he sang.

He swayed with the rhythms he was playing, a smaller version of the dance. His robe of pale sage green draped along his limbs as he moved. Eliani yearned to touch him, to be enfolded by those long arms, to feel his warmth against her. Never before had she longed so strongly for the sensations she had only heard about.

The dance ended in a roar of cheers and applause. Ishanen opened his eyes and smiled at the dancers' approval. His brow gleamed slightly from his exertions.

Eliani applauded where she sat, and when Ishanen resumed his seat and glanced at her, she smiled. His answering smile was more polite than warm, but still it raised a little thrill within her chest.

He took up a flute and played a long, mournful melody while the company gradually returned to their chairs. Eliani remained where she was, and no one challenged her for the seat. She knew it was greedy of her, but she could not help it. She wanted to be close to the bard.

Ishanen played and sang long into the night, and Eliani hung upon every note. Toward midnight some of the guests began to depart; she could hear her father's voice at the front of the hall quietly bidding them farewell. Still, many stayed on to hear the master bard from Southfæld whose presence here in Highstone was such a rare treat.

Governor Jharan had sent Ishanen from the court at Glenhallow to Highstone as a gift to his old friend, Governor Felisan. Eliani's father adored music; he was always urging minstrels to come to Felisanin Hall, but a bard of Ishanen's gifts was far superior to the musicians who usually performed there. Indeed, some of the local minstrels were in the audience, and Eliani knew that Ishanen had agreed to meet with them while he was here and teach them some of Southfæld's traditional music.

She wished she had enough talent to attend those sessions. She played a little on the flute, but poorly.

The circle around the bard grew smaller as guests took their leave. Luruthin pulled two empty chairs out of the way and drew a third closer. Eliani spared only a glance for him, enough to notice that he had not retrieved his bowl of nuts, for which she was thankful.

Her father came and sat beside her, smiling when she looked up at him. He rested an arm across the back of her chair. She loved him, but could wish that he had not chosen this moment to embrace her.

At last, only kin remained listening to the music: Felisan and Eliani, Luruthin and his parents from Clerestone. They were not immediate family—Suthini's mother and Felisan's father were siblings—but beside Eliani they were the nearest kin Felisan had save for a sister who had gone to live in Fireshore, and he had invited Lurunan and his parents to stay at Felisanin Hall during Ishanen's visit.

The fire had burned down to embers. Ishanen sat curled around his lute, head bowed as he frowned slightly in thought. At last he began a final song: "Skyruach," a ballad commissioned by Governor Jharan, a tribute to the many who fell defending Southfæld at the battle that had concluded the Midrange War.

Eliani glanced at her father, for he had been in the battle along with Jharan. He listened, but his gaze seemed distant and he did not smile.

Ishanen sang with eyes closed once again. Thus freed from fear of embarrassing him, Eliani stared to her heart's content, memorizing the planes of his face, the subtle colors of his skin, hair, and clothing. Pale colors, all. Only his eyes were dark, and they were hidden.

When the song drew to a close, no one moved or made a sound for a long moment. At last Felisan removed his arm from Eliani's chair and leaned forward.

"Thank you, Ishanen. You have given us a rare gift this evening."

The bard opened his eyes and smiled. "It has been my honor."

"We will let you rest now, for we expect more tomorrow."

Ishanen's smile widened to a grin. "I believe I know a few more tunes."

Suthini and Lurudon stood, and Luruthin joined them. While they exchanged goodnight wishes with Felisan, Eliani stepped toward the bard.

"May I help you carry your instruments to your guest house?"

Ishanen gazed at her, seeming to debate the offer. At last he gave a nod.

"That is kind of you. Thank you."

Giddy with delight, Eliani could not stand still. "I will fetch your cloak."

She dashed to the hearthroom and through it to the small chamber where visitors' belongings were stored, and fetched the only cloak remaining. It was silver colored, a cloth so fine and soft it felt like the feathers of a bird. She folded it carefully over her arm and carried it back to the feast hall, taking care not to let it touch the floor.

Ishanen was putting his flutes into a padded cloth case. He had already covered the lute and the harp in similar cases. They must all have been made by the same person, for they were all of a like green fabric, adorned with silver beads. Ishanen tied the flute case closed and glanced up at Eliani as he slid the drum into a padded satchel.

"Thank you." He took the cloak from her and put it on, then held out the satchel and the flute case. "Will you carry these?"

Eliani slung the satchel across her shoulder and held the flutes with both hands, knowing she must neither grip them too hard nor drop them. Ishanen settled the lute case at his back and picked up the covered harp. He stepped toward Felisan, who was still talking with the others. The governor turned and saw Eliani, then glanced at the bard.

"Let me have an attendant help you with your instruments."

"I can do it!"

Eliani stared intently at her father, silently imploring him not to interfere. One brow twitched upward slightly as he looked to Ishanen.

"Perhaps someone could help you with the heavier things."

Ishanen bowed slightly, his arms full of the harp. "Thank you, but I can manage, with your daughter's assistance."

Eliani's heart beat painfully hard. He *wanted* her help!

"Well, good night then, Ishanen. Rest well, and thank you again for the music."

Eliani led the way out of the hall, through the hearthroom and out into the star-scattered night. Autumn's chill was in the air and she wished momentarily that she had brought her own cloak, but excitement bore her on toward the high stair that descended from Felisanin Hall to Highstone's public circle. She glanced back at Ishanen, his hair made paler and eyes darker by the night.

"We could go around by the road if you do not want to take the steps."

"Thank you, but I believe I can manage."

Eliani preceded him down the stair, careful to keep both the drum case and the flutes from bumping against the rock wall. The steps were broad enough that two could walk abreast, but burdened as they were it was safer to go separately.

She looked back at Ishanen as she neared the foot of the stair. He came carefully, watching his footing, moving with an unconscious grace that thrilled Eliani.

She walked beside him as they crossed the public circle to

the guest house that had been given over to Ishanen's use during his stay. Luruthin's family had taken up the guest rooms at the Hall, and in any case, the guest house was more spacious, with a large front room where Ishanen would teach the minstrels on the morrow. Eliani wondered if he might allow her just to sit and listen.

She glanced at him, considering making this request, but her courage failed and she asked a less dangerous question. "Have you been to Highstone before?"

"Once, long ago. I was still an apprentice then. Oralan brought several of us here to play."

"Oralan ... I do not think I have met him."

"Doubtless you have not. He has not been back to Highstone, and that visit was long before you were born."

Eliani pressed her lips together, annoyed at the reference to her age. She was not so very young. More than halfway to her majority.

The door of the guest house stood open, and bright firelight gleamed out from the welcoming hearth. Eliani passed through the hearthroom into the main room, where a fire also burned. Candles stood alight in pewter holders on the large table at one end of the room.

Eliani set her burdens down and turned to help Ishanen, but he had already put his harp in a corner of the room. He took the lute out of its case and unfolded the small whitewood stand that had held it while he played other instruments up at the Hall. Eliani watched him prop the lute upon the stand, his long fingers gently clasping the fragile instrument.

He straightened and turned to her, smiling. "Thank you for your assistance."

She nodded, her heart beating rather quickly. "Is there anything else you need?"

"I think not. Your father was right, I look forward to resting."

"I could make you some tea ..."

"That is kind of you, but I do not wish for tea just now."

She stared at him, her chest rising and falling with each

anxious breath. This was not the scene she had pictured as they walked hither. She had thought that being alone together they would fall into cozy conversation, discover tastes they shared, and realize their mutual attraction.

This was not so comfortable as her imaginings. This was awkward. She wished to stay, wished to further her acquaintance with Ishanen, but he was not at all encouraging.

She took a step toward him. "Would you like some company for a while? I would l-love to hear more about Glenhallow."

"I will tell you more, perhaps, but not tonight."

"Well ... I enjoyed your singing. Especially the song about the weaver."

He smiled, moving toward the hearthroom. "Thank you."

"You know so much about love." She followed him, wanting to stay close to him though she knew he wished her to leave. "I want to learn from you, Ishanen!"

He paused, blinking. "About music?"

She gulped a breath, knowing she did not sound nearly as mature as she wished. "About love!"

He gazed at her, then raised a hand to her cheek. His khi was warm and gentle; his skin smelled faintly of resin. Eliani stood absolutely still, scarcely daring to breathe.

Ishanen smiled softly as he cupped her jaw with his long fingers. "You are a lovely child, but I would not pluck a flower before it has fully blossomed."

His voice was so quiet, almost a whisper, yet she heard all too well. She drew a ragged breath.

"I am not—"

"Patience, Eliani. Good night now, and sweet rest to you."

Somehow she had come to the hearthroom doorway. Ishanen pulled back the drape and held it for her, leaving her no choice but to go out. She should wish him goodnight, but her throat had closed.

She darted out before the tears could slip down her cheeks. She did not want Ishanen to see them. An unhappy gasp escaped her throat as she ran out into the public circle.

"Eliani?"

Not the bard's voice. Someone else had seen. Her face burning, she ran westward across the circle, between houses and up into the forest.

"Eliani!"

Luruthin. Her heart cringed and she sobbed, climbing the steep slope scattered with leaves and old needles.

"Eliani, wait!"

"Leave me be!"

She leapt for a pine branch and caught it, rough bark hurting her hands as she swung herself up into the tree. A short jump to the next branch around, then along it and onto the limb of a neighboring oak.

She could hear Luruthin on the forest floor, still pursuing her. She wiped her arm across her face and kept on, wanting to be alone.

Tree to tree she ran, pine to oak to greenleaf, sometimes leaping to catch a branch or cross a gap. Anger and humiliation burned in her chest, driving her forward. She fled without thinking, without caring, until she jumped onto a branch and heard a snarl and growl before her.

Eyes glowed at her from low along the branch near the trunk, reflecting faint starlight. The growl rose and fell again, but did not cease.

"Eliani! Do not run!"

She stood still, panting, staring at the creature she had not noticed in her haste. Night washed the color from its pale fur, but she knew it by its rounded ears and huge paws with claws gripping the branch.

Catamount.

"Stand tall, Eliani!"

Trembling, she did as Luruthin commanded, though she wanted to drop down to the branch and make herself small. She heard him climbing; he made little noise but enough that the catamount also noticed. The cat turned its head just before Luruthin appeared on the next branch around.

"Hah, cat! Yes, look at me, it is me you should fear! Eliani, get to the ground. Heigh there, cat, I am watching you!"

Eliani gulped, looking below. She was too high to jump straight down, but a branch below and to her right was within reach.

The cat snarled at Luruthin, ears flat. He was closer to it than she; too close. Fear for him pounding in her heart, she leapt lightly from the branch and caught the lower limb, then swung to the ground.

"Luruthin!"

"Are you down?"

"Yes!"

"Go back to the city. I will be right behind you. Run!"

Choking on a sob, she ran. The catamount's growl rose to a scream of rage. Eliani skipped to a halt, looking back in dread.

Footsteps pounded, then Luruthin appeared, running through the woods. Eliani sobbed with relief.

He caught her, spinning her around with the force of his pace, and held her shoulders as he peered into her eyes. "Are you hurt?"

She shook her head. Luruthin crushed her in a swift hug, then took her hand and pulled her toward home.

"Come on."

"W-wait."

"We must get back before a patrol is assembled to hunt for you."

Eliani cringed, wiping at her face as Luruthin dragged her along. She hoped no such notice had been taken of her flight, but if Luruthin had seen her...

What had he been doing in the circle? She had thought he and his parents would retire to their rooms at the Hall.

She had no chance to ask him, being occupied with avoiding tripping as he hastened her back to Highstone. As they neared the few houses at the west side of the circle, she heard voices raised in alarm. Her heart sank.

Luruthin pulled her forward, passing between the houses and into the circle. A handful of guardians were gathered there, three of them saddling horses. Luruthin went toward them.

"Eliani is safe!"

Heads turned at his call. Felisan hurried forward from behind one of the horses.

"Eliani! Thank the spirits!"

He caught her in his arms and held her close. She tensed, but did not squirm away.

"I am sorry, Father. I did not mean to cause alarm."

"What happened?"

"Nothing. I just ... wanted to be alone."

He held her by her shoulders and stared hard at her. Eliani swallowed. To forestall further questions, she glanced at Luruthin.

"I came upon a catamount—almost stumbled over it, and angered it. Luruthin distracted it so I could get away."

Felisan looked at her cousin. "Thank you, Luruthin."

Luruthin nodded, then met Eliani's gaze. "I am glad I was nearby."

Her father thanked the guardians and bade them goodnight, then put his arm around Eliani's shoulder and led her toward the stair up to the Hall. Luruthin followed.

Eliani could not keep from glancing toward the guest house. The door stood open still, and the fire on the welcoming hearth burned bright. The ground floor windows were lit with soft light as well, and she thought she saw a figure standing at the side of one.

She looked away, fresh heat in her cheeks. The bard wanted none of her; he thought her a child. Unhappiness welled anew in her chest and she stifled a sob.

Her father glanced at her, but said nothing until they had entered Felisanin Hall and retired to their private quarters. Stopping in the hallway outside his study, he turned her to face him.

"Do you wish to talk?"

Eliani shook her head. She stared at his feet, and at Luruthin's beyond. There was a scuff of dirt on one of Luruthin's boots.

"Are you all right, Eliani?"

She nodded, then looked up at her father's concerned face.

"I am sorry to have caused a disturbance."

He stroked a hand over her hair, then tousled it as he had done when she was a child. Eliani gritted her teeth.

"Well, rest you then. We will talk in the morning." He released her and turned to her cousin. "Luruthin, will you join me for a cup of wine?"

Luruthin glanced at Eliani, who silently pleaded that he not betray her. His gaze returned to the governor and he smiled.

"Of course."

She watched them go into her father's study, then slunk down the hall to her own chamber. She washed the dirt from her hands and rubbed away as much of the sap as she could, then took off the good tunic and legs she had worn for the evening's festivities and slipped into comfortable fleececod ones.

She lit the candles in the branch beside her bed and sat down to inspect her clothes for damage. Apart from one cuff where the embroidery was a bit frayed, they were unharmed. Her shoes had not fared so well; they were smudged with dirt and gummed with pine sap, probably ruined.

Eliani frowned at the slipper in her hand, thinking over her flight into the woods. Luruthin had seen her, which meant he had been near the public circle. Had he followed her and the bard down from the Hall?

Anger and embarrassment conflicted in her. She wished Luruthin would take less interest in her concerns, but had he done so tonight she would have been alone when she encountered the catamount. Not even in her most ungrateful mood could she regret that he had aided her then. He often annoyed her, but he had also been her true friend since they were both very young.

Highstone was not a large city, certainly nowhere near as large as Glenhallow. Children were rare enough among the ælven that Eliani had grown up with little company. Luruthin, living a day's ride away in Clerestone, was the nearest to her own age of anyone in the area, and because of that both Felisan and Luruthin's parents had encouraged him to make Felisanin Hall his second home.

Now, though, Luruthin was past his majority, while Eliani still suffered the endearments and caresses of those who thought her a child. She was not; she had seen much, and her father had encouraged her to sit with him when he was hearing petitions and managing the governance of Alpinon. She knew more than any child.

Sounds drew her notice: a door softly closing, a murmured goodnight, quiet footsteps. She waited until she heard both her father's and Luruthin's doors close, then slipped out into the hall.

Luruthin and his parents always stayed in the same rooms when they were visiting: two adjacent chambers across the hall. Eliani padded in her bare feet to Luruthin's door, then quietly opened it.

Luruthin turned toward her in surprise, his arms still in the sleeves of the tunic he was removing. He frowned, pulled it off and tossed it onto the chest at the foot of his bed.

"What?"

Eliani came closer, matching her whisper to his. "What did you tell him?"

He grimaced, then picked up a plain fleececod tunic from the bed and unfolded it. "That I saw you run across the circle and thought you were upset, so I followed."

"Did you tell him where I came from?"

Luruthin pulled the tunic on. "He knows you were at the guest house."

Eliani bit her lip. Yes, of course he knew. He had heard her offer to help the bard with his instruments. She felt heat returning to her cheeks, and turned away so that Luruthin would not see.

"Eliani ..." Luruthin's hand touched her shoulder. "Did he hurt you?"

"No." She shook her head, squeezing her eyes shut against the memory of humiliation.

"If he laid a hand on you unwelcome ..."

"No." Impatient, she faced Luruthin. "That is the trouble. I *wanted* him to touch me. He would not. He th-thinks I am too young!"

A small smile curved Luruthin's lips. "Well, you are two decades shy of your majority."

"You did not wait until your majority!"

He blinked. "We are not talking of me."

She stared at him, breathing sharply, remembering how she had laughed at him when he had first become interested in females. In the space of a year he had gone from wonderment and awkwardness to a confidence that she did not completely understand, and he had ceased to talk with her about it. She still resented that.

He put both hands on her shoulders. "Eliani, do you really want your first love to be a stranger with a pretty voice, who will leave again in a few days?"

She looked away, sullen anger filling her. He was right, and that annoyed her.

"Or would you rather it be someone who truly cares for you?"

She glanced back at him. "But there *is* no one like that who is willing to teach me!"

Luruthin's eyelids drooped, hiding his eyes, though she suspected she saw a gleam of amusement in them. His voice was quiet and serious.

"You will find the right partner, and when you do, you will both know it."

She swallowed and her hand curled into a fist. She struck it lightly against his chest. "I am not a child!"

"This bard ... awoke your curiosity. I see that. There will be others who do the same. Trust me, Eliani, you will have no trouble finding admirers. There is no need to rush."

"What need is there to wait?"

All humor faded from his gaze. His eyes, green as moss, lit with a strange intensity.

"Perhaps none."

His khi, so familiar she rarely noticed it, suddenly filled her awareness. A tingle of surprise went through her. Luruthin moved his head toward hers, slowly—giving her opportunity to pull away—but she held still as he kissed her.

His lips were soft and warm, a faint taste of mead lingering on them. The kiss ended too soon; she had been kissed more soundly by her eldermother.

Luruthin drew back and gazed at her, as if asking whether she approved. She stared at him, breathing shallowly, unsure what to do. After a moment he kissed her again, more urgently.

Fear and eagerness surged within her. Luruthin's tongue flicked forward, teasing, exploring. She had heard of this and wondered why anyone would like it, but was not so strange as she had thought and her body reacted to it in ways she had never imagined.

A fire kindled in her belly. Her arms slid around him, pulling him closer.

Luruthin's arms went around her, tight with the strength of his muscles. He kissed her deeply. She followed him as best she could, hoping she was doing right. His response seemed approving, but then suddenly he pulled away.

Had she done something wrong? He had never stared at her like this.

He was breathing as fast as she. He put an arm around her shoulders and pulled her toward the bed, then sat on it, drawing her down beside him. He kissed her neck beneath her ear, making her shiver. His whisper was hoarse.

"If you want me to stop, tell me. All right?"

Eliani nodded, then jumped as his lips pressed into the hollow of her throat. She hesitantly stroked his hair, then froze as his hand touched her breast—and stayed there.

He raised his head and kissed her again, hungrily. His hand squeezed and caressed her breast, creating sensations that stunned her. She returned his kisses when she remembered, but often she held still, her attention fixed on his touch and the feelings it roused.

His other hand slid inside her tunic, up her back, warm and firm and friendly; no, much more than friendly. This was her cousin, she recalled with amazement—her childhood playmate —but they were neither of them children any more.

Luruthin paused in kissing her to pull her tunic over her head, then dragged his own tunic off and pulled her to him. Warm flesh against hers; she gave a small gasp of delight. Luruthin froze and raised his head to look at her, putting a finger to his lips in warning.

She understood. His parents were in the next room; she must be silent.

He drew her up onto the bed, gently laying her back, and thrilled her by kissing her neck, her shoulders, her breasts. She bit her lip and clutched the blanket to keep from crying out. His hands traveled over her, warm and firm, caressing everywhere. He slowed, moving downward, his kisses becoming tentative.

Her loins lit with fire, and though he had not yet touched her there, she knew he would. She wanted him to. She wanted him to touch her everywhere at once.

He kissed her belly softly, slowly. His hands moved over her hips and she felt the tension of the waist tie on her legs release. His fingers hooked into the waistband and pulled the garment downward.

Shivers ran through her as his palms traveled down her hips. He sat up, one hand resting lightly on her belly. She looked at him and saw that he was hastily removing his own legs. He kicked a boot off and it thudded across the floor. Eliani smiled, holding back laughter.

In a moment he was back, his full attention raising heat in her flesh once more. He moved up to kiss her intently, then down again. His hands stroked her hips, her thighs, her loins.

Gently, so gently, he touched her more intimately. She held still, all her attention on what she was feeling. His fingers brushed the soft hair of her loins, then explored into it and stroked her tingling, tender flesh.

She caught her breath as he found the most sensitive place and caressed it. Shivers ran through her; he must know what he was making her feel. She reached for him, touching whatever she could find of him, wanting him to know that she did not wish him to stop.

When his hand withdrew she knew an agony of

disappointment, only to be relieved the next moment. He pushed her thighs apart and bent his head to kiss her there, raising waves of delight more intense than she had ever imagined. She abandoned herself to sensation, thrilling at what he was doing to her, wanting him to do more.

His tongue slid deep into her, surprising her, then returned to the delicious torment a little higher. His teeth closed lightly on her and she gasped.

He slid a finger into her, sending a flash of excitement from her hips to the top of her head. She wanted him truly inside her, not his finger but him, his maleness. Wanted the culmination of coupling but could not bring herself to speak, nor did she want him to stop what he was doing.

Her breath was ragged; she hoped it was not too loud, but she no longer had much control of it. Luruthin teased her into a fever pitch of excitement until she thought she could bear no more, then something tipped and spasms of pleasure went through her, blinding her, sending her soaring.

Gradually the sensation subsided, leaving her flushed with delight. She sighed as Luruthin's caresses became languorous. In his khi, though, the tension had not ended.

Slowly he withdrew, only to loom over her, arms to either side of her, his hair dangling against her chest. He kissed her, tasting salty and strange. She ran her fingers up into his hair, but he pulled back, watching her.

Her gaze traveled to his loins, where his maleness stood stiff and proud. Would he stop even now, if she demanded it? A part of her—the child that had always loved to tease him—was curious, but she would not try him so. She did not want him to stop. She wanted to feel all of him.

As if he had heard her thoughts, he lowered himself atop her, skin hot against hers. He kissed her as the strange hardness of his sex pressed against her loins. She jumped at the contact, still sensitive. He pressed himself against the wetness between her thighs and began to move back and forth.

Her body reawoke, the fire building swiftly again. She let out a soft moan and he silenced her with a kiss more intense than any yet.

His hands roved down her sides and slid under her. She waited, eager to feel him inside her.

Would they conceive a child? Unlikely, but possible, though she had not heard of anyone so young conceiving. If it happened she would welcome it.

He stopped moving and raised his head, catching her gaze. His eyes burned with a fire she had never seen and it thrilled her.

Holding her gaze, he pulled his hips back and she felt him press against her lower down. Heat flashed through her loins and she gave a small gasp of delight.

Their gazes locked, with infinite slowness he moved into her, deeper and deeper, stretching her, filling her with himself. She felt a pressure deep inside and knew that he had found her inner self, the part that must open to him if they were to conceive. Would he push into there as well?

He stopped, withdrew a little and pushed forward again against the barrier. A wave of indefinable sensation washed through her deep inside.

Luruthin closed his eyes. She watched his face as he began to move slowly, rhythmically. It felt lovely; he filled her and pressed deep inside her and sent flashes of delight through her.

A frown of concentration built on his brow as he moved faster, more urgently. She pushed back against each thrust, then closed her eyes, feeling the approach of another lightning spasm. Just as it reached her he gave a small grunt and thrust wildly, rapid and deep, almost but not quite causing pain.

Frantic spasms slowed to more tender caresses. Eliani breathed deeply, waves of bliss rolling through her. She stroked Luruthin's hair, his back, his hips. His arms tightened around her, then relaxed. They fell still.

She listened to his breathing, felt his heart pounding against hers, gradually slowing. His khi was blended with hers and that felt surprisingly good, not an intrusion at all.

They had not conceived. That was, after all, very rare. She knew a twinge of disappointment, and realized that if she were to conceive a child, she would much rather it be with Luruthin than with the bard.

How foolish she had been, dreaming about love from a stranger. She would not have been nearly as comfortable. Luruthin she knew; she trusted him, and he had proved himself more than capable of teaching her what she wanted to know. She reached a hand up and ran it down the center of his back.

"Thank you, my friend."

He lifted his head, eyes filled with tenderness now. He kissed her sweetly.

"Thank you, my love."

"Are we lovers?"

"Ah—yes, I believe this meets the definition."

"No, I mean ..."

Sudden embarrassment silenced her. Her dreams beyond initiation into the pleasures of sex had been vague, but they had included a continuation of the relationship. She had not thought of its impact on others, though.

Would her father be upset to learn what they had done? She could not bear to think of him angry with Luruthin, nor did she like the thought of pretending nothing had happened. That seemed deceitful.

She looked up at Luruthin and swallowed. She did not want to lose his camaraderie, but she wanted more of this closeness. She felt confused, and it made her insecure.

"Will we do this again?"

He smiled. "Oh, I dearly hope so. I have not taught you everything, you know."

"No?"

The smile widened to a grin. He shook his head, and kissed her soundly.

Eliani let go of her worries and wrapped her arms around his neck.

Recipe: Green Chile Roll-ups

New Mexicans know this party standard very well. It's easy and popular, and anyone can enjoy it. Just select the level of spiciness when you buy your green chile. Can't find green chile in your local supermarket? Order from:

http://www.newmexicanconnection.com

Ingredients:

    4 T chopped roasted green chile
        (or 1 4-oz. can chopped green chile, drained)
    1 8 oz. package cream cheese
    1/4 t garlic powder
    dash of salt
    flour tortillas

Preparation:

Let cream cheese warm up to room temperature. In a mixing bowl, blend cream cheese, green chile, garlic powder, and salt. Spread onto tortillas, leaving 1/2 inch around outer edge. Roll into an oblong, wrap in plastic wrap, chill at least 1 hour.

Unwrap chilled rolls, slice into 1/4 inch rounds, arrange on platter and serve.

Dawn's Early Light

"'She comes after the darkness—after the battle is over—and moves among the wounded, weeping men, a silent shadow bringing comfort and peace.'"

A lurch of the wagon caused Mr. Parker's pencil to scrape a vivid line across the page. He cursed the driver, then read what he had just written. Scowling, he tore the page from his pocket notebook and crumpled it.

They had reached division headquarters, an abandoned house crouched atop a small rise at the edge of the woods, with a couple of peach trees just blooming. Near the house were a few army tents and a jumble of wagons, forlorn in the absence of their owners. A couple of staff officers sat by a gently smoking fire, gazing across open fields to where Griffin's division had moved forward to defend their hold on the Orange Turnpike.

A sketchy line of barricades, hastily constructed after the previous day's fighting, marked where the division had spent the night after losing the battle. Reinforcements had become entangled in the undergrowth of the Wilderness and arrived far too late to be of any use. Mr. Parker had heard the details from an ordnance officer's aide at the Union army's headquarters.

He smiled, remembering with satisfaction the aide's chance comment which had alerted him to the presence, at Griffin's division's hospital, of the elusive Miss Tamer. He'd been only too glad to leave the swarm of reporters orbiting General Grant on the occasion of his first clash with Lee. Mr. Parker disliked being one of a crowd, and however his story on Grant might have outshone the others, it could still be obscured by their numbers.

He preferred to pursue a more unique story, even though it had cost him a night's sleep in a bumpy wagon.

The sun had climbed nearly to midday. Away to the south a hot fight had been raging since dawn.

Spring burgeoned in the Wilderness, green leaves peeking out along the tangled branches of young trees beyond the barricades. The ghosts of Chancellorsville still haunted those woods—believed by many to be cursed—and there was fresh blood beneath the spring branches.

The wagon stopped, its way blocked by some others which were being searched by a weary-looking guard. The driver began a heated discussion with one of the soldiers.

Mr. Parker put away his notebook and picked up his traveling case, and hopped over the wagon's side, his boots raising dust from ground whose springtime was marked only by a few trampled shreds of young grass. Abandoning the driver to his argument, he started toward the largest tent he could see, tucked away in the shelter of the hill.

It was, as he had assumed, the hospital. As he approached the wall of dirt-smeared canvas he began to hear moanings, and murmuring voices, and now and then a sob.

These were the men whose anxious families would hang

upon the words he was about to write. Mr. Parker squared up his shoulders, reminding himself to be a faithful observer, to seek the qualities above all that would move his readers.

He paused in the open doorway, gazing around the tent, filling his mind with detail which he would later transfer to paper: a bowl of bloody rags set aside and steaming in the chill spring air; an empty bed still bearing the impression of the body that had lain in it; hollow-eyed boys looking up at him as if seeking some explanation of their sudden grief. A good correspondent noted such things without letting them cut to his heart. He'd been accused of coldness by some. It troubled him not a whit.

A number of people were tending the wounded, but he saw no woman among them. A steward came up to him, dull eyes inquiring his business.

"I'm Ethan Parker, of the Times," said Mr. Parker. "I've come to request an interview with Miss Tamer. Is she here?"

The steward shook his head. "She don't give interviews."

"I've come quite a distance. If you don't mind, I'll ask her myself."

The steward shrugged. "She ain't here now. She worked all last night."

"Is the night shift her usual duty?"

A grudging nod was enough. "Thank you," said Mr. Parker. "I'll return this evening."

"Won't do you no good," said the steward. "The others—"

"I am not like the others."

Mr. Parker's gaze challenged the steward, who shrugged and turned away. Mr. Parker noticed a man staring at him from his bed, eyes deep in hollow sockets, full of fear and loneliness, almost pleading. It occurred to him that this man might be able to tell him a little of Miss Tamer.

The dark eyes tracked his approach. He bowed slightly. "Good morning."

The soldier nodded back, brightening the smallest bit.

"I wonder if I might ask you a question or two? I'm a journalist, and I've come to write about Miss Tamer."

"The Dark Angel," said the man thickly. "I know her, aye. She'll not come for the likes of me."

Mr. Parker glanced about and found a stool, which he drew up to the bed whose blankets draped limbs wasted by illness. Taking out his notebook, he met the bright gaze of the sunken eyes. "How often have you seen her?"

"Took sick on Wednesday. Seen her that night, and last night. But I've seen her before, too. At Chancellorsville a mate of mine was hit, and I come to sit with him after, and she were there. She come for him, at the end. I heard the next morning when I come in. Glad for him, I was."

"What does she look like?" Mr. Parker asked.

The question seemed to confuse the man, for he frowned, and stared into unseen distance. "Oh ... dark," he said at last.

Mr. Parker concealed his impatience. The fellow was no genius. A common soldier, and whatever wits he had were evidently affected by the progress of his disease.

"Is she a young lady?"

"She's not old. Well—don't *look* old."

"Have you ever spoken with her?"

"Oh, every night. She sits with me a while. She's good that way—sits and talks with each of us as can hear. She comforts us all, not only the ones that are chosen."

"What do you mean, 'chosen'?"

"Them whose time's come." The dark eyes wandered restlessly. "Them what's wounded, and bound for their maker. She comes special for them. She knows when it's time."

Perplexed, Mr. Parker gazed silently at the man for a moment. Perhaps he was too far gone in delirium to be of any use. Yet his words had an echo of something—some deep feeling—that might yet be captured.

The soldier's eyes burned deep in their sockets. "I wish she'd come for me," he muttered.

"Perhaps she will," said Mr. Parker.

The man shook his head, his lank brown hair clinging to his brow. "Not the sick. Never the sick. She's kind to us, but she only comes to them as won their death in battle."

Mr. Parker sighed, and scribbled a word or two. Not much sense to be got from this fellow.

"She even comes to them on the field." The man's voice began to rasp, and his fingers fluttered restlessly at his sides. "She finds them. Seen her walking the ground before the fight's over, I have."

We have crossed into nonsense, thought Mr. Parker. Closing his notebook, he stood up and nodded to the soldier.

"Thank you. You've been very helpful. I won't disturb your rest any further."

A shade of hurt entered the restless eyes. Mr. Parker turned away. There were others whose job was to comfort the dying. He had a different task at hand.

He tried questioning a few of the hospital staff but found them reticent, so he determined to wait for his chance with the "Dark Angel" herself. A few inquiries led him to a small A-tent which had been erected for Miss Tamer's use.

It was not far from the hospital, set apart in the shelter of a blasted tree. Mr. Parker dared once to call her name softly, but got no answer.

Setting his case down, he made himself comfortable against the tree trunk, and contented himself with sketching the tent and its environs. The sound of battle rumbled like distant thunder. A raven—possibly the only wild creature within miles —came to pose on the peak of Miss Tamer's tent, and Mr. Parker dutifully sketched his portrait.

When hunger awoke he pulled half a loaf of bread and a stale end of cheese from his case. Conscious of the nobility of the act, he offered a crumb to the bird. The raven peered at it, turning his head this way and that, then uttered a disparaging squawk and departed with a huffle of black feathers. Mr. Parker shrugged and finished his meal.

Perhaps he should go down to the fighting, but he couldn't conjure any enthusiasm for it. He'd been on too many battlefields, written too many vivid accounts of terror and glory, to be susceptible any longer to their thrills. He wanted a new view of the weary war, and after months of searching he thought he'd found it in Miss Tamer.

Rumors were unreliable, of course, and he had too much self-respect to perpetuate war-born myths. Wild tales of bad luck haunting other journalists who'd sought out Miss Tamer he dismissed out of hand. It was war, and bad luck came to many. A journalist, if he was any good at his job, took risks as great as or greater than those of a line soldier. Some died. That was the way of things.

Mr. Parker gazed at the little white tent, pondering the little he knew of its occupant. Miss Tamer, while hard to find, seemed determined to be otherwise dull and ordinary despite the wisps of lore that followed like mist in her wake. No great family claimed her, no noble statesman was her patron. She was thought to be of humble means, and some said she had taken to nursing for the meager support offered by the army.

Everywhere she'd been in the past year, the same tale followed again and again. Miss Tamer was an angel come to Earth. Miss Tamer's touch soothed away all cares.

What was it she did or said that was so magical? She gave comfort, was all he had learned so far. That seemed too simple a thing to spawn the reverence with which soldiers spoke of her. Others sat with the sick and dying, watched through the long lonely nights. Why did Miss Tamer's name above others lift the hearts of soldiers to a state of awe?

⚭

The rumbling shuffle of many footfalls awoke him. Sitting up, Mr. Parker heard more than saw the shifting dark mass of soldiers on and around the road. Now and then a glint shone off a rifle barrel or a bayonet. Griffin's division was returning to their breastworks.

Fires flickered among the midnight trees beyond. The tent before him was dark. As he sat up and glanced toward the hospital, a skirted figure appeared silhouetted by the glowing canvas, paused at the door, then went in.

A sharp breeze made him shiver. He picked up the notebook

and pencil which had slipped from his lap, and regarded Miss Tamer's tent.

"Miss Tamer?"

But it was she he had seen entering the hospital, he was certain. A little flush of exhilaration ran through him as he did what he should not do; two steps brought him to Miss Tamer's tent, and he pulled the flap aside.

A bare cot, a single trunk, clothed in shadows. No light, no pictures, no possessions. Mr. Parker glanced behind him, saw no one watching, and stepped inside, letting the canvas fall.

In the dimness he edged forward to the trunk. His heart jumped as his boot scraped against it, and he bent to grope for the clasp. Locked, of course. Probably nothing but a spare dress or two anyway. Disappointed but not surprised, he slipped out of the tent, retrieved his case, and started down the slope to the hospital.

The place was busy now with comings and goings, new wounded being brought in, and the muffled horror of the surgeons' tables hidden by a breastwork of screens. Mr. Parker stood to one side of the door and gazed down the long rows of wounded. The bed of the man he'd questioned earlier was now occupied by an amputee—scarce seventeen, he judged—moaning softly to himself.

Farther down the tent Mr. Parker spied a head of glossy dark hair bending over one of the beds. He stepped into the busy aisle and edged his way toward her.

"Miss Tamer?"

She made no reply. Her hands, long-fingered and pale, continued to spoon soup into the mouth of her patient from a rough wooden bowl.

"My name is Parker, Miss Tamer. I'm a journalist."

"I believe you were told I do not speak to journalists," said the woman, her voice unexpectedly deep, and with an odd lilt. European? he wondered.

Mr. Parker stepped 'round the bed, the better to see her across it. The weak light of a lantern overhead cast stark shadows on the planes of her face. Not precisely young, but certainly not old. Not a beauty, though there was something compelling about her—a sense of hidden strength, perhaps.

Her movements were smooth and unhurried, her dress and countenance unremarkable. Eyes, which she kept on the boy she was feeding, were dark and rather large.

"I'm here to bring your story to the thousands who will take hope from it," Mr. Parker said, setting down his case.

"I have no story worth telling. I am merely a nurse."

"I have heard you compared to Miss Barton."

A scowl crossed Miss Tamer's face, replaced at once by a stillness almost unnatural. Her gaze followed her spoon from bowl to the wounded boy's lips and back again.

"Miss Barton is a genius of organization," she said. "Her efforts have comforted thousands. It is her story you should write."

"Miss Barton's story is well known," said Mr. Parker. "I am looking for something different."

"Different? What could be different? It is the same everywhere, Mr. Parker. War is always the same."

"I intend to bring my readers a story of hope, ma'am," he said. "I want to tell the story of a woman whose kindness has made her beloved."

"Then tell it," said Miss Tamer. "You must surely have the talent to create such a tale. Journalists are always making up pretty lies."

"But I want the truth."

"The truth is not pretty," she said, meeting his gaze at last. "The truth is not the story you want!"

Her eyes, glinting anger, remained locked with his for a moment. Mr. Parker felt something stirring within, and found himself strangely moved to smile. Then she looked away, dispelling the moment's intensity.

"The truth," she said quietly as she offered her patient another spoonful of broth, "is that many of these soldiers will die of their wounds, and many more will die of sickness, and it will not stop while the war continues."

Mr. Parker glanced at the soldier—a rosy-cheeked farm boy,

like hundreds he'd seen swallowed by the war—wondering how he liked this blunt evaluation of his chances. The boy seemed not to care. His attention was fixed on his nurse.

That was it, Mr. Parker realized. It was this woman's personality, her air of carefully controlled feeling—passion, a better word perhaps—that made her so memorable, all the more so to men who were hurt, frightened, in pain. They would naturally turn to a figure of such strength. Who better to support them at the hour of death?

A prickle of excitement crossed the back of his neck. His fingers itched to be at his pencil and paper, but instinct warned him Miss Tamer would not tolerate them. Instead he watched her quietly, his story evolving in his mind.

It would not be the platitudinous fluff he'd expected to write. A portrait of words, rather—a sketch of this fascinating woman, who preferred stark truth to frills and embellishments, whose uncompromising spirit drew hopeless men like moths to a flame—

Miss Tamer rose abruptly, the empty bowl in her hand, and left without a word. The soldier gazed after her in seeming content.

Mr. Parker watched her pass along the crowded aisle and slip behind a screen, then turned curious eyes to her patient. The blanket, he noticed, was wet with blood. The boy's face was pale, and his eyes very bright.

"Did you know she is called 'the Dark Angel'?" asked Mr. Parker.

The soldier's eyes flickered. "She'll come back," he whispered. "She'll come back for me."

A sudden, fierce jealousy swept through Mr. Parker at the words, uttered in absolute surety. Leaving the sufferer, he plunged into the aisle once more, earning a curse from a steward, and hurried after Miss Tamer.

The screen behind which she had passed concealed a small workspace in one corner of the huge tent. Jars and bottles lined makeshift shelves of graying wood, and papers littered a small camp desk. No one was there.

She had slipped out. With a muttered curse, Mr. Parker left the hospital, glad to leave its stench and noise behind.

The night was cool, but the darkness was broken by the restless army. Fires flickered in the Wilderness, and rifle fire stabbed and crackled through the dense growth like lighting in a nearby storm.

Climbing the slope away from the trouble, Mr. Parker saw a dark, skirted figure approaching a tent near the farmhouse. He quickened his steps.

An officer joined her, to whom she stood talking until she noticed Mr. Parker's approach. The officer's head turned as well.

"Miss Tamer," began Mr. Parker as he reached them.

"This is the fellow that's annoying you?" said the officer. "Shall I have him escorted to the rear?"

"That would only increase his curiosity," said Miss Tamer. "Better to ignore him. You will see to my request?"

"At once," said the officer. A major, Mr. Parker thought, if he'd seen the oak leaves aright in this dark.

Miss Tamer walked away, and as Mr. Parker tried to follow the major's hand against his chest stayed him.

"I'll honor her wishes," he said before Mr. Parker could protest, "but you'd do yourself a favor by leaving. This is no place for civilians."

"I see plenty of civilians here—"

"Just a word of caution," said the major.

"A threat, you mean," said Mr. Parker. "You have a personal interest?"

The major did not answer at once, and Mr. Parker knew he'd struck a chord. A lover, perhaps? Lucky man.

"My interest is in the welfare of this division," said the major at last, a thread of anger in his voice. "Miss Tamer is good for morale. She is supported for that reason—"

"Oh, supported is it?"

"—by the entire staff. Including, I may add, General Griffin, who will not appreciate hearing that she's been chased off again by another damned journalist."

"She's leaving?"

Mr. Parker was struck with sudden dread. The major reached for his arm as he turned away, but Mr. Parker shook him off and ran down the dark hillside to the tree whose bare limbs scratched at the night.

"Miss Tamer?" he called again at the tent. Still no light inside. He listened, trying to stay his breath, then flung the canvas open.

The trunk was still there, the blanketless cot still erect. It gave him no comfort. She'd slipped through his fingers, and unless he found her before dawn she'd be gone, aided by that cursed major to seek refuge in some other corner of the vast Army of the Potomac, where it might take him days to find her again.

The pounding of his heart at this thought was so intense it surprised him. It was not, he realized, merely the desire to pursue this story. It was the desire to win over her suspicions, to prove himself more than the hackneyed sensationalists who had given her a disgust of journalism, to convince her that his intellect and principles were on a level with her own. He glanced up at the smoldering woods.

"She even comes to them on the field."

Mr. Parker set his bag behind the tree and started toward the breastworks. It would be the last place one would ordinarily think to seek her, and he knew deep in his soul that she had the courage to take this risk.

A part of his mind chittered in worry: ridiculous to think a woman would go toward the fighting—at night, no less—and how could he think he knew what she'd do when he'd scarcely met her? But he'd learned long ago to trust his instincts, and the feeling was too strong, as if there were an invisible connection drawing him to the field.

Mr. Parker prowled the breastworks for a quarter mile to the north, where they ended in a dense stand of trees, and as far again along the south. Ignoring surly glances from the field officers, he peered at what little he could see of the woods beyond the works. Had he glimpsed the dark bell of a skirt he would not have hesitated to venture past the lines, but he saw only trees, heard only men's voices.

Hooves pounded up from behind. Soldiers' heads turned, and before long sharp orders rang out and the men left their shelter to form up again on the road. Mr. Parker stood at the works and watched them march down toward the enemy, feeling as weary and hopeless as they. His instinct had failed him. He felt a fool, and he disliked feeling so.

"She'll come back for me."

Understanding crystallized. Without daring to think it through—for that would be to risk losing his insight to the cold bonds of logic—he turned and ran back toward the hospital, crossing the open fields and panting as he climbed the slope toward headquarters once more.

It was late. No sounds issued from within the hospital tent save the haunted moans of dreaming wounded. Mr. Parker paused in the doorway, glancing toward the soldier's bed where he'd met Miss Tamer, and froze at a sight that struck straight to his gut.

Miss Tamer, seated gracefully beside the bed with her dark skirts flowing about her, had taken the boy's hand in both of hers and brought it to her lips. They sat motionless, the wounded boy smiling dreamily up at his nurse, the lady's dark lashes veiling her eyes as she pressed her kiss deep into his palm. Mr. Parker's loins responded at once to the sight, and a soft moan escaped him.

She heard, though it was only the tiniest sound. Her head shot up, eyes flashing anger, pale cheeks flushing even as she rose and flung the boy's hand away in a single movement. She moved to the aisle and ran away down it, her skirts flitting over the feet of the wounded like the shadow of a cloud.

"Wait," called Mr. Parker, his voice jarring in the stillness as he stumbled after her.

By the time he reached the spot where she'd been, she had vanished behind the fearful screens of the surgeons' domain. He glanced down at the farm boy, whose white face still wore its beatific smile. The eyes gazed blankly upward, and Mr. Parker realized with a sudden surety that he was dead.

His gaze traveled to the hand which Miss Tamer had honored with her caress. In the palm a little pool of dark blood had welled.

Mr. Parker's stomach did a slow flipflop. He looked at the wall of screens, questions rising, scraps of legends remembered, too fantastic to be credited. He strode toward the screens and stopped there.

Surely there was some rational explanation. The thought died as quickly as it had sprung, replaced by the gut knowledge that he had found something truly rare—so rare few could accept it—a creature of myth walking the sacred soil of Virginia.

He stepped through the screens, past empty surgeon's tables stinking of blood, out the back of the hospital into the darkness. She was waiting for him now, he knew. It was almost as if he could hear her thoughts. She was waiting to kill him.

Deep into the woods he followed. She was no fool, she would draw him far away from the hospital before she struck.

Bad luck to journalists, he thought, understanding now her dislike of the press. But he was no ordinary journalist.

The night was old, it would not last two more hours. From the direction of the road he heard the army's rumble and clatter, then a sudden shatter of rifle fire announced a fresh battle. He turned toward it, though the formless pressure in his mind protested. By effort of will he continued walking south, attempting to force her to meet him.

His thoughts became jumbled, battered by what he now knew was her summoning and by the sound of the fighting. Fires were burning in the dry forest, sparked by the rifles, licking at young trees and old skeletons from the previous year's battle.

A spent ball hissed past him and thudded into the earth. The cries of the wounded drifted among the bare branches. No hell could be more ghastly.

"I want to talk to you!" he shouted, and suddenly there was a deeper darkness before him.

She stood clothed in shadows, pale face, dark lips, bright eyes glinting. "Still?" she said, mocking hatred in her voice, and a sneer showing sharp, white teeth.

"Yes," Mr. Parker managed to say.

"Then you're even more a fool."

"No," said Mr. Parker, struggling to gather his thoughts. "I want to know why."

She took a step toward him, fire-tossed shadows of bare trees dancing across her face. His body responded to her approach with a very real physical excitement. He knew he should flee, but his feet remained rooted.

"Why do you work in the hospitals?" he said.

"Obvious," she answered. "Ease of supply."

"No," said Mr. Parker. "If that were all, you would keep to the battlefields. Less risk."

"I am no carrion eater," she said sharply.

She was very near, now. Mr. Parker's heart jumped as she reached up to brush his cheek. Her eyes, veiled by long lashes, followed her hand's journey down along his throat.

"Compassion," he said, his voice tightening. "You care about them."

The dark eyes flickered. "What nonsense. I *consume* them, Mr. Parker."

Her hands on his neck were warm. Almost hot. He so wanted to close his eyes, and abandon himself to the pleasure of her touch.

"That boy," he said, struggling to speak. "He died happy."

"As will you," she murmured.

"What if I told you I am no threat to you?"

"Ah, but you are a professional liar."

"What if I said I—admire you? I do," he insisted. "In all ways."

The dark eyes rose to meet his, glinting amused surprise. The fires were getting nearer and he could see her face quite clearly now.

"I could help you," said Mr. Parker. "I could travel with you, keep the gawkers away. I could offer you my name—"

She laughed. "I tired of that game a century ago."

"Or not, then," said Mr. Parker. "Give me a chance to prove my esteem for you."

"You esteem an illusion, Mr. Parker. You esteem what you want me to be, not what I am."

"Do you not abhor pain?"

"Pain and I are old acquaintances."

"You once caused it, perhaps?" said Mr. Parker, conscious of her fingertips, which had come to rest in the hollow of his throat. "And now you make up for it by easing the deaths of the doomed. By saving them pain."

"What pretty stories you tell," said Miss Tamer. "And what a pity—"

A wail climbed into the smoky sky above their heads. Miss Tamer's eyes widened at the sound: a human voice, raised in inhuman terror and pain.

"You do care," whispered Mr. Parker.

"Oh, God, help me!" cried the voice. "Help me, I can't! I can't—"

Miss Tamer's eyes flitted, searching the woods, now hazy orange-lit by fire and smoke. Mr. Parker looked past her to the edge of the blaze, where a dark lump was heaving on the ground.

"Over there," he said, nodding.

She glanced at the figure, a wounded man, unable to walk, unable to escape the fire that now lapped at his clothing. Her eyes flicked back to Mr. Parker.

"It would take too long to kill me," he said softly. "Let me help instead."

Her lips parted. "I could kill you in an instant," she whispered, the words perfectly clear in his ears despite the fire's roar. Then she spun away from him and hurried toward the struggling soldier.

Run, he thought, but could no more have left her than struck her. That in him which admired her now moved him to follow, to see what he, too, could to do help the suffering soldier. It occurred to him, as he put up a hand to shield his eyes from the glare of the fire, that he would never have done so before.

Miss Tamer knelt at the man's side, heedless of the furnace-heat. She took his face in her two hands and murmured to him as Mr. Parker joined her.

"Here, let me lift him."

"No!" she said fiercely, eyes remaining locked on the man's face. "He is too badly wounded," she said.

Mr. Parker glanced at the soldier and saw she was right. His skin crawled at the sight of the man's leg, nearly severed, the ground beneath it soaked in blood yet still smoldering with the stink of burning flesh.

The man's face was serene. He no longer cared that his body was slowly being consumed by the flames. All he cared for was the tender touch, the soft voice which he could not possibly have heard over the fire, the sweet dark eyes. Mr. Parker saw bliss in the poor fellow's gaze, the moment before a sharp twist of his head ended his life.

An expression of satisfaction flooded Miss Tamer's face and sent chills down Mr. Parker's spine. Stumbling back, he became aware of the wild pounding of his heart and the oppressive heat of the fire. All around them the woods were ablaze.

"We're trapped," he shouted to Miss Tamer, then coughed.

"No." She rose and brushed her hands, unconcerned. "*You* are trapped."

She thrust her arm toward a blazing tree nearby, and the flames shied away. Mr. Parker stood sweating, eyes streaming, choked by smoke.

Fool, he thought as she slowly walked toward him. *This is how the others died.*

He wondered fleetingly if the hospital staff knew. He felt certain they did not. Too many god-fearing Christians among them, they would not have tolerated Miss Tamer had they known.

"You asked why I work in the hospitals," she said as she approached. "I will tell you, Mr. Parker. I abhor waste."

Darkness flowed about her in a sphere. The smoky flames looked pale and sickly through the thick air around her. As she neared him, Mr. Parker felt its coolness envelop him.

"A-and pain," he stammered.

"Pain does not interest me," she said. "I outgrew the need for such thrills long ago. Pain is also a waste."

"So you feed on the doomed in order not to waste the living," he said, struggling to conceal his fear. "That sounds like compassion to me."

"I have no such noble motive, Mr. Parker. I like my comfort as much as anyone. No one is suspicious of wounded men's dying in hospitals."

"I cannot believe that is your only reason," said Mr. Parker.

If he could keep her talking, he might yet escape. He dared to turn away, guessing she'd prefer to kill him face to face. The fire's heat smote him, but he took one step away from her.

"Why can you not believe it?"

There was annoyance in her voice as she came up beside him, bringing her cool shadow with her. Mr. Parker's heart leapt with fearful joy. He took another step forward.

"You are too powerful," he said, not daring to look at her. Another step; she followed. "You need fear no mortal authority."

"You overestimate our strength."

They were walking now, strolling through the inferno, two acquaintances conversing, with flames flickering out beneath their tread and springing to life again after they passed. Mr. Parker fought down an hysterical urge to laugh.

"I think it would be difficult to overestimate you," he said. "I think you do not credit your own good. You comfort more than you kill. I spoke with a sick man who said you visited him daily."

"I would hardly escape notice if I did not assist in the wards."

"Hard work for one who likes her comfort."

"Consider me a shepherdess, Mr. Parker. Not one of those dainty, lacy creatures in the paintings, but a real herder who sees her flock for the resource they are, and who doesn't weep on butchering-day."

Mr. Parker thought he saw the flames thinning ahead. It took an effort of will to maintain his slow stroll.

"The soldiers would not adore you so if you were as cold as you say."

"Simple men are superstitious," said Miss Tamer. "They know I ease the pain of dying, and that is all they want to know."

"They call you an angel."

"Does that shock you, Mr. Parker? Do you think it blasphemous?"

"No. Were you a nurse—before?"

"I was like you, Mr. Parker, very much too curious for my own good. It was my downfall, in fact."

A strange lurch of his heart made Mr. Parker stop walking. Against better judgement he turned to face Miss Tamer, unable to form the question in his mind.

"Do not fear," she said with a slight, sad smile. "I am not bitter and I have no desire to spread my disease."

Mr. Parker felt something too close to disappointment for his liking. He turned away again and was surprised to see the hospital ahead, a mass of canvas against indigo sky. They had come out of the worst fire. Here it only licked at the trees through clouds of black smoke. If he ran—

"But you know I cannot let you live," said Miss Tamer behind him.

Mr. Parker felt a sudden wave of cold wash through him. He could not take another step. He scarcely had the strength to breathe.

"At least I can look forward to a pleasant death," he said in a whisper as she came up beside him once more.

"That's your good fortune. I've no choice in that respect."

A voice was raised in the hospital, a steward calling for assistance. Miss Tamer's eyes narrowed.

"Come."

She took hold of Mr. Parker's wrist. Her hand was cool and dry, and very strong. She drew him away from the blaze and the hospital, to a clearing in the woods at the foot of a small hill.

A thin, bluish haze of smoke softened the lines of bone-white trees. Flowers bloomed here, a scene worthy of the beribboned shepherdesses Miss Tamer had scorned. Mr. Parker saw that she was frowning slightly.

"I do not like doing this," she said. "If I thought I could trust you—"

"You can," he said, "but you cannot trust the others. They'll keep coming, and you will have to kill the ones who figure it out. You really don't like killing, do you?"

"None of us likes killing, Mr. Parker. Why do you think so many inflict pain? It is an expression of our own agony."

"You don't inflict pain."

"It stopped when I stopped fighting what I am."

"So you do have a choice."

His hand came up to touch her face. The skin was soft and cool. His fingers traveled to her hair, smooth and neat, as if she hadn't just walked through a maelstrom. She was almost pretty, here with spring flowers at her feet and the dawn's early light just touching the treetops above her head.

Mr. Parker froze, staring up at the golden light flickering among new, green leaves. Morning had stolen upon them, cloaked in smoke and fire.

Miss Tamer's gaze followed his, then her head whipped around to the east, where rays of light spread upward from the hilltop. The shadow in which they stood was a twilight island in the sea of morning that flooded the forest, rising second by second.

For the first time he saw fear in her face. She turned on him, dark eyes flashing.

"Very clever, Mr. Parker!"

He felt sick. He glanced around in desperation, then looked back at her angry, accusing stare.

"Hide!"

She looked astonished, then laughed. "Where?"

Sunlight touched the hem of her skirt. She flinched away toward the center of the hill's shrinking shadow.

"It is too late," she said.

"I didn't—"

"Go back to the hospital."

Unnatural stillness had returned to her face. It was as if a door that for a moment had begun to crack open was suddenly closed again.

"Tell them to move the ward, or they will lose it to the fire," she said calmly.

Mr. Parker seized her hand, tears stinging his eyes, but she pulled away from his grasp. She snarled, sharp teeth glinting in the growing light.

"Go!"

She turned her back on him and stepped up to a sapling, wrapping her strong fingers around its trunk. She stood facing west, where the forest was blue-gray and hazy with smoke. She had turned her head away, yet he still heard her whisper.

"Do not watch."

But he was a journalist. And, she was dying because of him. How could he not watch?

Rifles crackled in the distance. Mr. Parker felt the sun's heat strike his shoulder, and clamped his teeth on his lip as the light spilled over the hilltop.

She turned her head toward him at the last moment, dark eyes afire with bitter amusement. Then he was blinded; a flash of light followed by a hair-raising skriel. When he could see again he ran forward, but found nothing, only a snowfall of ash drifting against the sapling's bark in the sunlight.

✿

It was many hours before he found the time and the courage to approach the little A-tent beneath its gnarled tree. He was bone-weary, having spent the day helping move the hospital away from the fire. Now he intruded once more on Miss Tamer's tent.

Silent, empty. Bare cot—she must never have used it—and the trunk.

Mr. Parker broke the lock, and was not surprised to find that it contained merely earth. He had thought there were no more tears in him, but one fell on the soil as he leaned over it to place a handful of battered peach blossom—stolen from the headquarters trees—inside.

An approaching rumble made him hasten to shut the trunk up again. Stepping outside he saw a wagon lumbering to a halt. The teamster climbed down and gave him a suspicious glance, then pushed past him into the tent.

"Go along," said the man. "You're not wanted here."

"Where are you taking that?" Mr. Parker asked as the man lifted one end of the trunk and began to drag it out of the tent.

"Never you mind. Damned nosy busybody."

"She won't be there."

"I follow my orders, damn you. Either help, or get out of the way."

Mr. Parker stepped aside. Useless to attempt explanation, just as it was useless to think any story he could write of Miss Tamer would ever be believed.

Yet—

Mr. Parker helped the teamster lift the trunk into the wagon. Then he sat beneath the tree, reached for his case and pulled out his pocket notebook.

It didn't matter, after all, whether his story was believed. He knew what his readers wanted, and the last thing any journalist would do was to let a good story go to waste.

Kind Hunter

The hunter paused near the end of the tunnel, gathering himself against emerging. He had not been to this place before, but he knew he would not like it. Already the unnatural smells and the roaring, constant cacophony were hammering at his mind. Had his quarry not been here, he would never have come.

A brush of soft warmth against his calf. "Stay close, Shade," he said softly. Golden eyes glanced up at his, flash of green in their depths. Shade didn't like it here either.

Bad place. Torril go home? queried the cat.

No.

Torril shifted the case that carried his bow and pulled his hood forward, covering his ears. This was a city of mortals; he must not be recognized. His kind rarely walked among humans now, and to be noticed would have undesirable results. A deep breath, and he started toward the light.

A musician sat at the tunnel's end strumming a guitar, soft chords hanging in the air, lonely, aching. For a moment Torril wished for his flute, but he'd left it behind when he'd taken the kind hunter's oath.

He dropped the change from his train fare into the open case and walked on, not bothering to query the man's mind; humans were too busy with their own tumbling thoughts to heed gentle questions. There would be birds, maybe mice, dogs and cats he could ask. Some would have seen his quarry.

gray skies outside, but brighter light. Torril shaded his eyes. This was the older part of the city, built of brick and stone rather than glass and steel, still too stark for his comfort. Pavement separated his feet from the living earth, isolating him. A carved stone cross towered over the walk, a symbol abhorred by the

189

creature he hunted. A good omen? Perhaps.

Pigeons sat atop the cross. Torril greeted them silently.

Do you know of a nightwalker hereabouts?

Nightwalker, no. Night we sleep. Food? Food?

No, I'm sorry.

Feathers whipped at the air. Torril walked on.

Cold. The gray buildings seemed to suck the life out of him. No green anywhere near them; they were traders' halls full of dusty books and such. Torril pulled the lacings of his hooded coat tighter to hoard his warmth.

The coat looked enough like the current fashions of mortals for him to escape notice, though no mortal had formed it. His surviving sisters had woven the cloth and wrought it into coat, tunic, leggings. He remembered their hands in the dance of its making, dappled by green-gold sunlight, while he sat apart carving the arrows that now lay in the case with his bow. The essence of his sisters' gentle touch remained in the caress of the fabric against him.

He smiled softly, sadly. Perhaps he would see them again, if all went well. Perhaps.

Humans hurried along the sidewalks, and Torril fell in among them, leaning forward to keep his face hidden and to lessen his appearance of height. Shade ghosted at his feet, stopping now and again to sniff at interesting crannies and doorways. A shopkeeper shouted unwelcome and batted the cat with a broom. gray hackles rose. A hiss, and he darted between Torril's feet to explore some friendlier spot further on.

The sun was too deeply veiled to be seen, but Torril knew he had less than a quarter-day before dark, when the hunt would begin in earnest. He would do well to find shelter before then. He glanced up at the grayness, troubled by the thought of a storm, and hurried on.

In a lace-curtained window a small, flat-faced dog sat on a cushion. Its eyes watered. It was staring at Shade.

Where are trees? Torril asked.

Downhill, the dog answered. *Cat there—careful.*

Cat's a friend. Many thanks.

The dog opened its short muzzle to bark as they passed. The window-glass muted the sound. A circle of mist appeared before the dog's face, then faded.

The next cross-street sloped downward. Torril turned that way, scenting grass on the cold breeze. His steps quickened. He had not seen a free-growing thing since leaving home that morning, and after the rattling train ride and the noise of this man-city he craved peace. Shade scampered ahead toward a small park—a haven—at the foot of the hill, and Torril had to force himself not to run after.

Trees, their green leaves singed with yellow, whispered welcome. Autumn was coming, and summer things would soon slumber. Torril stepped onto the grass and sighed as its aliveness tingled at him through his boots. He walked straight to an old oak and laid his hands on the rough bark, felt its sleepy strength flowing into him, closed his eyes.

Thank you.

The tree's glow washed through him slowly. He drifted as if under a sea of golden warmth, drinking in renewal, peace, life. Then through the depths a sound came to him, distorted; a cry.

Reluctantly he took his hands from the trunk, stepped back, blinked his eyes open. The cry became clearer. A human child, sitting on the ground near a bench where two women chatted. Young enough to hear; Torril touched its mind gently.

Trouble?

Toy! Toy!

Torril glimpsed bright colored triangles in the infant's mind. The child stopped wailing and looked straight at him, empty-handed, hopeful.

Shade?

Here. Bushes. I smell mice.

Find this, Torril asked, sending the toy's image to the cat. With gentle urging, Shade abandoned his hunt and went to a holly bush near the human child. Rustles followed; a many-colored ball rolled out toward the child, who grabbed it tight.

"Ba!"

One of the women looked up. Torril faded close to the tree

trunk, cloaking himself in rustle-green breeze.

"Ba!" cried the child, pointing at him and beating the toy with its other hand. The woman looked toward Torril and tree, saw only tree, and picked up the child.

Torril smiled to himself, turning away. So far from his own people, it was good to have helped a small one. His race bred slowly, their numbers diminishing as the mortals' increased. With every forest cleared to make way for farms or towns it grew harder for his kind to survive. His own sister—Tana, the youngest—had recently died in childbirth.

Tana. Lightning and terror; a pale face streaked with rain and tears. The memory swept all pleasure from him, cold anger filling its stead. He became aware of the man-city's towers fringing the park. With a shiver he moved on, away from the women and the child, deeper into the park toward a small cluster of trees that might shelter him until dark.

A pathway led past the little grove; willows and ash, grouped to form a pretty backdrop for a small pond. They had gone untrimmed a while, the willows dangling long trails of leaves into the water. Small shrubs at their feet offered a few last blossoms to grace the harvest season. Torril left the path and entered the tiny forest, inhaling deeply of the green smells.

Shield me? he asked.

A swell of well-being answered him. The green, growing things of the world had no words, nor clear-shaped thoughts. Feelings were their language. He had not realized how sharply he would miss them until he'd left his forest home.

His hand went to the band of white cloth at his brow; the kind hunter's badge. Not until he had completed the task he'd sworn to would he remove it or return home. A kind hunter's oath set him apart from his people. Killing was not their way, yet killing was sometimes necessary, and he had chosen to seek this kill on behalf of his kin.

Shade burst from beneath dark, glossy leaves, a tiny mouse in his jaws. Fierce eyes glowed then vanished, gray tail twitched welcome. Torril sat on the first thin layer of fallen leaves beneath an ash, and took bread and fruit from the pouch at his waist. His sister Alia had made the bread that morning, and handed it to him in silence. No one spoke to a kind hunter; he stood outside the circle of his people, apart from his kin, until his task was finished.

The bread tasted good. The apples were still tree-crisp; he cut them into slices with the small knife he wore at his waist. A fierce little tooth, that knife. He had traded a quiverful of his best arrows to have Yoren dip it in molten silver. Its edge was not quite so keen since, but would deliver a more bitter sting to his prey.

He finished his meal, cleaned the knife, and leaned back against the ash. Around him the grove's strength glowed softly, calming him. He opened his case. Bow and quiver were ready in a few moments. He laid them across his lap, leaned his head back, and inhaled sleep with the musty dry scent of the leaves.

◈

Darkness clung in sharp corners formed by the buildings of the street. Tall man-houses, squared-off blocks built of smaller blocks, marched in straight lines as far as Torril could see.

Here and there a small tree or bush, imprisoned in a man-made pot, formed a beacon of life in the bleakness. Shade roamed near, questing for game in the shadows. Torril listened to his thoughts, ready to interpose questions before the cat made his kill.

Torril's quarry was here, that was certain. Shreds of rumor led to this dark section of the town, always the thoughts tinged with fear.

Though Torril had never sighted his prey, there was no question about the creature's nature. Terror and blood by night were the trademarks of his kind, and these things echoed in the minds of the small creatures of the city, rippling outward from this district. Torril listened to their wisps of thought, some nearer, some stronger and more distant, a murmuring stream.

He chanced upon a hollow in the flow—a curious calm— and stopped to listen. No such eddy would ever occur in the life-filled forest. That was the trouble with forests. Too many layers on layers of living things. In a man-city it was easier for a hunter to isolate his prey, to control it, to....

Realization, revulsion, a moment's touch of hunger and hate. Torril wrenched his mind free and shut away all thoughts, reaching out a hand to steady himself, finding cold stone. The creature had sensed him, perhaps knew now he was hunted. Torril felt the ghost-touch of a powerful mind questing, seeking him. He sat at the foot of a building, willing the thoughts to flow past.

A bump against his shin. Reach out a hand to stroke warm fur. Shade mewed a query, and Torril opened his mind enough to hear the cat.

Go now? Go home?

Not yet.

Bad thing near.

Yes.

Eyes open, the world retreated into gray and brown blocks once more. Torril got to his feet, shook off dark feelings and started on, deeper into the heart of the man-city.

Shade did not roam far ahead now, but clung to Torril's ankles. Their way took them down narrower streets, not as well-kept, not well-lit. Keen eyes in the dark caught tiny movements in the shadows; Torril queried briefly, sensed a rat's fear of Shade.

Nightwalker near?

Hunts. Hunts.

A skitter and the rat was gone. Shade made no move to follow but stayed close, eyes wide, fur fluffed and angry.

Torril slid an arrow from his quiver and set it noiselessly against the bowstring, calling the shadows to cloak him. Shadows of stone and brick were less accommodating than forest shadows; it took an effort to bend them to his will.

Tana, he thought, seeing her weary, rain-soaked form stumbling toward him through the woods, weeping with joy and sorrow. For her sake he would do this, kill one of the creatures who'd caught her, enthralled her, defiled her. A life for a life; that was the kind hunter's oath.

Breathing too fast. Torril focused on clearing his mind, on silence, on hearing and seeing.

The pavement was damp now; a moist night. Tang of blood on the heavy air, fighting the city smells. Shade growled soft and low, and fell back behind Torril's feet.

The hunters turned down a street lit by strange colors—red and orange and the brilliant pinks of summer flowers—glowing unnaturally in windows and over doorways. For all their weird illumination the street was still dim. Though the night was more than half gone, mortals strolled the walks or stood in clumps at corners here, restless and sullen-looking, the lost or becoming-lost.

Torril held his bow as close as he could and wrestled the shadows to conceal him, knowing he could not continue so for long. The effort was costing him some of his alertness, and it was Shade's hiss that brought his attention to two figures disappearing around a corner a short way ahead; a male—tall and dark, somewhat slender—preceding a ginger-haired female in high boots and a short skirt. They seemed clouded by shadows; a skill Torril's folk shared with the nightwalkers.

His scalp tingled. This was his quarry.

How much better it would be to meet him in a forest glen instead of this dead city. But of course, the creature knew that; it was part of the reason nightwalkers tended to live in the cities of men.

Torril saw cat-shelter behind a discarded box. He flashed the image to Shade and told him to wait there, then crossed the street alone, following the nightwalker and his victim. Down an alley, dim and still, each step that brought him closer to his quarry weighing on him.

To kill a being of high intelligence was wrong. That was the rule he'd been taught, and, in part, it was the kind hunter's justification, for the nightwalkers had no such philosophy and caused great destruction among the world's thinking races. Yet this did not ease the trouble in Torril's mind. Was he not now, in his quest to slay this creature, sunk to his own level?

Tana. She would be avenged. A life for a life, or his kind would be overrun. The blood-seekers preyed on mortals as food, and on the elven kindred—

There. In a dark doorway; the beast was toying with his prey. The ginger-haired female stood over the lean form reclined on a clutter of rubbish. A nightwalker's eyes could mesmerize his prey into performing any unnatural act. Avoid the eyes, Tana had whispered to him, her cold hands gripping his shoulders, rain dripping from his hair onto her cheek.

He let go his cloak of shadows and silently nocked his arrow; pure oak, sharpened and hardened in the fire of his hatred. Move aside, woman, he thought, though only to himself. The nightwalker must not hear him.

She did not move aside but leaned closer instead, straddling her companion, bending her head to his. Torril surpressed his frustration and stepped out, seeking a clear shot. The dark-haired man moaned, a sound which lit acid flames in Torril's heart.

A plish—soft boot at the edge of an unnoticed puddle— betrayed by his own inattention. Furious with himself, Torril raised his bow for one desperate shot as the woman looked up at him.

Blood on her lips! On *her* lips! Eyes of ice stabbed even as he flung himself away. The arrow clattered on the pavement behind him.

Stop!

Yes, he must stop—all would be well if he stopped—the feeling filled his whole being, yet he ran on. Away from the command, from the desire to submit, from terror; back toward the garish lights and the mortals.

Hurt? Torril hurt?

Come!

He did not pause to look for Shade. The cat was in no danger, or not near so much as Torril.

As he distanced himself from the nightwalker his senses returned. Mortals stared, some called out words unclear, unimportant.

The quiver bounced crazily at his hip, arrows rattling as he ran through the streets, not bothering to hide, always seeking the brighter lights that he knew his enemy would shun. The huntress would not wish to spook her herd; he would be safe among them for now.

With fire in his throat he stopped at last, leaning against comfortless stone, gasping and shaking. A clay pot at the foot of stone steps held a young tree captive; he grasped the slender trunk and drank its small life in a heartbeat, then grieved.

He had never before consumed a tree's life. Bad fortune. When he returned home he would plant a sapling in its stead.

When he returned home. Easy to say, but not so simple to achieve. He must first kill the nightwalker, and the nightwalker was a female, and that changed everything.

Tana. Lend me your strength, sister.

This was not the creature who had captured Tana, tormented her, caused her death. No matter; a life for a life was the oath, and it was hard enough to hunt a nightwalker without inquiring its identity. He would kill this female because she was at hand, and because he must or be doomed himself.

"Hey! What are you doing there?"

Torril came out of his thoughts with a start, and found himself leaning against the steps with one hand around the dead tree's trunk and the other gripping his bow stone-hard. A human male in dark clothing, with badges and weapons of office adorning his person, was speaking at him angrily.

Torril let go the tree and backed away, hiding his bow in shadow. The mortal took a step toward him, then Shade ran between them, purring and stropping against Torril's legs.

He reached down to scratch the cat, watching the mortal from the corner of his eye. The man seemed to relax. While Shade flirted with the mortal, coaxing him to bend and pet, Torril slipped into shadow and away.

Down an alley, over a fence, back in darkness. Deep breath of freedom. He needed to replenish his energy before he could finish this hunt. He needed green, but he dared not open his mind to inquire where to find a mass of trees, for he was both hunter and hunted now.

He found his way into a neighborhood of tall houses with small gardens, separated from the street by a low wall of bricks. Torril stepped over it into a patch of sanctuary; vines just starting to flame with autumn, clumps of tame flowers, and evergreen bushes shorn to peculiar shapes.

He sank to the ground, leaned against the vine-covered wall —eyes nearly closed but watchful lest the mortals behind their stone blocks should wake—and caressed leaves with either hand, drinking deeply of the garden's strength, yet not too deeply. Control; that was the difference between the nightwalkers and his people. Control and compassion. He would kill no plant, waste no life. He took only what each could spare, reaching through the soil beneath him to the roots of the neighboring gardens.

A shudder passed through him as he slowly let go the tension that gripped at his shoulders. Shade joined him with a rustle and thump, flicked his tail in greeting, and padded to a bush to explore its smells.

The nightwalker was searching for him, Torril knew. Fear prickled up his arms as he thought of facing her again. *Avoid the eyes.* Yes, but what if she chose not to mesmerize him, merely to kill? Immortals still bled; she could strike from behind, and consume his life in moments.

Pray that she does, if she catches you.

Tana had not been so lucky. Nearly a year had gone by from the time she was taken until her escape. She had been given up for lost by her kindred, and then one morning, early, in the midst of a howling rainstorm—

Torril pushed himself to his feet. No rest, not until she was avenged. His kin had spent a year in hell. He would waste no more darkness.

Street emptied into silent street. The gardens left behind, there was no more life around him, only the dark, dead eyes of the mortals' dwellings. Shade followed in silent resignation.

Ahead at a crossing, a single tree, gnarled and scant of leaves. A bird sat upon a twisted branch, and Torril dared a query.

More trees?

His answer was a raw squawk as the bird took wing. It cried again, circling, then dropped toward him. Shade's hiss came as one with his realization—too late, both—she transformed as she fell toward him, naked and horrible.

Eyes! Torril rolled aside, scraping a knee against the hard street, flinging up his bow arm to ward her off.

He heard the wood splinter as his arm was struck painfully to the ground, the nightwalker's weight atop it. Free hand to his waist for the knife; a slash, a hiss, and the weight was gone.

He staggered up, keeping his gaze away from her face, and wound up staring at pale breasts instead. Ice-tipped, yet they stirred something in him.

Her body was firm, her waist slender, hips a welcoming bowl. She raised a bleeding hand to lick the cut he'd given her, and his eyes flicked to her face before he could check them, glimpsing a smile. He tore his attention away and looked at the knife in his hand; cold silver, harsh under the dim chemical lights of the mortals' city.

She's not attacking.

The thought didn't comfort him. The blade in his hand began trembling. She smelled good.

The broken bow dropped to the ground. She stepped over it, bare white feet on rough pavement. He could hear her breath, she was that near.

You're a pretty one.

Her thoughts were too strong to be blocked. Torril aimed a blow with the knife and watched in horror as his hand gently yielded up the blade to his enemy instead. She turned it this way and that in the light, sending glints off the blade, then dropped it on the ground.

Look at me.

With all his being, Torril resisted. He kept his eyes on the ground, saw her place a dainty foot between his boots.

Lustful imaginings flowed through his unwilling mind and aroused an urgent response from his body. He strove to move his feet, her soft hissing laughter mocking him, her hunger washing through his thoughts, tainting them.

How wonderful it would feel to take her, here, now, under the black night while the stupid mortals slept in their dead houses. How delightful to become hers, to hunt no more and care no more, to live only for their mutual pleasure, days, weeks, years of it. She was beautiful, she was strong, she would bear strong children.

Not by me!

In desperation he wrenched a foot away from the pavement. He stumbled backward, nearly falling, a hand thumping into his quiver and his back coming up against something hard.

The tree. With a wordless cry he sucked its strength—all of it, years of growth, season on season of strength—and in one vicious thrust repulsed the nightwalker's mind.

His hand drew an arrow and he flung himself forward, stabbing up beneath her ribs with the slender oak shaft, feeling it crack as her shriek filled his senses, wild elation sweeping through him. Deeper, deeper he pushed the broken arrow through the blood that slickened his hand. She clung to him, howling, weakening, falling.

He let go the arrow. No more than two handspans protruded from her body, heaving as she gasped her last breaths.

He looked in her eyes then. Beautiful, dark eyes; they had no more power to control him. They accused him instead, and he knew he would remember them always. That was the price of his oath.

The life faded from her face. She no longer saw him, no longer was something to fear. Death drew a dull film over her eyes.

Torril's senses returned all at once; he felt the coldness of the predawn air in his lungs as he breathed sharp and fast, heard the dry rustle of dead leaves overhead, smelled blood. He picked up the knife, reached down and gathered the nightwalker's ginger hair in one hand, and severed it from her head with one stroke.

He faced the hoary tree whose life had saved him—the tree the nightwalker had perched in to hunt him—and saw its leaves had turned paper-white. He draped the tresses over its branches; at dawn they would crumble into ash and blow away along with the nightwalker's body, leaving no trace of her existence.

He looked down at her again; a pale, broken girl, slim like an elf-maid, reminding him uncannily of Tana in her funeral-boat. He'd stood in the rain and watched the river take his sister and her child—the child Tana had killed with her own hand—the infant got on her by her nightwalker captor. Slaying it had been her last act before death claimed her, that stormy dawn.

No hint of rain now. He kicked gently at the nightwalker's body with a booted toe. He had not wanted to hunt—and had dreaded killing—one of his own kind, however distantly related. They were more alike than he'd realized, perhaps. In the end, he had enjoyed it.

Shade came out of the shadows, padded silently to within an arm's length of the nightwalker's body and sniffed the air, then hissed softly.

Bad thing. Go home now?

Torril pulled the white band from his brow and dropped it beside the pale body.

Yes.

Emancipation

The Custodian of Oporto's Island stood in the darkness of his house, listening to the growing murmur of voices in the Grove of Malamalama outside. It was not a feast day, when a large attendance might be expected at Nightfall, but the woods were full of people.

He knew they had not come just to watch him perform the

evening ritual. How he wished his father still lived; his father had loved the ceremonial aspect of the office of Custodian, while he himself dreaded it.

He donned his green robe and the tall feathered headdress that weighed on him so. A tight knot of fear was growing in his stomach, for he alone was ultimately responsible for the sacred rite of Maintenance, and that responsibility was about to be challenged. He went to the door of his house, and as he stepped through the curtain that covered it, the drumming began.

Malamalama, the island's axis, glowed bright with captured sunlight, its near end terminating in a shielded pole in the center of the ceremonial clearing outside the Custodian's home. Dancers—men and women in the traditional garb of the hula kahiko, their hair and arms decked in the leaves and flowers of the island—waited around the pole, ready for Nightfall to begin.

Among the ti trees at the Grove's edge and back into the woods beyond were the island's people, dozens upon dozens of them, more than he had seen at any ritual in months. The Custodian glimpsed his counterpart, the Governor, among the growing throng, and his belly tightened at the sight of her.

How often had he silently wished for her presence at Nightfall—his favorite hour—the beginning of the time when lovers could tryst in shadowed groves and not be observed by curious eyes from across the island's sphere. How often had he dreamed of dancing for her alone, then taking her hand and leading her among the waterbelt's gardens with the gentle night to cloak them.

It was not to be. She did not come as Hoku, the sweet, laughing playmate of his childhood, but as Governor of the island, in the people's name, to put an end to Night.

The Custodian took his place at the foot of the dais that held the Focus, and the rolling drums burst into rhythm. He chanted an ancient prayer to Pele, his hands echoing the words while the dancers swayed in the clearing surrounded by tall palms and bushes heavy with fragrant blossoms.

When Pele had been duly honored, the ipu players began a faster rhythm and the Nightfall dance began. It was centuries old, one of many dances that kept alive the sacred heritage of Maintenance on Oporto's Island, or Moku Wina as the island was called in the chants.

Through graceful gestures the dancers told the story of Moku Wina's creation, how Oporto enticed Pele to come away from Earth and hollow out an asteroid, filling it with all the best things from Earth for the pleasure of his Guests. Dancing hands told how the great mirrors outside caught light from the distant sun and fed it into the island through Malamalama, source of all blessings, and how Oporto had decreed the order of days and nights. As his hands led the story, the Custodian's eyes watched the Governor standing at the clearing's edge, waiting.

The chant ended and a hiss of gourd rattles began; the dancers knelt while the Custodian came forward to perform the ritual of Calibration. He kept his eyes on Hoku as he danced up to the pole and turned the key that sent beams of light shimmering toward the four sacred shrines around the clearing.

His green robe flowing around him in graceful folds, he danced to each one in turn—Hi'iaka, Poliahu, Laka—passing his hands through the light and verifying its centering in the target on each shrine. As he came to Pele's shrine he looked up, thinking a silent, hopeless prayer to the goddess whose rituals he had faithfully performed, and in whom he had never believed.

She did not answer him. Shadows flickered over her image as his hands danced through the light, then he turned away, returning to the pole and shutting off the Calibration light before approaching the Focus.

The music intensified as he climbed the steps. Before him was the Focus that brought light into the island and sent it glowing along Malamalama; a large, ornate lever, completely unnecessary in a mechanical sense, but vital as a symbol of Maintenance. As the Custodian stepped toward it the drums suddenly stopped, and he heard what he had been fearing since the ritual began.

"Wait, Manuel."

He turned to face Hoku, the Governor, his life-long friend,

who had come up behind him. She did not smile, but stepped between him and the Focus, her red robe brushing the grass-covered dais.

"The Council has made a decision," she said, turning to face the people crowding the Grove. Her formal tones carried easily through the clearing and beyond. "Oporto's Island has been dominated for centuries by the rituals of Nightfall and Dayrise. We treasure our heritage, but we are not savages, or children. We do not need lies to control us, or darkness to inspire us with fear. We are an enlightened people.

"Nightfall is a wasteful practice. Every time the Focus is shifted away from Malamalama, precious light is spilled into empty space. We can use that light to better our lives."

The Governor turned to the Custodian, and he saw that her eyes were hard. "The Council has voted to eliminate the process of Nightfall, effective immediately."

The crowd roared approval, and the Custodian felt a sinking in his chest. "That would violate Maintenance procedures," he said over the din. "The Manuals clearly state—"

"The Council consider the Manuals open to interpretation," said the Governor. "We have the right to reevaluate procedures when the good of the people is in question."

"The Manuals were given to us by Oporto," said the Custodian. "To deviate from their instructions will place the island and its people in peril!"

"The Council has debated this," said Hoku, her face a careful mask. "We have concluded that to take the Manuals literally can place us in danger of misunderstanding their metaphorical intent."

"Maintenance must be performed," said Manuel, hoping he sounded firm despite his growing desperation.

"Manny," said Hoku, her voice dropping to a whisper, "don't make it hard on yourself. You haven't got a choice." For a moment her eyes poured warm sympathy into his, then she raised her arms, the folds of her crimson caftan sliding down to her golden shoulders as she turned to the people now crowding into the clearing and called out, "Henceforth, we live in light, not in darkness!"

A cheer went up among the people, and the Custodian's courage crumbled. He gazed out over the crowd in worry. Here and there a mournful face stared back at him, mostly dancers or his acolytes, the Maintenance technicians. He was their spiritual leader, and they looked to him for guidance in this crisis, but his heart was empty. He had said all he could think to say.

The Council ruled the island, and he must bow to their authority. He turned his eyes away from his followers and watched in numb despair as Hoku placed a hand on the great lever of the Focus. She borrowed two gestures from the dance; "light" and "forever." The cheers grew louder.

Hoku beckoned to a Watcher—one of the guards serving the Council—and posted her on the dais to prevent any attempt to shift the focus. Then the Governor stepped down from the dais and passed into the crowd, touching the hands they reached out to her, moving away under the continuing daylight.

The people followed, all but a few faithful who watched the Custodian expectantly as he slowly descended the steps. He stopped in the middle of the clearing and gazed at them, sensing and sharing their fear.

"What will happen, Manuel?" a young dancer asked him, her worried face framed in the leaves and fresh flowers of her headdress. "Will Pele punish us?" Her eyes pleaded for reassurance.

Others gathered around with soft and frightened voices. The Custodian raised his hands to ward off their questions.

"I will appeal to the Council," he said.

It was inadequate, he knew, but it was all he could offer. His followers exchanged doubting glances. He spread his arms in the wavelike gesture of blessing, which seemed to comfort them a little.

"Go home," he told them. "Close the curtains on your windows and doors. Bring night into your homes, and Pele will know you are faithful."

"Thank you, Manuel," they answered, the words rippling in a whispering wave through the small group as they drifted out of the clearing toward their homes.

He watched them go, their hands flashing in the spaces between leaves, speaking in silent, worried gestures. When they had passed out of sight Manuel went into his house and changed his ceremonial garb for light cotton, then went out— barefoot so he could feel the island with each step—through the Grove and down the path that led to the waterbelt.

It was his custom to walk along the belt every evening after Nightfall, enjoying shadows and the soft sounds of water as it travelled endlessly around the island's center; here a trickling stream, there a clever waterfall, lakes like jewels, some with stars flashing underfoot through viewbays lapped by their blue- black depths. The stars were barely visible now, obscured by the continuing daylight.

Manuel stopped and glanced up at a viewbay overhead just as the sharp glint of a mirror's edge passed it. Malamalama glowed steadily bright with the light which should have been diverted for night, some to replenish the great storage cells, the rest to pour off into space.

Music began somewhere nearby, and wild shouting; the people celebrating their freedom from darkness. Suddenly Manuel needed to sit down.

He went to the nearest bench and lowered himself onto it with the weariness of a man many times his twenty-four years. A jasmine bush caressed him with its heavy scent.

How had it come to this? He was Manuel, descended from a long line of Manuels, the Custodians of the island since the time of the Separation, when Pele had returned her attention to Earth where Hi'iaka was making war on her.

It was then that Oporto's children had lost contact with the children of Earth. It was then that Oporto had created the Council, and set into law the Days and Nights of Moku Wina. It was then that the first Manuel had accepted the lifetime post of Custodian, and pledged to train his successor so that the island would always be cared for. And so it had been, until now.

Manuel searched his heart for the source of his failure. He had studied and preserved the Manuals in whose honor he was named, faithfully performed all of the Maintenance rituals—of which Nightfall and Dayrise were the most important—listened to his people and striven to answer their needs. He had tried to hide his own doubts, yet despite his best efforts, the people had begun to question the old ways.

Some said the gods were not real, that Pele would never return to the island to reclaim her lost children. A growing number said the only true power was the people's own, and that no ancient system should dictate to them. Such ideas weren't new—Oporto himself had faced opposition, as had Custodians through the centuries—but never before had a Custodian failed to perform Nightfall. Manuel knew the vital importance of the ritual, of Maintenance, for the island's continued well-being, but he did not know how to impress it on those who saw Maintenance merely as superstition.

"Manny?" came a soft voice behind him, and his muscles tensed.

He didn't answer, but listened to the sound of sandals on the path, the swish of crimson cloth. A hand touched his shoulder and he flinched, then looked up at Hoku, unable to keep a stab of resentment from his eyes.

"I thought I'd find you here," she said. "May I join you?"

"Shouldn't you be at the celebration?" he said bitterly, hating himself as the words left him, for of all the people on the island, Hoku was the one he least wished to hurt.

She gave him the fleeting smile that always made his pulse a little faster; Hoku, heart's friend and gentle leader, daughter of Governors, descendent of Guests as shown by the reddish sheen of her hair. Though most everyone on the island was of mixed blood, the Governor's line still bore the distinctive features of Oporto's heritage.

The Council were children of Guests also, while Manuel's night-black hair proclaimed his descent from Staff. The two groups—Guests and Staff—had shared the governance of the island since the time of Separation; their children ruled after them and kept their names alive, each following his or her parent's path. Dancers and technicians fulfilled their birthrights,

Hoku performed her function, and Manuel, until today, had performed his.

Hoku sat beside him on the bench, her hand still touching him, gently making circles on his shoulder. A tiny shudder went through him, despair mingled with release of the tension knotting his back.

"It isn't you, Manny," she said, bringing both hands to bear on his shoulders. "I swear it isn't. You've done everything you should. We have simply outgrown the need for night. Like you always said, these rituals are just symbolic—"

"Night is not just a symbol!" said Manuel, turning to face her. "Night is the time of rest, of replenishment—"

"On Earth, yes. In primitive societies, yes," said Hoku, "but we're beyond that. For centuries people have worked through the night—on Luna, on the stations, even on Earth—and still lived happy lives. There's no need for us to huddle in darkness half the day when the sun's light is available to us all the time."

"If there hadn't been a need for Night, Oporto wouldn't have built the Focus," said Manuel. "He wouldn't have created Nightfall."

"He made Nightfall for the Guests from Earth, so they would feel at home," said Hoku. "And as for the Focus, we control the flow of light, it doesn't control us!"

Her eyes were beautiful, full of righteousness and something else—something dangerously like pity—that stung him and made him turn away. "I don't want to argue with you," he said.

"No," she agreed softly.

They sat in silence for a moment, Manuel acutely aware of the warmth of her hands on his back. He had loved her from childhood, wanted her from youth, but the Custodian and the Governor were counterparts, working together from a distance, living at opposite ends of the island, close and at the same time standing apart.

Never since the island's creation had a Custodian and a Governor joined. It was thought that such an alliance would threaten the balance of power.

Manuel glanced at Hoku. Perhaps she was right. Oporto's people were enlightened; perhaps endless day would enrich their lives, and it was only his selfish love of starlight that made him long for the night. If so, then the skeptics who denounced Maintenance as superstitious nonsense were justified, and the Custodian's function was meaningless.

Except it wasn't meaningless. It was necessary. Beneath the rituals were the foundations of the island's vitality.

Rising abruptly, Manuel paced a few steps away. "I wish to address the Council," he said.

"They won't change their minds," said Hoku.

"It is not for the Council to interpret the Manuals," said the Custodian formally. "Their meaning requires study—years of study—for which I have been trained and the Council have not. It is my duty to advise them." He turned to face the Governor and saw a sadness in her eyes; his words had built a wall between them.

Hoku sighed and stood. "Very well. I will inform the Council of your wish. You may address the next meeting."

He nodded silent agreement, gazing at her with an inner ache that was all too familiar. She raised a hand to her heart in the gesture of family-love, gave him a sad little smile and turned away, her sandals whispering on the path, red robe flashing through the leaves as she left him in the sharp light of day.

❧

Lehua came for Dayrise, and Manuel was both glad and sorry. He had not spoken to her since before the last Night. Hoping to resolve the conflict, hoping he could make the Council see his viewpoint, he had gone to their meetings and reminded them of Oporto's word, which threatened dire consequences if the people failed to perform proper maintenance.

His words had disappeared like raindrops into a lake; the Council would not be convinced. His failure to reach them weighed on his spirits, and though it pleased him to see Lehua among the sparse group gathered in the Grove of Malamalama for Dayrise, he did not look forward to speaking with her.

There were only a handful of dancers this morning, and the flowers they wore were a bit brown at the edges. One musician beat out the Dayrise dance on the ipu, and Manuel chanted words of joy without much enthusiasm. It was hard praising the return of light when Malamalama was already shining brightly.

He finished the song, moved to the Focus where the Council's Watcher stood silent guard and pantomimed shifting the great lever upward, then turned to watch the worshippers drift away. Lehua waited for him by his house, the whiteness of her hair as it brushed her shoulders making her cotton Maintenance garb seem dim.

Lehua—Chief Technician of Moku Wina, mother of Lehua and Manuel—was a grand old dame, stout as a nut and just as tough. No one cared to cross her. Manuel wished he had inherited some of her tenacity; no doubt he would have dealt better with the Council if he had.

He remembered her strong hands around his waist, lifting him up to a Maintenance shaft for the first glimpse of the systems that were his heritage. The hands were gnarled now but still strong, and she held them out to him with a smile.

"You look tired, Manny," she said.

"It's hard to sleep. Come inside, share my breakfast."

Manuel held the curtain aside for his mother and followed her into his house. It was dark; he had formed the habit of keeping the windows covered. He pushed aside a curtain to let some light in, and brought cushions and fruit to Lehua.

"We haven't seen you in Operations lately," she said as she settled herself.

"I've been busy," said Manuel, cutting slices from a ripe mango. He handed her a piece and ate one himself, let its musky sweetness fade on his tongue. "You would send for me if there was any problem."

Lehua bit into a date and chewed slowly. "Have you been down at the Hotel?"

"Not since the last Council meeting."

"What has kept you so busy, then?"

Manuel laid down the knife and wiped the stickiness from his hands with a napkin. "I've been—searching."

"For?"

"A way to make the Council hear me. A way to...."

"To believe in what you are doing?"

Lehua's voice was gentle, but the words cut. Manuel had never been able to hide his true feelings from her, but she had not said a word about it ever before.

Always loving, always accepting, Lehua. Now even she saw the danger that lay in his failure. He could not look into her eyes.

"What would my father have done?" he muttered.

"Your father never faced this kind of challenge."

"You mean the Council."

"I mean the doubt."

He straightened and looked at her, and the pity in her eyes was worse than all the rest. Manuel hid his face in his hands, but the smell of mango clung to them, inescapable as the daylight. He got up and went to the window.

Outside children were playing tag in the ceremonial clearing, something that would never have happened when he was young. The place had lost its holiness, or the people had lost their sense of it. Or perhaps it had never been holy.

"Why did Manuel III make Maintenance into ritual?" he said angrily.

"You know why," said Lehua. "The people were losing interest, and he feared the procedures would be forgotten. He set them to music and dance in order to preserve them."

"He made them a religion, and now we may lose them altogether!"

"Merely because you lack faith? No, Manny. The island is more important than your personal crises."

Like a slap in the face, the words sobered him. He turned to his mother, who sat quietly watching him.

"It seems hopeless, I know," she said. "But you will find a solution."

"You believe that?"

"I know it. These are good dates." She leaned forward, helping herself to another. "Do you remember Hoku's womanday?"

Caught off guard, Manuel blinked. "Yes—"

"She gave you her ti lei. All the boys on the island were courting her, and she gave it to you. I see you still have it," she said, gesturing to where the dried loop of twisted ti leaves hung from the wall above his bed.

"I don't think—"

"She loves you, Manny. Why don't you marry her?"

"The Governor and the Custodian can't marry," said Manuel, more sharply than he'd meant to.

"Can't? I never heard that. You young people place too much importance on your functions."

"You were just telling me my function is more important than my beliefs!"

"Well, that's true," she said placidly, reaching for another date.

Frustrated, Manuel began to pace, the woven mats beneath his feet creaking softly. "How can I go on lying to the people I'm supposed to serve?" he demanded. "It's hypocrisy!"

"Maintenance is not a lie, Manuel. You know that."

"But it's all tangled up in mythology! How can I expect the people to believe what I don't believe myself?"

"They don't need to believe. They need to have faith." Lehua got up and walked to the window, where she stood watching the children outside with a soft smile. "They need to know in their hearts that they aren't alone, that there's a whole universe beyond the island," she said.

"What if we are alone?" said Manuel.

"Why do you still do the Communications ritual, Manuel?" said Lehua. "We haven't had a signal from Earth in four hundred years."

"That doesn't mean we'll never get one."

Lehua's smile widened. "Exactly. You know we might get a signal someday. You know we are not alone. You don't believe it, you *know* it."

She turned from the window and reached out a hand to comfort him, a gesture that sent him back to boyhood. Manuel came to her and sighed as her strong arms enfolded him.

"That's what faith is, Manny," she said into his ear. "It's knowing. Believing is worrying that something might not be true; faith is knowing it's true even if you can't see it. You've got faith, my son. You just have to decide in what."

Manuel gave an exasperated laugh. "Any suggestions?"

"Yourself?"

Lehua leaned back to smile at him, then patted his shoulder and started toward the door. "I'd better get over to Operations. Akamu and Keoni keep arguing about when to reschedule rainfall."

"Lehua—"

She stopped, and Manuel caught her hands in his, squeezing tight. "Thank you," he said. "I hope your faith in me isn't misplaced."

"Of course it isn't," she said, kissing his cheek. "You're Manuel."

"It's just a name, Mother."

"Is it?" Lehua's hand pulled back the curtain over the door. Light spilled in, framing her so he couldn't see her face, setting her hair aglow. "You know, they say a Manuel once saved the Earth," she said.

He could hear the smile in her voice, and smiled back as he watched her walk down the path to the clearing. She patted a child's head, gestured her respect to the four shrines, and disappeared into the trees.

Manuel turned back to his empty house. The uneaten fruit lay on its plate among the cushions. He walked past it to his bed and took down the ti lei from the wall, imagining its making years before, Hoku's pretty hands folding and twisting the long ti leaves into a supple, glistening rope on the morning of her womanhood.

He remembered the glow in her face as she had proudly danced alone that day, the ti lei gleaming between her small breasts, and the voices of dozens of boys begging for the gift.

And he remembered his feeling of silent triumph as she had tossed it into his hands.

The lei was dry and brittle now, lifeless, faded with age. He wondered if the same thing had happened to their love.

It was not a trivial question. They both needed successors. Adoption was a last resort for those who truly could not have their own children; it was everyone's duty to pass on genetic heritage as well as function. Perhaps Lehua was right, and it didn't matter that a Governor and a Custodian had never married.

He raised the lei to slip it over his head, but it had dried too narrow, hanging on its peg, and he didn't want to break it. Such a fragile thing now, though it had once been strong enough to bind a man's hands. He hated what had happened to it, just as he hated the change the Council had imposed. Sometimes he even felt he hated Malamalama, source of all blessings.

Bad thoughts. Manuel shook his head to get rid of them, but he knew they would not go away.

He was angry, he realized, not just at the Council but at Hoku personally, for standing against him. She had chosen to oppose him, and none of his arguments or entreaties seemed to move her.

He reached up to hang the lei back on its peg. Its faded green was only a little darker than the grasses of the wall. In time, it would blend in completely. Manuel wondered if he would someday forget it was there.

◈

"You must check the systems again," said Councilor Haveland, fanning himself vigorously in the heat of the Council Chamber. "There is clearly a malfunction."

"There is no malfunction," said Manuel. "All environmental systems are operating at peak capacity—"

"Nonsense!" said Councilor Gary, wiping moisture from his brow with a fine kerchief edged in Councilor's yellow. "If the systems were functioning properly the island wouldn't be three degrees hotter than normal!"

Manuel's fist tightened around a handful of his robe and forced himself to reply calmly. "It is increased demand that is causing problems. Continual day is placing strain on our cooling systems—"

"Then increase their power," said Councilor Petra. "We have the light, let's use it!"

"It's not quite that simple," Manuel began.

"Manuel, we understand your wish to make a point," said Councilor Haveland testily, "but you've made it. The island needs its Custodian to keep the systems in order. You and your descendants will continue to have a place of honor. Now fulfill your function—get the island back to normal!"

"The island can't be normal without Night!" said Manuel, his hands emphasizing his statement with the gesture meaning "night."

"Do the Manuals say night is necessary?" asked Gary.

Manuel clenched his teeth. He'd been expecting that question; he'd spent hours searching the Manuals for just such a reference, hoping to use it in support of his arguments, but he'd found none. The Manuals were written by the Oporto and the Investors, children of Earth, who took night for granted.

"Not in so many words," he said, "but references to nighttime functions make it clear—"

"I know of no functions that cannot be as easily performed in day," said Gary, stifling a yawn.

"The advantages of daylight outweigh the difficulties," said Petra. "We are increasing our quality of life. With continual work shifts we have more space for our workers, we can produce more food and allow people to have more children—"

"All of which will increase the demand on our physical systems," said Manuel, "and they're already overburdened!"

"Manuel," said Hoku, who had been silently observing the discussion, "is it possible to increase power to the physical systems?"

Manuel turned to her, frustrated by her neutral mask. "Yes, but—"

"There!" said Gary in triumph. "He admits it! I move the Council require the Custodian to increase power!"

"We can't maintain an increase indefinitely!" said Manuel, but his protest was lost in a chorus of agreement from the Councilors.

"So ruled," said Hoku, her voice putting an end to the clamor. "Manuel, you have the Council's instructions." Her eyes were hard, and Manuel swallowed angrily, then turned and left the chamber without another word.

Outside the Hotel the air was oppressive; hot and damp, as if the island had been doused in the steam from a battle between Pele and her sister Hi'iaka. A slight stink of rotting vegetation made Manuel frown.

He stripped off his robe, under which he wore Maintenance garb—light, close-fitting cotton for the sacred work of Holding Up The World—but even this thin clothing seemed too much in the heat of the endless day. Manuel glanced at the nearby pole of Malamalama, terminating in the Civic Plaza, exactly opposite to the Grove of Malamalama.

Across the plaza was the Governor's house, flanked by ti trees and stately palms. Oporto himself had once lived there. Now it was Hoku's.

Feeling a sudden tightness in his throat, Manuel turned away and started back toward Operations, on his side of the island. He jogged most of the way back, passing fields of flourishing new crops and others that seemed pale and withered.

Workers looked up at him, some with weary eyes; he was not the only one having trouble sleeping in the constant light. Feeling helpless against their misery, he jogged on past the fields and between flowering shrubs that had dropped their blooms, strewing the path underfoot with flashes of faded color.

Arriving at Operations with a sheen of dampness on his skin, Manuel slowed to a walk and wiped at his face with his robe. He would need a fresh one for Nightfall, and wondered how much time he had before the ceremony.

It annoyed him, having to check. Ordinarily he would have

known by instinct how many hours of light were left, but he couldn't count them now, no matter how closely he shuttered his rooms against the incessant daylight.

He strode into Operations with the robe slung over one shoulder and headed for the control room, where he found a cluster of technicians gathered. "What's the status, Lehua?" he said, joining them.

Lehua glanced up from her console, grimacing as she wiped perspiration from her face with a brown hand. On the screens around her frantic images conveyed stress on the island's systems.

"We're at maximum on environmental control," said Lehua. "Power use is up thirty percent, ambient humidity up eighteen percent, water use up seven percent. And the temperature's still rising," she added unnecessarily.

Manuel leaned toward the screen, knowing what he would see. Though the Council blamed the island's woes on system failure he knew there were no malfunctions. He and his technicians had been searching the complex environmental systems for days—even for nights, though he disliked putting his staff on the continual shifts that the Council promoted—trying to find a problem to correct, but there were none.

The Custodian rubbed his sweating chin, thinking of Oporto's warning to his children of the consequences of failing to perform Maintenance: crops withering, lakes drying, fighting among the people. He had not thought such plagues would actually occur, yet without doubt they were beginning, and only weeks after the Council had first denied his pleas to reinstate night.

"What shall we do, Manuel?" asked Kaleo, a young tech whose dark eyes were tense with worry.

Manuel glanced at Lehua. "I've been given orders by the Council," he said. "We must make a change."

He gathered the technicians into a circle and led the chants of purification that preceded all major Maintenance functions. Feeling Lehua's eyes on him, he hurried through the song, his hands weaving the air in the gestures of blessing.

Then he looked up at Lehua. "Increase power to environmental systems by ten percent," he said.

One of the techs took a sharp breath. Lehua moved toward her console, pausing to look back.

"We'll be drawing on reserves," she said.

Manuel nodded. "I'll inform the Governor," he said, glancing at the screen. "After Nightfall."

He stepped back, breaking the circle, and as he glanced at them the techs avoided his gaze. Their silence followed him away down the hall.

Few people paid any attention to the Nightfall and Dayrise rituals any more; even his own technicians had lost faith. Often as not he performed the ceremonies alone, but he did so without fail. He was Manuel. If he stopped performing the rituals, he would cease to be Manuel.

As he strode down the corridor he heard the surge of new power into the environmental control system, sensed the change of air pressure as fans picked up speed, felt a breath of coolness as he passed beneath a vent. Welcome as it was to his body, the change only increased his anxiety, for now the physical plant was supplementing the fire of Malamalama with stored light from the great power cells. When their reserves ran out, the island would have no other source to meet its demands.

He went to his house and permitted himself the luxury of a shower. The water was lukewarm, slightly stale. Donning a fresh green robe and his ceremonial headdress, he went out to the Grove of Malamalama and found the clearing empty.

No dancers, no singers, no drummers. The only person in sight was the Council's Watcher, standing on the dais between him and the Focus. With a sigh Manuel walked to his place at the foot of the steps, and stood alone in the silence.

Closing his eyes, he listened to his own breathing and the distant sounds of activity muffled by the woods. He could almost imagine a miracle, a crowd of followers waiting breathlessly for him to lead the ceremony. He laughed at himself; easy with eyes closed.

Easy to mumble incantations and trust in omnipotent gods

to take care of you, but he believed—no, he knew—that Moku Wina's people were their own caretakers, and he was responsible for seeing it was done.

Manuel opened his eyes and stared at the shielded pole that marked Malamalama's terminus. Above where the shielding stopped, at a level distant enough not to damage the eyes, the axis gleamed with brilliant daylight. Malamalama, source of all blessings, was after all just a machine.

Sometimes he thought of going through the Manuals and removing all reference to ritual and worship, but when he tried to picture himself performing the functions of Maintenance without the gestures of blessing and reverence, it felt wrong. He was his father's son. He had spent his life training to perform the rituals of Moku Wina's heritage. His feelings, even the Council's decision, didn't matter. Maintenance must be performed.

In a voice barely above a whisper he began the chant to Pele. He did not believe she was creator of Moku Wina, or protector of Oporto's people. He remembered arguing with his father over the dedication to Pele. His father had told him it didn't matter what he thought; Pele must be honored because that was part of the ritual, part of Maintenance.

He danced alone, chanting softly, hands flowing through the air and his bare feet gripping the soft earth of the island. He danced not for Pele, but for his father.

He followed the dedication with the Nightfall dance, then in silence he performed Calibration, his hands cutting knife-like through beams of light. One of the mirrors was slightly off-focus, and he sent a command signal to its driver to adjust. Every bit of light was needed now.

Finally he shut off the Calibration light, and ascended the dais to stand before the Focus. He stared at the lever, carved with symbols no one believed in any more.

"Manuel," said the Watcher, startling him. It was Puna, the woman who had first been posted on guard over the Focus.

"Yes?" he said.

To his surprise she stepped aside. "I think you were right," she said, her eyes bright with worried tears. "The Council shouldn't have stopped Nightfall. Please complete the ceremony."

Manuel caught his breath, and reached out his hand shivering with an instant's joy at the thought of shifting the lever and plunging the island into Night. Instead he grasped the Watcher's shoulder.

"Thank you, Puna," he said, "but the Council would see it as an act of war. There must be a better way to bring back the night."

"How?" asked Puna.

It was a question that had filled him with despair for many days. "Pray," he said helplessly. "Pray for guidance."

It was the best answer he had, and it was not enough. Feeling defeated, he turned away to descend the steps.

"May I pray with you, Manuel?" Puna asked.

Surprised, Manuel stopped halfway down the steps and looked back at the Watcher. Her eyes pleaded, and Manuel returned and took her hands, then began the chant he thought she was most likely to know; a chant to Pele, a simple song, one of the first learned by every child on the island. Puna sang with him, stumbling over some of the words, but when the chant was finished she smiled.

"Thank you, Manuel," she said, looking up at him shyly. "I would like to sing with you again."

Touched, Manuel nodded. "Tomorrow, we'll sing again."

"Thank you," she said as he stepped away. "Thank you, Manuel!"

Puna's voice followed him through the clearing and into his home. As the curtain fell closed behind him he suddenly realized he'd been doing everything wrong. He had been working alone—shutting himself away in solitary darkness, shielding his technicians from responsibility, trying to fight the Council singlehandedly—when what he needed was to add the people's voices to his. It was not his faith that mattered, but theirs.

Even if Pele was just a symbol, she stood for Maintenance,

and he knew beyond doubting that Maintenance was necessary. Night was necessary too, and there were others who wanted its return.

If he could win back the people's support, the Council would not be able to ignore him. How many days in the unending day he had wasted! Tossing his headdress onto the bed, he caught his long robe in one hand, went back outside, and began to run.

The first people he encountered were field workers, tending new crops. "Nightfall has passed," he told them. One or two sneered, but he ignored them. "I know your work shift kept you from attending the ceremony. I came to offer a prayer for those who wish to join me."

They stared silently at him, and Manuel could feel the heat rising to his face. "Maybe some of you miss the Night, as I do," he said. "Maybe you would like to have it back."

"You won't get it back," said a worker, turning away.

"Maybe not," said Manuel, "but I will pray anyway."

The workers looked at each other, then one put aside her shovel and came to him. Others followed, and Manuel led them in the same children's chant he had sung with Puna.

"We'll sing again at Nightfall tomorrow," he said. "Everyone is welcome."

Moving on, he made the same offer to everyone he found awake, Staff and Guests, at work or at play. Some ignored him but many did not, and each time he joined hands with a new circle and began to chant, he felt the strength of the people flowing through him.

He walked all through the hours of night, returning to the clearing for Dayrise. When he reached it he found a small crowd of people waiting for him, many of those he'd sung with in the last few hours. Among them were a dozen or more dancers, decked in wreaths of fern and flower woven by their own hands, and musicians enough to perform the Dayrise chants. Manuel led the ceremony, then sang the children's chant again with the people and sent them into the day with blessings while he continued his mission.

He lost track of time as he walked all the paths of the island, seeking to sing with as many of its two thousand people as he could persuade to join him. He surprised his technicians by leading them in a chant of celebration he had not sung since the beginning of endless daylight, and laughed inside at their astonishment. They must think he had gone mad, and perhaps he had, but at least he was doing something.

His legs and feet were aching with weariness by the time his wanderings brought him to the Council Chamber. It was empty; the Councilors were busy elsewhere, and he stood in the Chamber's center and chanted a song praising Night while the Watchers at the doorway stared. Then he went outside and crossed the plaza to the Governor's house.

"Hoku," he called, standing outside her window, swaying a little with weariness. "Hoku, come sing with me."

He received no answer, and with a laugh he sat beneath her window. He plucked a leaf from a ti tree nearby and tore it into strips, fingers clumsy as he twisted them together, one end held between his toes and the pungent juice making his hands sticky.

He began to sing, not a chant this time, but a song of love, a courting song. He had sung it softly to himself a thousand times, alone in the darkness of his room, with Hoku's face shining in his imagination. Now he sang it out loud, heedless of who might hear, his hands caressing the air now and then before returning to the rope-weaving.

Manuel had gone mad, the people would say. It might be true, but if so it had happened long ago.

As he sang of starlight on the island's waters he became aware he was not alone. He kept his eyes on the twist of leaves in his hands and tied its ends together as he finished the song, then turned to see Hoku herself, in Governor's red, with the Council behind her.

"Manuel," she said in a voice that matched the sadness of her frown, "what are you doing?"

Rising to his feet, Manuel held out the bracelet he had made. "This is for you," he said.

Hoku's hand came up to take the circle of dark, glossy green.

As she looked up at him a flash of regret replaced the frown, and all his anger melted.

"Come sing with me, Hoku," he said softly, taking her hand. "We haven't sung together since we were children. Analani e— remember?"

"Manuel," said Hoku, "you are not yourself. You need some rest—"

"We all need some rest," said Manuel, laughing. "That's what I've been telling you! Never mind, come and sing! All of you, come sing!"

He beckoned to the Council as he led Hoku by the hand down the path toward the far pole and the Grove of Malamalama. They followed, probably with the idea of preventing him from doing anything they disapproved. It didn't matter to Manuel. He squeezed Hoku's hand as she walked beside him on the path.

"I love you, Hoku. I don't think I've told you that in years," he said softly. "It's more true now than ever."

Hoku didn't answer, but neither did she pull her hand away. She walked on beside him, gazing at the path beneath their feet, the bracelet in her free hand.

They crossed the waterbelt on Manuel's favorite bridge, and long before they reached the Grove they began passing through a great crowd, hundreds of people, more than Manuel remembered seeing all together in many years. The people reached out their hands to him as he passed, and he touched their fingers with his own.

When he reached the ceremonial clearing he led Hoku up to the steps before the Focus, with the Councilors close behind. The voices of the people filled the clearing, some questioning, some cheering Manuel. He smiled, then held his hands up for silence.

"People of Moku Wina," he said aloud, smiling, "many of you have sung with me today, and my heart is filled with gladness. Sing again with me now."

He led the same song—the children's chant to Pele—a song with no significance toward day or night. It was the voices chanting together, the hundreds of hands moving in unison, that mattered. He heard Hoku's voice join the others, and saw her lovely hands rise in gestures of happiness and love, the bracelet of ti leaves circling one slender wrist.

At the end of the chant the people cheered, and the ipus began to play the rhythms of the Nightfall dance. Voices from the woods joined Manuel's in the chanting; he saw the hands of the people echoing the dance.

Those who didn't know the song chanted "Po, Po"—calling for Night, Night—and kept up the chant while he performed the dance of Calibration.

The voices rose higher as he approached the Focus. The Council clustered on the dais, and he faced them, smiling, with open arms.

"Councilors," he said, "you honor your people with your presence at the Nightfall ritual." He saw Councilor Haveland ready to speak, and continued. "I thank you for what you have taught us in the time since the last Night. You have shown us what we can accomplish by using all of Malamalama's blessings. That is a good thing, but now we are using more light than Malamalama can give us. Now we are using the reserve power from our storage cells. The island needs to sleep, just as we need to sleep."

A roar of agreement went up from the crowd, so strong it surprised Manuel. He glanced at the people, then at the Councilors, who looked uncomfortable. Manuel went on.

"You have given us the freedom to work through the hours of Night. Now I ask you to give us the freedom to rest. Can we not offer our people both choices?"

Hoku was frowning slightly. "What do you propose, Manuel?" she asked.

"Change is a good thing, as you have taught me," said Manuel. "On Earth the days change in length. I propose a new system that will allow us to have longer days some of the time and longer Nights some of the time, as on Earth. Then we can still achieve more without exhausting our light completely."

The Councilors exchanged glances. "We must discuss this,"

said Councilor Gary.

Manuel nodded. "I will bring a plan to you tomorrow," he said. "My staff and I will determine the most efficient use of the energy at our disposal."

"Agreed," said Hoku, glancing at the Councilors. "In the meantime—"

"In the meantime," said Manuel, lowering his voice so that only the Councilors would hear, "we're depleting our reserves to run the environmental control systems. Let us have a Night to allow them to recover. You can call it a holiday if you like."

He watched their faces anxiously. The Councilors did not look pleased. "Shall I ask the people what they wish?" he said softly.

Hoku glanced at him with sharp amusement. "I don't think that will be necessary," she said. "Councilors, the Custodian's words make sense. Any opposed to declaring a holiday?" When none spoke, she turned to the waiting people and raised her arms. "People of Moku Wina, your Custodian has made a wise suggestion. The Council will meet tomorrow to review a new plan for the use of Malamalama's blessings. In celebration of this, we declare a holiday from now until Dayrise. Let torches be lit to honor Pele, and let Night fill the island so that the torches can be seen by all!"

A cheer broke from the crowd, and accompanied by the roaring of drums, Manuel stepped up to the Focus, placed his hands on the ornate lever, and shifted it downward.

Darkness surrounded him, a black so deep he felt an instant's primal fear of blindness. Then the light of stars penetrated the viewbays, and the cheering rose higher as torches were kindled and began to dance through the woods, scattering away from the clearing. Manuel stood gazing at the stars for a moment, then turned away from the Focus.

His eyes were still adjusting, but he knew the shadowed figure standing still before him was Hoku. He smiled at her through the Night.

"Well said, Governor. You are very good at your function."

"And you are good at yours," said Hoku. "This will be a

good change, I think."

Manuel could see Hoku's hand, pale against the shadows of her robe. He reached out to take it, and led her slowly away from the others, down the steps to the clearing.

"I have another change to propose," he said. "Won't you walk with me by the water?"

Rocket Boy on Call

The last message he'd received from GGL was tagged "urgent," so he hadn't taken time to clean up, but as Sonja glanced up from her desk he wondered if it was a mistake to report fresh out of the cockpit. She looked so righteous in her pristine white business uni with turquoise accents, he felt downright slimy.

Her eyes were glassy until she shifted focus to him; then her gaze flicked down and up, taking in the full length of him. He pulled back the hood of his flexsuit and ran a hand over the short, unwashed stubble on his scalp.

"Tasha said ASAP," he said, trying hard not to stare.

Long-boned, with just enough curves, and a Scandinavian complexion made more pale by living in a shielded environment, Sonja woke the hunger in his long-isolated body.

"She had to take a call. Finish your report?"

He handed her a data chip, and she fed it to her desk.

Her eyes went distant again.

He glanced around the compartment, which was amazingly stark given its size. Though only Sonja was here at the moment, she shared the workspace with her two partners—both equally hot—and he knew it served them not only as a business office but as a research lab. He wondered if they had a daily service come in to keep it this clean.

Sonja nodded a couple of times as she scanned his report, then ran her hands over a virtual keypad.

"There you go. Thanks for a job well done."

"My pleasure." He verified the transfer of credit to his account, and sent back a receipt.

"Ready for the next assignment?"

He stifled a sigh. He was tired and sore from chasing down

the pirates that had been siphoning bandwidth from GGL's client. The fight had been quick but exhausting. It wasn't just his ship that needed a recharge.

"What is it?" he said.

Sonja worked her keypad again, then took the fresh chip her desk spat out and handed it to him. "You're to track down a lost colony. Here are the specs."

"Last known location?"

"All in there, along with projections of the most likely trajectories. It won't be easy; last contact was over a century ago."

He whistled. "Talk about cold."

Sonja shrugged. "It's an inheritance claim, and the courts are demanding proof of demise. Give it your best shot. You'll be paid for your time, with a nice bonus if you find them."

He slid the chip into his cuffband. "Okay if I start tomorrow?"

Sonja raised an eyebrow, as if surprised he would need any down-time. "Fine with me. Maeve is off with the client, discussing strategies for bringing the colony in once you find them."

"Assuming they want to come in."

"That's outside our scope."

"If they're not in default, they're not obligated."

She shrugged. "We'll deal with that when we get there."

He nodded, watching the gentle ancillary waves the gesture had raised in her flesh. He had to swallow a sudden mouthful of saliva.

Sonja had turned her attention back to her work, but when he didn't move to go she glanced up at him after a moment. "Something else?"

Took him a couple of seconds to work up the nerve. "Yeah. How about dinner? My treat."

That pale eyebrow rose just a fraction. How could a woman be hotter than Sol and colder than a comet's tail all at once?

"Thanks, but I never mix business with pleasure."

"What if I turn down the lost colony? Then it's not

business."

A tiny frown creased her brow. "But that would hardly put me in a mood for pleasure."

He sighed. "Right. Seeya," he said, turning to go.

"Joe."

He stopped. Turned. "It's Joseph."

She nodded. "Sorry. Joseph."

She didn't say anything more. Her gaze traveled his body, with more curiosity now. A slow smile widened her pink-frosted lips.

"Maybe after you're done with this contract, and before the next."

Oh, mama. He grinned, tossing off a salute as he turned and headed out.

"You're on."

Recipe: Cheater's Chicken Chile Soup

In New Mexico, chicken chile soup is a staple of comfort. After a long, hard day, or if the weather is cold and nasty, there's nothing like a hot bowl of spicy chicken soup to warm up the body and soul. This recipe is a way to make chicken chile soup as fast as possible.

Ingredients:

    1 medium onion, chopped
    2 T vegetable or olive oil
    1 lb cooked chicken
    6 c chicken stock (or canned broth)
    1 16-oz jar of your favorite salsa
    1/2 c tortilla chips, crumbled (optional)

Preparation:

In soup pot, saute onion in oil. Cut chicken into bite-sized pieces. When onions are translucent, add chicken and stock. Bring to a boil. Add salsa and, if desired, tortilla chips. (The chips will make a thicker soup.) Heat to boiling, then serve with warmed soft flour tortillas.

Arroyo de Oro

He was beautiful. An angel's face—soft brown hair framing chiseled cheeks, skin so fair it seemed never to have seen the sun, and the sweetest almost-smile on his lips—that was my first deader.

He was found at 10:47 am in one of the less-frequented hallways of the Rainbow Man Hotel and Casino, right near the hologram of the Blue Corn Maiden. See, every morning at 11:00 the Maiden speaks—a recorded blurb about her role in pueblo religion—which is what the tourists who found him came to hear. But I doubt they caught a word.

By time I got there it was almost 11:30. I left the field office as soon as the call came in, but downtown Albuquerque is a long way from "Arroyo del Oro." That's what they call the strip. It runs right up the Sandia Reservation on the north edge of town, and it rivals Las Vegas for glitz.

I got on the freeway and headed north, feeling pretty unhappy about the assignment. I am not a cloak and dagger kind of girl. Numbers I can do; my background is in accounting, and I naturally expected my job with the FBI would entail investigating bank fraud and money laundering and that sort of thing.

When they sent me to New Mexico after graduation I figured I might also have to handle some shady across-the-border deals, but murder investigations I was not expecting. This murder, however, had taken place on the reservation and was therefore under Federal jurisdiction, so I got tapped to help check it out.

The directions said to take the Tramway Exit and turn toward the mountains. Serious mountains, too—bare granite jutting up over the city—pretty stark for a girl used to wheat fields and rolling green hills. There was not much green here to speak of at all, and as if it wasn't enough that the land was brown, these people had to make most of their buildings brown, too. I had been in town all of two days, and was already wondering how soon I could transfer back east.

I reached the exit, turned toward this gigantic arch, all neon, that said "Welcome to Arroyo de Sandia," and drove under it. It was like entering another world.

Hotels lined the street, neon-traced towers crowding right up to the sidewalks, flashing and glittering even in midday. Hotel Sandia, Hotel Bien-Mur, Hotel Kokopelli, each with its own casino.

Traffic crawled, blocked by herds of tourists on foot walking up and down in sneakers and shorts with big plastic cups in their hands. More tourists in rented cars sat gawking at the glitz and OK, I did a little gawking myself, especially when I got to the Rainbow Man. Big, flashy entrance with a gigantic neon figure on the hotel tower above it. It was a kachina; I had learned that much, having seen bunches of kachina dolls in the airport.

Kachinas are sort of minor deities, only not exactly. This one's head was a mask, with black rectangles for eyes and some feathers and horns and things. The feet were pretty normal, but the body between them arced in an enormous rainbow that put head and feet on the same level. Gorgeous.

I stared at it too long. The red Camaro behind me had to lean on his horn before I realized the light had changed.

I parked on a side street that was a box canyon of slab-sided casinos. All the glitz was out front on the Arroyo. I hurried back toward Rainbow Man's entrance and went into what I thought was the lobby, but it turned out to be the casino, and I immediately got lost.

The place was a labyrinth; big rooms full of light and color and this incessant circus music. Took me a few minutes to realize it was the slot machines. Man, I don't know how anybody can stand that sound all day long.

I wandered around a while, thinking I had to be getting close, but every time I thought the crime scene should be around the next corner there was a restaurant instead, or a bank of elevators. I never saw so many little hallways and fountains and things.

And everywhere—in corners and crannies, and odd little coves—were these holograms of kachinas. Life-sized, so life-like they were scary. They bothered me, mostly because I knew that kachinas had some kind of religious meanings of which I was entirely ignorant.

Well, I broke down and asked for directions. Twice. By the time I finally found the crime scene I had lost a significant measure of my professional cool, and a crowd was already gathering.

I had my hand clamped around my badge, and flashed it to the first cop-looking guy I saw—a huge man—Hispanic or Native American, I wasn't sure. He was wearing a gray wool suit, mildly rumpled, that looked pretty nice even on his bulk.

He took one look at me and said "More feds? We got Chase here already."

"I'm Agent Sandra Marsh," I said, pocketing my badge. "I'm here to assist Special Agent Chase."

"Armando Mora, BIA PD," he said, sounding bored. His face was a mask of stone. He glanced away and shouted "Arnold, get the damned spectators out of here, will you?"

Some men in brown Tribal Police uniforms started shepherding the crowd away, and the big guy went to help while I was still trying to remember what "BIA" stood for. That's when I spotted the yellow tape and the deader lying behind it on his back, his blood pooled around him like a mantle.

A woman was kneeling beside him, black "FBI" windbreaker proclaiming her an evidence tech. Standing over him was a hologram; the Blue Corn Maiden. She was wearing a black dress and moccasins, and a shawl, and a mask painted blue with black rectangles for the eyes. Her hair was black too, done up in a kind of Princess Leia do on the sides of her head, and she was holding a basket filled with ears of corn.

I ducked under the tape, and got up close to the deader. Man, he was gorgeous! Late 20's, very slender, dressed in silk trousers and a shirt that had to have been tailored: the model/actor type. His eyes were closed; unusual, perhaps done by the killer. I knelt beside him, and the tech glanced at me.

"Shot, or stabbed?" I asked.

"Stabbed, I think. Nobody reported a shot."

She picked up his hand—long delicate fingers—and began slipping a plastic bag over it. I looked at that serene face again, wondering who had destroyed such beauty, and why. I'm not ashamed to admit wishing I'd met him alive.

"Do we have an ID?" I asked.

"Alan Malone," said a rich, deep voice to my right.

I glanced up and found myself staring at the Blue Corn Maiden, but she couldn't have spoken in that masculine voice. Just past her a tall man in a worn leather jacket was leaning against the wall, taking an unhurried drag on a pipe.

The coal glowed angry-hot as he pulled on it, at odds with

the calm blue of his eyes. High forehead, big crooked nose, looked vaguely northern-European. He was staring kind of absently at the body, jaw cocked a little to one side and a muscle or a vein pulsing on his temple underneath the thinning hair.

I stood up. "Special Agent Chase?"

He unfolded a lanky arm to shake my hand, then took the pipe from his mouth. "Welcome to New Mexico," he said. "I hear you've just arrived."

"Yes," I said, straightening my shoulders a little. Yeah, I was defensive. Every cop I met was giving me the cool treatment, and this guy was no different.

"You'll find Albuquerque is very different from Quantico. He's a singer," he said, gesturing toward the deader with the pipe. "Was, I mean. Worked here, in the Kachina theater. Two shows a night, dark Tuesdays."

"Dark?"

"No show. It's their only day off."

It was Wednesday. "So he was killed coming in this morning?" I said.

"Probably. Except that this hallway is nowhere near the theater entrance."

"Between it and the parking lot?"

"Not really," said Chase. "There's an exit nearby, but there are closer ones to the theater."

The BIA guy came back from shooing off the gawkers, and walked up to Chase. "How soon can we get him out of here?" he said.

"Easy, Mondo," said Chase. "Did any of the staff see him alive?"

"Not so far. We're still talking to the buffet people. The manager's bitching—it's almost time for lunch to open."

Chase glanced past the Corn Maiden. "The line forms out there?"

"Right there," said the big cop, nodding his head. He got an extra chin with each downward thrust of his jaw.

Chase looked down the hallway, then back at Mondo, and got this gentle little smile. "Maybe you should find a screen, then," he said. He turned to me. "Shall we go look at the theater?"

"Sure," I said. I followed him back the way I'd come, walking fast to keep with his long stride, knowing I would most likely get lost again trying to find my way through the casino alone.

"Um, Special Agent—"

"Call me Chase," he said.

"OK. Do you happen to know where there's a restroom?"

"Should be one right over here." He led me past some craps tables to a bank of restrooms tucked in a corner, and said "Meet you back here."

He was nowhere in sight, however, when I came out. I waited, looking across the casino, watching the tourists gamble, listening to the clatter of slots paying off.

"I am Buffalo," boomed a voice beside me.

"Jesus!" I said, jumping.

A hologram set off in a little alcove near the restrooms had come to life: a big guy in a huge furry headdress-robe thing that went all the way down his back. In one hand he held a rattle which he started to shake. Distant drums throbbed.

"I am the gift of the Great Spirit," he said. "I give the blessings of my body to the people...."

"All set?" said a voice behind me, and I jumped again.

Chase had come out of nowhere. He hadn't been in the men's room, and he hadn't come across the casino, and the only thing behind me was a wall.

"Shit," I muttered. My heart was pounding.

"Sorry," said Chase. "Didn't mean to scare you."

He sucked on his pipe, and glanced at the hologram giving its spiel. Then, just as I was really beginning to wish I was back in Quantico, he turned those blue eyes on me and smiled.

It transformed him. Suddenly he wasn't just another tired cop, but a human being full of love and joy, sharing something fun with me, simply because I was a fellow human. Swear to god, his eyes actually twinkled.

He grinned at me, and said "They give me the willies, too!"

I managed a smile in return. Chase took off toward the

casino again.

We passed more slots, poker tables, holograms of course, some kind of big wheel-of-fortune thingie, and still more slots. I followed Chase through an acre of blackjack and up a half-dozen steps to some closed banks of doors labeled "Kachina theater" in orange and green neon. Two big holograms with antlers and bits of pine branches hanging off them stood on either side. Chase knocked at the center doors, knocked again, then pushed them open and we went in.

Dark. After all the noise and light of the casino, I felt like I'd stepped into some underground cavern. The doors fell shut with a muffled whump, sealing us off from light and life. I peered hard at nothing, trying to adjust my eyes.

A gust of wind hit my face with an audible "whoosh." In the distance something pale moved.

My neck hairs prickled; I stared at it until I discerned a bird flying, flapping great, lazy wings, glowing white against the darkness, growing closer, larger. An eagle; no, an eagle kachina with long, feathered wings strapped to arms that filled the width of the room as it rose toward us, enormous, majestic and terrible.

I could hear the flap of the great wings, feel their wind wash over me. It flew overhead and vanished, leaving me drenched in silence.

"Sorry to interrupt," said Chase pleasantly beside me, "but we need to talk to someone connected to the show."

"Tickets at the concierge desk," an irritated voice returned from the darkness. "Sorry, no visitors. You'll have to leave the theater."

I noticed a dim row of aisle markers on the floor. My eyes were adjusting. Chase was now a shadow nearby.

"We're not visitors," he said. "We're with the FBI. If you'll bring up some lights and talk with us, we'll try not to take up too much of your time."

Mutterings, indistinguishable. I glanced over my shoulder at the doors.

The faint seam of light between them flickered; a silent

shadow passing. My skin prickled with the sense of someone unexpectedly near, and I was still peering after the shadow when the lights came up hard, making me blink. There was no one there.

"Thank you," said Chase.

I followed him down the steps to where three men were sitting in a booth; two Native Americans and one Anglo. The natives both had that ageless, flat, round face that looked like it hid centuries of secrets; they stared at Chase with dark, watchful eyes. The white guy was around forty, with frizzy, graying hair in a ponytail and a pair of headphones around his neck. He looked pissed.

Chase flashed his badge. "Any of you know Alan Malone?"

"Yeah," said the white guy. "The little shit's late."

"Well, yes, as a matter of fact," said Chase gently.

He was halfway through explaining before I noticed the pun. Cop humor. I gave him a look but he seemed not to notice, except that a corner of his mouth twitched a little. The others didn't have a clue.

"Oh, man!" said the Anglo, his eyebrows going up. "Oh, shit! Joe, call Ben and tell him to get down here!"

One of the natives nodded and started up the aisle at a jog. "Joe," I wrote in my pocket notebook, starting a list of people to interview.

"Can I have your name, sir?" I said.

"Huh? Oh, sure. Stauffer. Daniel. Jesus, when did he die?"

"We're not sure yet," said Chase. "When was the last time you saw him?"

"Monday night. Final performance of 'The Wild West'."

Stauffer turned out to be the director for the Kachina theater. He alternated between puzzlement over Malone's death and dismay at its impact on the upcoming premiere, and some kind of excitement that I didn't fully understand.

A few other people connected with the show emerged from various parts of the theater. Most of them, to my surprise, were white, not Native American. A couple were Hispanic.

I took down names while Chase encouraged Stauffer to chat

about Malone and the show. It sounded spectacular; from the way he was talking the eagle we'd seen was nothing. Live performers interacting with holographic gods, acting out the legend of creation. State of the art physical simulation effects. When Stauffer offered Chase a pair of tickets, I felt a stab of envy.

Stauffer glanced past me, and I turned to see Joe coming back. I suppressed a shiver; hadn't heard the door.

"He's coming," said Joe.

"Good," said Stauffer. "Jesus. OK, let's set everything up for the opening number again. Tom, recalibrate the soundtrack for Ben."

"Who's Ben?" Chase and I asked in unison.

"He's, um, Malone's understudy," said Stauffer.

"Hey, Danny," yelled a stage hand. "Somebody's made a mess of the props!"

"Shit!" said Stauffer, pulling off the headphones and starting down the aisle toward the stage.

"We'll get out of your way," said Chase.

Stauffer paused. "Yeah, I'm sorry—"

"So are we. We'll be in touch."

I followed Chase up the steps. As he opened the door the casino's noise struck me like thunder.

I paused, gearing up to plunge into that chaos of light and sound. I'd always been kind of curious about Las Vegas or Atlantic City, but now I was beginning to lose interest. The people sitting at the slots all had this kind of weary, hope-against-hope expression as they fed the machines gold tokens from their plastic cups. False gold, false hopes. Seemed everything around here was false.

"Let's go talk to the manager," said Chase, raising his voice over the circus music. "You should meet him."

"You know him?"

Chase nodded. "Been working pretty closely with all the managers in the Arroyo. Setting up good relations, so they'll cooperate when there's a problem. Lets them know we're watching out for trouble."

We passed several craps tables and some banks of blackjack tables I hadn't previously seen. "Are all the casinos like this?" I asked.

"Like what?"

"Uh—this big, I guess."

"Pretty much," said Chase, heading up a half dozen steps.

At their top the red carpet gave way to marble floors and velvet ropes. We were suddenly in the hotel lobby, and the noise of the slots diminished behind us as we crossed it. I sighed with relief. Chase led me past a bank elevators and down a hall.

Another kachina stood a little way ahead. This one was male, wearing a green mask with feathers on top and a white kilt-thing. His bare torso was painted black with green and yellow designs.

"This way," said Chase's voice behind me.

Turning, I saw him standing at the foot of an escalator discretely tucked into an alcove. I'd gone right past without even seeing it.

We rode up to a floor blessedly silent: not a slot, not a video game, not a scrap of neon. Even the carpet was more subdued. A small brass sign pointed the way to Meeting Rooms.

Chase led me through a set of carved double doors into a plush reception area. I mean, seriously plush. Leather sofa and chairs. Bronze planters full of calla lilies. Expensive art on the walls.

"Good afternoon, Mr. Chase," said a smiling Native American receptionist.

"Hello, Sally. This is Agent Marsh. Is Kyler still in that meeting?"

"All day. Can Emily help you?" said the receptionist.

"Sure," said Chase.

He sat down on the leather couch and invited me to join him. I did, feeling a flash of the little kid's trepidation at sitting on the grown-up furniture.

Chase's fingers tapped the shiny brass of an ashtray standing next to the couch. The pristine sand had been shaped by some modern magic into a relief of the Rainbow Man's mask.

"Mr. Chase?" said a soft voice to our right.

A woman walked out of a side hall and up to us, a pretty Native American with a long waterfall of black hair spilling over the shoulders of her cream-colored suit. She looked vaguely familiar, I thought. Chase stood up and shook her hand.

"Ms True-hee-oh," he said. (I learned later from Mondo that it's spelled 'Trujillo.') "This is Agent Marsh."

She shook my hand with dry, warm fingers. "I'm Mr. Kyler's assistant. How can I help you?"

"Can you give us a room to conduct interviews?" said Chase. "We're investigating the death of Alan Malone."

Sally the Receptionist's eyebrows went up, and she glanced at Ms. Trujillo, whose face showed a flicker of pain. The latter opened one of the heavy doors and led us out into the empty hallway.

The escalator hummed quietly at our feet. Ms. Trujillo led us down a hall flanked on one side by meeting rooms and the other by a wall of glass. The windows overlooked the hotel's swimming pool, a huge affair with a waterfall, lots of landscaping, and a couple dozen tourists courting melanoma.

She took out a keychain and opened a door to a small room dominated by a conference table. Masks on the walls acted as sconces, light gleaming behind their eyes. I didn't like them; they made me feel like I was being watched.

"You can use this room for your interviews," she said.

"Fine," said Chase. "Have a seat, please. I just have a few questions."

Ms. Trujillo sat down across the table from us. "I'm sorry," Chase added. "I understand that you and Malone were close."

"We were good friends," said Ms. Trujillo, her voice barely above a whisper.

"Not lovers?" Chase's voice was gentle, but his eyes watched. I was glad I wasn't the one being questioned.

"Friends," she said firmly.

"When did you see him last?"

Ms. Trujillo's eyes got far away, and she didn't respond for a moment. Then she blinked, and sighed.

"Sunday there was a Corn Dance at the pueblo. He always came to the public dances."

"Any trouble between you?"

Her eyelashes fell over her eyes—black slits—then she looked up at Chase. "No."

"No disagreements?"

"We understood each other. He was very interested in our ways. He studied them. He knew them well."

"Where were you this morning?"

"In my office. Sally can tell you."

"Thank you," said Chase. He leaned back in his chair. "Can you get us a list of everyone who works in the theater? I know they're having a rehearsal, but we need to start interviewing—"

"I'll have Sally make you a copy of the roster," said Ms. Trujillo.

I suddenly realized why she seemed familiar. She reminded me of the Blue Corn Maiden.

"Ms. Trujillo, did you pose for any of the kachina holograms?" I asked on impulse.

A flash of scorn in her eyes surprised me, then her lids half-hid them and her face became a mask of calm. "Those are actors," she said flatly.

"Well, you might have done one for fun—"

"No," she said. "I didn't pose for them." She looked from me to Chase, then stood up. "I've got some calls to make," she said. "Is there anything else you need?"

"Just that list," said Chase.

"Sally will bring it to you. Would you like some coffee?"

"Yes, thanks," said Chase.

She left, sable hair swaying. I glanced at Chase, who gazed at the doorway long after she was out of sight. She *was* pretty. I suppose if I were a man I'd stare after her, too.

Chase took off to find out about the autopsy, leaving me to spend the rest of the afternoon interviewing Malone's co-workers with the masks glaring down like a row of judges. Mondo fetched dancers and stage crew and waiters for me to grill. Dark-eyed natives from catering looked in now and then, silently refilling water and coffee, and once leaving a plate of dull but nourishing sandwiches.

Through the interviews I began to build a picture of Malone. They all agreed he was talented, well-liked, and would be sorely missed.

No one could think of any reason someone would want to kill him. No one could even think of anyone who disliked him.

He had no ex-wives, estranged lovers, or creditors. His drug use was confined to an occasional joint backstage. He didn't gamble, drank moderately, never fought except for disagreements with Stauffer over staging and such.

His family lived back east, and he spoke of them lovingly and infrequently. Yes, they'd been notified. The mother was flying in to claim her angel boy.

Chase called around five to tell me the ME's opinion; Malone had been stabbed several times in the back with a thin, straight-bladed knife, possibly a stiletto. The killer was right-handed and no taller than Malone. Time of death between 9:30 and 10:30 a.m., and how was I doing with the interviews?

I told him fine, fine. Actually, I was pretty discouraged.

I hung up and looked at the list Sally had brought. Check marks ran down three quarters of the page, with gaps here and there where some folks had not yet come in to work. A number of those I'd interviewed had alibied each other, and I'd established that Malone had been alive and well when he left the hotel after Monday night's performance. Beyond that I hadn't learned much.

The door opened, and Mondo stuck his head in. "Got the director for you finally. And the understudy. Which one you want first?"

"Understudy," I said. I was getting ticked at the director, who'd been putting me off all afternoon, so now it was his turn to wait. "Hey, Mondo—did the victim's car turn up?"

He nodded. "In the parking garage. Nothing useful in it. Nothing in the apartment either."

"OK, thanks." Malone's life was too clean. This was not going to be easy.

Mondo let in a sharp-dressed, slick-haired stud whose every move said "gay." He sat down across from me while I ran a finger down my list.

"Good afternoon, Mr...."

"Hanes," he said. "Benjamin Hanes."

"Mr. Hanes. Where were you before nine this morning?"

"With my voice coach. Every Wednesday."

"All morning?"

"'Til eleven. Then I had lunch with a friend, and then Joe paged me and I came down here. I guess I got here around one."

"You hadn't been here before that?"

"No, thank God! Poor Alan!"

"What was your relationship with Alan Malone?"

Hanes laughed. "Purely professional. Alan was depressingly straight. We all used to—"

"You were his understudy," I said.

"Yes."

"So you stood to gain from his death."

His cheerful mask slipped a little. "I resent that," he said with a laugh, but instead of sounding light he sounded sullen. "I would never hurt Alan."

"I see. Do you know of anyone who would?"

"I can't imagine. Everyone adored him. Even Miss T, and she doesn't much care for the rest of us."

"Why not?" I asked.

"Doesn't like the new show, on account of the kachinas. Doesn't like the holograms either."

Now that was interesting. Maybe Ms. Trujillo had wanted to stop the premiere.

"Did she argue about the show with Malone?"

"Not that I know of. He knew how she felt, and she knew he had to work."

So dies a promising lead. I felt like I'd reached for a door, only to have the handle melt away under my hand.

I asked Hanes a few more questions and got nothing useful, so I freed him and called for the director. They passed in the doorway and exchanged a glance that told me something more about Hanes.

"Thank you for taking the time to come up, Mr. Stauffer," I said. "I know you've been rehearsing all day."

The director looked haggard and pissed as he sat down. Coming in he'd looked worried. It had been a long day and I didn't feel like pussyfooting around, so I said "You and Mr. Hanes are lovers, right?"

He frowned at me, then shrugged. "Yeah. You keeping a list of everybody Ben's slept with?"

"Not yet. Where were you this morning before nine?" I said.

He sighed. "In the theater, setting up for the premiere."

"When did you arrive?"

"I never left last night. I crashed upstairs."

I hadn't expected that. "In a hotel room?"

"Yeah. There's usually a couple free. Mr. Kyler lets us use 'em if we're crunched for time mounting a new show."

"Was anyone with you?"

"Ben went home. He wasn't anywhere near the place until this afternoon."

"That's not what I asked."

Stauffer's frown deepened a bit. "Steve Clay shared the room with me. He's on an errand right now, be back in about an hour."

"What's the errand?" I asked.

"Somebody dicked with our props, and there's one missing. He's getting a replacement."

A chill ran down my back. "What kind of prop?" A knife, perhaps?

"A rattle."

Oh.

"Did you like Alan Malone?" I asked, for lack of a better question.

"Sure, I liked him. He was a decent guy. Saw things his own way, of course. All actors do."

"But you're glad Ben has his part now, right?"

Stauffer sat back, as if he'd been waiting for that. "Listen, Ben's got a lot of talent"—he dropped his voice with a glance at the door—"but he's no Alan Malone. Yeah, I'm glad he's getting a shot, but if you think I'd kill Alan to give it to him, you're crazy."

There was not much more to say. I got the names of his alibis for the morning, and let him go back to the theater.

It was almost six by now and Mondo was looking hungry, so I called it a day. With my notes under my arm I headed back down the escalator in search of dinner, grateful to be up and about even if it meant running the casino gauntlet again.

I swear they were moving the walls. The place never looked the same twice, except that it all looked more or less the same. Slots, slots, tables, slots, and holograms. I noticed one I'd seen before—a guy painted red all over with a big, snaggle-toothed snout on his mask—and made a mental note of the landmark.

I was making progress; the casino still disoriented me, but it didn't seem quite so huge. I had almost gone past the Blue Corn Maiden before I recognized her and stopped.

The little hallway was empty. A damp area of recently-shampooed carpet was the only sign of disturbance.

I stared at it, feeling a crazy stab of loss. Blue Corn Maiden still stood guard over the spot where Alan Malone had died, but the casino had already forgotten him.

Well, I wouldn't. Someone that handsome—and, apparently, that nice—deserved justice.

Looking up at the hologram, I had no idea why I'd thought she was like Ms. Trujillo. Her hair wasn't loose, and her face was a mask. I reached toward her, my hand passing through the air where she was and was not. My fingers seemed to disappear into her basket of corn.

"There you are," said Chase's voice behind me, making me jump again.

"Damn it," I said. "Quit sneaking up on me like that!"

"Sorry. What were you doing with the hologram?"

I looked up at him, then on impulse I stepped into the hologram and turned to face him.

He shook his head. "Doesn't work. You're just blocking the projector. Watch."

I moved aside, and when Chase stepped into her place the

Corn Maiden vanished. We found the projection equipment in the wall behind her, and played a little more with the image, figuring out how it worked. We concluded the hologram could hide a small object—my notebook disappeared nicely into her feet—but nothing as big as a person.

Still, the back of my neck tingled, as if some dormant hunter's sense had awakened. I fumbled with the projectors, squinting to see past the bright beams of light, and spotted a small red button.

Flute music blasted out of the speaker in front of me. I jumped back, and the hologram flicked into existence, raising the basket of corn in her arms.

"I am the Blue Corn Maiden," she said. "I guard the seed of the sacred corn, and watch over the young plants as they grow. I am the keeper of our gift from the gods."

"What did you do?" said Chase, as the Corn Maiden gestured in different directions with her basket.

"Pushed a button," I said.

"You must have found a test mode."

The flute music subsided, and the Corn Maiden resumed her normal frozen stance.

"Chase ... would you mind blocking the projectors again? I want to check something."

"Not now," he said softly. I turned and saw Ms. Trujillo coming toward us.

"Agent Chase, I'm glad I caught you," she said. "I had a note from Daniel Stauffer asking me to give you these," she said, handing him an envelope. He took it, and pulled out a pair of tickets.

"They're for the 7:00 dinner show," said Ms. Trujillo. "Is that all right?"

"Fine," said Chase. "Want one?" he asked, turning to me and making me blush, because of course, yes I did.

Ms. Trujillo smiled briefly at us both, said "Enjoy the show," and headed back into the depths of the casino.

Chase held out a ticket. I glanced up and saw him smiling. I guess I was more tired than I'd realized, because that smile hit me straight in the chest.

"Thanks," I said, taking the ticket and hoping he hadn't noticed how red I was getting.

"Be warned—I'm going to talk about work," he said.

Chase led the way back into the depths of the casino. I saw the buffalo guy coming up, and noted that he was near a large bank of slots with a neon eagle above them. Across from him was a doorway.

Now, I was pretty sure that that was the same wall I'd been standing by earlier, and there had not been a door in it, and there had not been a hologram in front of it either, but now there was. I stared at the kachina, which had curving antennae and was painted head to toe in black and white stripes. He was wearing a black kilt and holding what looked like a handful of grass. How I could have missed him earlier I don't know.

Chase went through the doorway into a fern bar. He made a bee-line for a table of executive-types, one of whom looked up and grinned.

"Chase! Pull up a chair! Who's your friend?"

"Agent Marsh. She's assisting me in the investigation," said Chase, turning to me with a nod. "This is Mr. Kyler."

"Agent Marsh," said a big, friendly rancher-type, standing up to shake my hand. "Pleased to meet you."

His smile was the painted-on kind you see on politicians and other salesmen. He said names around the circle—they turned out to be the Rainbow Man's Board of Directors, every last one of them white—and offered to buy us a drink. We sat in padded leather chairs and I sipped at a beer while Chase settled into a glass of Irish whiskey.

"Terrible about Malone," said Kyler. "We were just discussing it. Terrible. He was a great draw."

"Maybe the new guy won't cost so much," said a silver-haired dude with a Texas twang. "You always used to gripe about how expensive this kid was."

"Yeah, but he was good," said Kyler. "Pulled in the crowds. Gotta keep those patrons coming in. You'll wind this thing up nice and quiet, won't you, Chase?"

Chase shrugged and sipped his liquor. "Do what I can. Murder is never tidy, though."

The talk turned to the casino and a new hotel Mr. Kyler was planning further up the Strip. Most of it was about negotiations to lease the land from the pueblo. Boring stuff.

After a few minutes I excused myself, promising to meet Chase at the theater at quarter to seven. I went past the elevators and up the discreet escalator to businessland. There was something I wanted to check without Chase around.

I pushed against the heavy double doors, half expecting them to be locked, but they weren't. They creaked a little as I poked my head in. Sally the Receptionist looked up from her desk.

"Oh, hello," she said. "Did you need something?"

I came in, letting the doors fall shut behind me. "I just have a couple of questions, if you don't mind. Were you leaving?"

"In a few minutes. Have a seat."

I watched her tidy up some papers on her desk. She had a round face and short, curly black hair. Smiled easily. A mama type.

"You're working late," I said.

"Because of the board meeting," said Sally. "I had to get tomorrow's agenda straightened out. Things got off schedule today."

"What time did Mr. Kyler get here this morning?" I asked.

"Around eight, I think," said Sally.

"Did you see him come in?"

"Yes. He and Mr. Parker came in together. They went out again, but I'm not sure when."

Parker was one of the guys I'd met in the lounge. I made a note.

"What time did you get here?"

"Mm—ten to eight, I guess."

"Was anyone else here who might have seen them?"

"Emily was in her office. She spent the whole morning on the phone."

"Ms. Trujillo? Is her office near his?"

"Yes—let me show you."

She got up and led me down a wide hallway. The plush carpet deadened our footsteps. Sally waved a hand toward an open doorway.

"That's Emily's office, and this is Mr. Kyler's."

I didn't get to Kyler's. Behind the desk in the corner of Ms. Trujillo's office stood a kachina hologram. It was a woman, with a white mask and towering stair-step headdress—decked in feathers and carved wooden flowers—a red shawl, and a white skirt. I stared at her.

"That's the Butterfly Maiden," said Sally. "They did a pretty good job on that one. At least I think so. She's Hopi, so I'm not sure."

"What's she doing in Ms. Trujillo's office?"

"Mr. Kyler gave her to Emily. He pretty much gives her what she wants."

"She wanted this?"

Sally nodded. "She asked for it Monday. I'm not sure why—she doesn't really like them. Mr. Kyler wanted them because there was some unhappiness when this hotel was built. It's the only hotel in the Arroyo that's not Indian-owned."

"So he decided to add some Ind—some Native American culture."

Sally nodded. "Emily tried to talk him out of it, but he went ahead with it. The holograms were created by Dan Stauffer and his staff, using local actors. Some people got very angry."

"Does it make you angry?"

She hesitated. "They're not really kachinas," she said slowly. "They're more like the dolls—something you could use to teach about the kachinas—only these aren't very accurate. I guess I would like it better if they weren't here, but I want to keep my job, so I don't say anything."

How many others feel that way, I wondered? I reached through the image, skin tingling, and found the projector on the wall behind. As my hands blocked the light the image vanished, and I glanced at the floor. Nothing there.

"Are you and Ms. Trujillo from the same, uh—"

"Pueblo?" said Sally. (I'd been about to say "tribe.") "Yes, we're both from Sandia."

I looked through the doorway at Kyler's office across the hall, then back at the hologram. Butterfly Maiden bothered me.

"Tell me about Sandia," I said.

"We're one of the smallest pueblos. Less than five hundred. A big family, really."

"I heard something about a dance—"

"Oh, the Corn Dance. Yes, it was just a couple of days ago."

Corn Dance. Corn Maiden. A connection?

"Was Alan Malone there?" I asked, remembering something Ms. Trujillo had said.

"Oh, yes. He's been coming to all the dances this year. He likes to pick up the feel of them, for the new show."

"Did he have any enemies in Sandia?"

Sally's eyes widened a little. "No—everyone liked him. Even the elders. He's—he was—always very polite."

I stared at Sally's flat face, feeling like I was forgetting to ask some basic question. Something like, "Did you kill the guy?"

I didn't think Sally was the murderer, though. Besides the fact that she and Ms. Trujillo had both been upstairs all morning, she was just too nice. She let me stand there a full minute before she started to fidget.

"This is Mr. Kyler's office," she said, stepping across the hall.

I peered into a huge room with big picture windows. The late sun was slanting through orange anvil clouds outside, and the Arroyo was really beginning to sparkle. I could see a corner of the Cibola Hotel across the street, all gold-glitter glitz.

Kyler had a hologram too—the Rainbow Man, of course—along with other bits of expensive art and a desk made out of some huge gnarled tree trunk. On it sat a Rainbow Man kachina doll: foot-high, carved wood, like the ones I'd seen at the airport.

"Is there anything else you wanted to see?" Sally asked.

"Yeah," I said, giving up. "A photo of Alan Malone."

I followed her back to the foyer, and she dug up an eight-by-ten glossy and two show flyers, one for "The Wild West" and one for "Pageant of Creation."

"We'll have to re-do that one, I guess," she said, handing them over.

"Thanks, Sally," I said. "You've been a big help."

I went down to the theater, which I found by a somewhat roundabout but effective route of buffalo-guy to neon eagle to red snout to black-with-rabbit-ears to antlers. The casino looked exactly as it had at midday—bright lights, lots of color, lots of noise—and I realized there were no windows and no clocks anywhere.

Made sense, I guess. If you're a casino owner you don't want your customers thinking about how late it is.

The theater was open and I was promptly seated in a booth, one of the best seats in the house, for the simple reason that it faced the stage. The tiers above and below the booths were jammed with narrow tables perpendicular to the stage; people sitting there would have to turn their heads to see the show. Cram in the customers, make big bucks.

The stage was hidden behind a glittery blue curtain. In front of it a giant hologram hung in midair: the Rainbow Man's mask, with black rectangle eyes.

I took out Alan Malone's black and white glossy, held it in both hands and stared at it long and hard. His eyes—which I had only seen closed—had been blue or gray or some other light color; they almost looked clear in the photo. His smile was intensely charming.

Gorgeous boy, everyone's darling. Why did you die? And who closed your eyes against the night?

I looked at the "Wild West" flyer, dismissed it, and picked up the one for "Pageant of Creation." The eagle kachina we'd seen earlier was on the front page, along with a full-length photo of Alan Malone all in white.

I opened the flyer, activating a snap-holo, the gimmicky kind you find in greeting cards. The eagle again, soaring across the page before winking out.

Not a cheap flyer. Too bad they'd have to redo it. Alan Malone had clearly been the star attraction; his face and name were all over the brochure, along with slogans like "Discover

Sandia's Ancient Mysteries" and "Journey through the Indian Myth of Creation."

I wondered why Malone—obviously talented but undeniably white—was the star of a show about Native American mythology. Circumstance, maybe. Malone probably had a contract with the hotel, and the show had been designed to attract tourists. Plug star into show and you have an instant hit, right?

"Looking forward to the show?"

I looked up at Chase. He sat down across from me and leaned across the table. "What do you have?" he said.

I told him the results of my interviews. He nodded and said I'd done well, which was nice of him.

"No one has a clear motive," I said. "Did the weapon ever turn up?"

Chase shook his head. "Mondo's boys spent the day going through every trash can and dumpster on the premises," he said. "They're starting on the neighboring hotels."

I sighed. "No weapon, no motive, no suspect. So far we don't have much of a case."

"It's early yet," said Chase. "And we have a potential suspect. You said Stauffer had motive."

"Yeah, and when I pointed it out he agreed, and then denied killing Malone. He's got three alibis for this morning, unless we can break them."

Chase took a thoughtful sip of his drink.

"There's another potential suspect," I said. "Mr. Kyler."

"Hm. I don't think Kyler would."

"Remember his partner saying he complained about how much he had to pay Malone?"

"Yes." Chase swirled the ice in the bottom of his glass, peering into it as if he saw something mystic in there. "It doesn't seem a strong enough motive."

"How about this? He gives his assistant expensive art for her office, but she was close to Malone."

Chase raised an eyebrow. "Love triangle? I don't think so. He's devoted to Marie. Mrs. Kyler. Besides, he has an alibi."

"We haven't established that yet—"

"Don't have to. It's me." He looked up at me. "I was here at eight-thirty. Kyler asked me to breakfast."

"Why didn't you say so?"

He sighed. "I should have. I'm sorry."

I watched him frown into his glass, and wondered how close a friend Kyler was. Our dinners arrived, and I remembered something I'd wanted to ask about. It was kind of an embarrassing question, but I figured what the hell.

"Chase—you know the lounge we had a drink in? Near the stripy guy?"

"Yeah?"

"It, ah—wasn't there earlier. This morning. I think."

Give him credit, he didn't laugh. He just cocked his head and gave me that intent, puzzled look.

"Wasn't there?"

"There was a blank wall there—"

"Oh ... that's a security feature," said Chase.

"Security?"

"It's a hologram. The hotel uses them to discourage people from entering areas that are closed—"

"Ladies and gentlemen," boomed a voice from the house speakers, "the Kachina theater is proud to present Pageant of Creation, starring Benjamin Hanes!"

The lights went out. The kachina mask glowed for a second, then faded and the place went pitch dark. Then I heard a "whoosh" that made my scalp tingle even though it was familiar.

The pale speck of the eagle dancer began to grow in the black well of the stage. The audience gasped as it flew overhead.

The stage lit up with flying holograms of kachinas—I counted a dozen before I lost track—along with live performers dancing to the rhythm of a row of drummers in colorful garb. The music and the images increased in speed and intensity until they became a maelstrom of sound and color. Then the place went dark again, and another pale spot began to glow in the depths of the stage while the drums rumbled low and a voice began chanting.

The image took form; a man, all in white, arms outstretched. It grew larger than life, and brighter, reaching out over the audience, and I gasped as I realized it was Alan Malone's ghost in the second before it vanished.

Chase must have heard me, because he laid a hand on my arm. The stage lights came up on the singer—all in white, raising arms draped in a cape of white feathers—Benjamin Hanes.

"They didn't have time to re-record the hologram," Chase said in my ear. I nodded, still feeling a weird shiver.

There were more holograms of Malone—he was inextricably part of the show, and I felt grimly privileged to watch his final performance. In one number Hanes sang a duet with Malone's hologram—something about twin brothers journeying to the sun—truly spooky.

Hanes was good, but he didn't have Malone's charisma. This was only a ghost of the show it would have been.

Even so, I enjoyed the hell out of it. Lots of color, beautiful use of holography and sensory effects. When the lights came up for intermission I clapped 'til my hands ached.

Chase's applause was more reserved, so much so that I asked if he disliked the show. He frowned, and said "The performance is fine. I'm just not sure about the content."

"What about it?" I asked.

"Well, it's a mish-mosh, and some of those Indian chants—"

"You mean Native American."

"I mean Indian. They call themselves Indians, so I do too."

I felt myself blushing. "I'd been given to understand 'Native American' was the accepted term."

"Maybe the eastern tribes prefer it. My friends would laugh if I called them Native Americans."

Our waiter brought us dessert, which was a scoop of something white (not ice cream) in a puddle of something brown (not chocolate). I took a bite, and pushed the rest away. It was like everything else in this place—a sham—not what it looked like.

"Not going to eat that?" said Chase. He had already inhaled

his. He gestured toward my plate with his spoon, and I handed it over.

"Oh, hey," I said, watching him dig in. "There's something else we should check. May not mean anything, but Stauffer said somebody stole one of the props."

"A knife?" said Chase, eyes sharp.

"Nope. A rattle."

"Rattle? What kind?"

"I don't know." We'd seen dozens of rattles in the show.

Chase dropped his spoon on the empty plate and stood up. "Let's go ask."

"Ah—in the middle of the performance?"

"Why not?"

One thing about Chase, he didn't waste time. We went down the aisle and climbed a half-dozen steps at the side of the stage. Backstage was crammed with towering racks of lights and projectors.

Chase found the props girl—a sharp-faced Hispanic I'd interviewed that afternoon—arranging things on a long table. He flashed his badge.

"Could you tell us about the missing rattle?" he said.

"How about after the show?" she said. "I'm kind of busy."

"Was it the same as these?" said Chase, picking up a rattle from the table.

"Hey! Put that down!"

Chase did. "Was the rattle that was stolen like this?"

"Yes, it was, only it wasn't stolen, it was broken."

"Broken?"

"Somebody rummaged through the props last night, and they broke one. So if you don't mind—"

"What's that one?" I said, pointing to a smaller rattle that we hadn't seen onstage. Unlike the others, it wasn't painted. A single white feather was tied to it with a leather thong.

"That's Alan's. I mean Ben's. Don't touch it, please," she said as Chase reached for it. "It's fragile."

"Lucky it wasn't broken, too," said Chase.

"It wasn't here. Alan asked me to keep it locked up."

Chase and I looked at each other. "Why?" I asked.

"He said it was special—Uncle Joe Vigil gave it to him."

"Who's—"

"Five minutes," said a guy in black, brushing past us.

The props girl gave me a pleading look. "I really can't talk now—"

"We'll come back after the performance," I said. "Please don't leave."

"Can't. There's another show at ten."

I pulled out my notebook and tried to scribble in the half-dark while I followed Chase. "What name did she say? Vee-heel?"

"Joe Vigil," said Chase. "He's about the oldest guy at Sandia Pueblo."

He stopped. Dancers were pouring out of a bright doorway in a stream of colored feathers, heading for the stage to start the second act. When they'd cleared out Chase went on, but I stayed.

Down the hall, in an open doorway, Emily Trujillo was arguing with Benjamin Hanes. I got as close as I could without entering the hall, and heard Hanes say "—didn't give it to me."

Then he started toward me and I ducked back, and nearly tripped over one of the racks of lights. Hanes came out and went onstage. I waited for Trujillo, but she didn't appear, and I glanced back down the hall just in time to see her go into Hanes' dressing room.

"Chase!" I hissed.

I couldn't see very far; figured he'd gone back to our table. The show was about to start again. The rational thing to do would be to go back to my seat. So I went down the hall and knocked at the dressing room door.

No answer. I waited, knocked again, then opened it.

The room was empty.

I stepped in and pushed the door closed behind me. I was getting pissed off. This whole place was a lie, and as soon as this damn case was over I was requesting that transfer.

"Ms. Trujillo?"

There were no other doors; not even a closet, just a rack of costumes in one corner, some of which I recognized. The feather cape was there, white plumes flickering slightly in the breeze.

Breeze?

No fan in the room. There was an air duct in the ceiling, but when I reached up toward it I felt nothing. I held my hand over the feather cape, and caught a whisper of air coming from behind the costume rack. I pulled it aside and reached a hand toward the bare wall behind it. It went through.

"Shit!"

I took a deep breath and stepped through the wall. Weird feeling—all my imagination, of course—but only ghosts and superheros are supposed to walk through walls.

I was in a short, dark corridor. Light at the other end, and carpet that looked like some part of the casino, but no sign of Ms. Trujillo. I went toward the light, stepped out into it and stopped cold. Across the hall and down a few feet stood the Blue Corn Maiden.

"Jesus."

I turned around, and found myself facing a blank wall. Reached out, and through; another hologram. Security feature, Chase had said. I remembered my confusion over the lounge. They *were* moving the damn walls!

Things started clicking in my brain. Private entrance to the star's dressing room. Alan Malone had a perfectly good reason to be in the hall by the Blue Corn Maiden; he was on his way into the theater.

The killer was someone who knew about the concealed corridor, maybe even hid there. Didn't look good for Daniel Stauffer. Then again, Kyler might have known it was there; his assistant certainly did. For someone who didn't like holograms, Ms. Trujillo sure knew a lot about them.

Oh.

I started through the casino, trying not to run. I crossed the lobby and passed the elevators, then hopped on the escalator and took the steps two at a time. The doors to the office were gone; a solid wall now stood at the top of the escalator. I put a hand through it and felt the carved doors behind. They were unlocked.

Dark. I felt around on the wall for a light switch, then gave up and started down the hallway. Arroyo-light from the picture windows in Kyler's office spilled across the carpet.

Kyler had an alibi. Stauffer had three alibis. And Sally the Receptionist said Trujillo had been on the phone all morning. On the phone, talking to no one. Just sitting at her desk.

I nearly tripped myself getting to Trujillo's office. Butterfly Maiden still stood in the corner, glowing in the dark room. It hadn't occurred to me before to wonder why Trujillo had put the hologram *behind* her desk, where she couldn't see it. I fumbled with the projectors, found the button, pushed it, stepped back.

Butterfly Maiden vanished. In her place, seated in a holographic desk chair and murmuring into a holographic phone, was Emily Trujillo in her pretty cream-colored suit.

"Holy shit!"

I stopped thinking at that point. All I knew was that Trujillo had killed her very dear friend, and that I had to find her. I tore out of there and back down to the casino, but of course she was nowhere in sight.

I headed for the theater, intending to get Chase. The maitre d' let me in and I stood in the dark at the back of the house, waiting for my eyes to adjust so I wouldn't fall on my face on the steps.

The stage lights were low. Hanes was alone, kneeling in front of a holographic fire, chanting low and loud, unaccompanied.

Some small movement to my right caught my eye; I saw a pale shape moving down the far aisle, and a shiver went down my back. I went toward it.

Hanes chanted louder and waved his arms over the fire as if casting some magic spell. A darker shape loomed between me and the pale blob, and my stomach lurched as I hurried toward them both, touching the backs of chairs and shoulders, whispering "Sorry, sorry," and trying to keep half an eye on the stage.

Hanes reached into the false fire, brought out the little plain rattle I'd seen on the prop table, and raised it over his head. At the same time a pale arm was raised ahead of me, and I saw it was Emily Trujillo's arm, holding a gun. Then the shadow between us blocked it.

I screamed "No!" and the gun went off, and all hell broke loose.

I ran the last few feet between me and Trujillo, barked my shin on something, cussed as I saw the shadow-shape crumple. The gun went off again, flash nearly blinding me, screams all around not the least of which was Benjamin Hanes shrieking like a lunatic and blowing out the house speakers.

The Quantico boys would have been proud. More by feel than by sight I tackled Trujillo, sat on her and took the gun away.

The house lights came up. On the floor nearby Chase lay bleeding, looking very surprised. I stared down at Trujillo, and managed to refrain from smacking her.

Her black eyes were narrowed to slits—like the rectangle eyes of the kachinas—then she closed them. She never gave in, even then.

She was charged with premeditated murder and assault with a deadly weapon. She hadn't hit Hanes, and I still think she never meant to. Her second shot shattered the rattle that Uncle Joe Vigil—the oldest, and incidentally the most senile man in Sandia Pueblo—had given to Alan Malone.

Mondo told me it had been a ceremonial rattle, and it should never have been seen by a white man, much less taken from the pueblo. But Alan Malone was a charmer; he made his living making people like him, and he'd fooled even Emily Trujillo.

She'd brought him to Sandia, and doubtless she felt responsible when he took the rattle. I wondered what he'd said when she asked for its return, and if he'd actually realized what it meant to her and her people.

I went to her arraignment, which was really just the usual, but I'd promised Chase a full report. He was stuck in the hospital for a few days, and maybe another junior agent would have resented being sent to fetch chocolate and ice cream and jelly beans, but I had learned something.

Of all the masks I'd encountered, Chase's was the easiest to see through if you bothered to look. His was just shyness, and underneath it was a wonderful being.

I stayed at the back of the courtroom, so Trujillo didn't see me until she was being led away. The eyes she turned on me were flat black, with no more emotion in them than the Blue Corn Maiden's black rectangles.

She had her own mask. We all do.

It's my job to notice little things, though, and as she looked away, I saw the flicker of grief. Maybe for Malone, maybe for a deeper loss, or maybe more than one.

No regret, though. She'd done what she felt was necessary to make things right.

I went away sad, but satisfied. I had seen the gentle and determined soul who had taken Alan Malone's life, and then reached out to close his eyes.

The Folsom Suit

Sunlight, gray and chilled by stone walls, moved the stale air when the closet door was opened. The souls within the suit stirred.

A jacket and trousers, plainly cut and made of sturdy black broadcloth, were accompanied by a simple tie and white shirt. No other clothes resided in the tiny closet at the end of the long, gray corridor. Most days the suit hung in darkened silence, alone with the echoes of its past.

A man named Cox reached for the hanger, his face set in something just short of a grimace. He carried the suit out into the corridor lit by a pearly December dawn and paused to examine it.

The suit, which had once been good but was now desiccated and weary-looking, dangled limply from the wooden hanger. It had been worn many times, though never twice by the same man.

Still, it was aging. "Good thing it doesn't have to last much longer," Cox muttered.

He shut the closet door and turned away, carrying the suit with him down the corridor. No more than a dozen strides were required to take it to #1, where he handed it in to Lambert.

"There you go," Cox said. "Make it quick."

The suit's souls fluttered like trapped moths. Mutterings, the voices of men, echoed from the stone walls.

"—Yeah, time's a wastin'!"

"—You heard the man, Maxie, don't dawdle!"

"—Hurry, hurry, I can't wait to move up!"

"Shut up, you," Cox shouted down the corridor. For emphasis he struck his heavy stick against the iron bars. "No talking!"

The whispers ceased, and the souls within the suit subsided. Max Lambert, the man in #1, hooked the hanger onto his light and began to put the suit on.

The shirt was too big for him. The jacket was tight across his shoulders, drawn taut by the strength in them—dangerous strength—all too easy for him to use for destruction. The snapping of a bone, perhaps. The staving of a skull.

The souls shivered in sympathy, flecks of memory firing into momentary brilliance. The hair on Lambert's neck rose.

His hands were inexpert or perhaps affected by the cold. He fumbled at the necktie until Cox, waiting outside, lost his patience and came in to tie it for him.

"Gonna give me one of your special custom neckties, eh, Coxie?" Lambert's grin was sickly.

"Yeah, that's right. Now get out of here."

Cox herded Lambert into a nearby room that was brighter. A white sheet hung on one wall, reflecting back the daylight.

Lambert sat on a worn wooden chair in front of the sheet to have his picture taken. As the photographer fussed and fiddled with his equipment, Lambert began to sweat, his sour musk seeping through the shirt and into the fabric of the suit. He tugged at the necktie and sighed.

At last the photographer told him to hold still, and with a flash immortalized Lambert's image in the suit. The man turned to Cox. "Last one," he said, with a trace of sadness.

Cox gave a derisive snort. "Don't tell me you're feeling sentimental."

The photographer shrugged. "No. It's just—history, I suppose. You could call this a historic moment."

Cox hauled Lambert to his feet, grinning as he began to tie Lambert's hands in front of him. "How do you like that, Maxie? You're a historic moment."

Lambert's eyes narrowed. "Swell."

The souls buzzed. The suit prickled like a stabbed hornet's nest.

"All, right, move it," Cox said.

They went out to the corridor and down the long row of men. Some peered out at them, others pretended not to see. Cox paused beside a locked door, holding Lambert in check until the guard opened it.

"Go ahead and put Schofield in number one," Cox told him. "Might as well get them all moved up."

The guard nodded. Cox pushed Lambert through the door, and the guard locked it behind them.

Lambert's fear was heavy in the air, now. The suit's souls swam in agitated spirals.

Cox took him through more doors, past more guards, and outside at last into the cold sunshine. Lambert swallowed as he looked at the tall wooden platform that awaited him. The motion sent a shudder through the souls.

Cox's stick prodded the suit in the back. Lambert slowly began to climb the wooden steps. The suit rode awkwardly on him, trousers creeping up his legs a bit by the time he reached the platform. No one pointed this out, and Lambert didn't bother to adjust the trouser legs.

Cox had followed him up, and now stepped forward to check his handiwork. Lambert waited, sweating despite the cold.

The souls remembered—in their broken, scattered way—this platform, this place. Their agitation grew. Lambert flinched as if flies were at his ears, though no flies lived in December.

"Come on, Maxie." Cox beckoned, his tone almost kind, now.

Lambert stepped forward. Cox slipped the rope around Lambert's neck and adjusted the knot.

"Give you a nice, clean break, Maxie," he said gently.

Lambert's parched lips parted. "Thanks."

"You're my last one, I guess. You're lucky. That gas room is just a horrible thing. I seen it when I went down to San Quentin last week."

Lambert said nothing. The souls were screaming now, flying through their prison of black cloth so fast that his skin prickled all over. Lambert closed his eyes.

Cox stepped back and nodded to the man on the lever. The trap fell, the rope went taut, and Lambert's neck snapped.

Cox let the others do their jobs, waiting while the executioner took down Lambert's body and the prison doctor certified his death. His own job was done, except for one detail.

He followed Lambert's body back into the gray stone prison and waited while the suit was stripped off it. He had the bucket ready as usual. No one wanted to handle the suit after a hanging; the prisoner always soiled it.

The black jacket, trousers, shirt and rumpled necktie were tossed into the bucket. Cox picked it up, sneering at the smell of excrement, and hesitated.

Usually he would take the suit to the prison laundry to be cleaned for the next execution. Lambert had been the last at Folsom, though. The other twelve on Death Row were being moved to San Quentin.

Cox gazed down at the suit, thinking of all the custom neckties, as the other guards called them, that he had made for its wearers. He was good at it. He did a clean job. There had only been a couple who deserved to swing a little before they went.

He looked up out a window at the winter sky, all glazed over with thin clouds. The air had a shimmery look to it.

He carried the bucket down to the incinerator room. The man working the furnace glanced up at him and gestured toward the heavy iron door. Cox nodded and the man opened the hatch. Heat roared out at him. He swung the bucket so that he wouldn't have to touch the suit. The jumbled black and white cloth flew into the furnace and blazed instantly.

The furnace man slammed the door. Cox glanced at him.

"Well. That's that."

Cox left, going back to Death Row to help move the other prisoners up. The next in line was always in cell #1, and there were thirteen cells on the row. Cox had always thought that a pretty hokey joke.

Above the stone walls, a wisp of paler smoke climbed skyward as the souls that had been imprisoned for so long, and one that had dwelt in the suit for mere moments, soared free.

♠

Ninety-three men were hanged at Folsom Prison between December 13, 1895 and December 3, 1937. Many of them were photographed wearing the same suit for their execution.

Draw

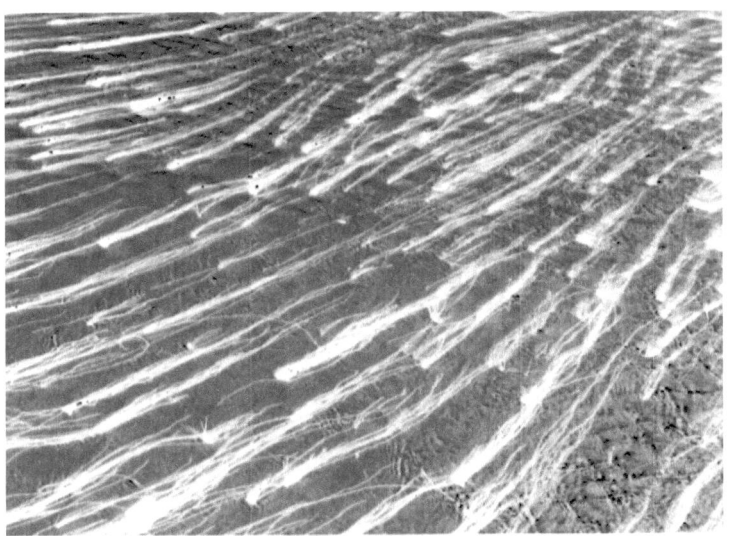

Dimitri noticed the time counter was way past 21:00, and paused his Robo-Warriors Invasion game. Dad should have been back from his rounds by now.

He took off his headset and gloves and looked around the apartment like maybe he'd missed something, but he knew Dad would have said hi when he came in. Would have rubbed his head and probably thrown off his score.

Dimitri got up and went to the big observation bubble that stuck out into the ocean from the living room. There was a cushion in it and he knelt on it, his breath misting on the cold surface of the bubble as he leaned against the thick plex, peering into the dark water outside.

It was night up top, and the light from the apartment only

reached a short distance past the window. He could see sand drifting around on the ocean floor, stirred by the ever-restless current, and he could just see the edge of the kelp beds beyond the nearest pump, fading into the blackness.

He shivered and backed away from the bubble. He was old enough not to be scared of the ocean, but at night it still bugged him sometimes. He didn't like being alone in the apartment at night.

He took his comcard out of his pocket and stroked it, then said, "Dad." Held the card to his ear and waited, but his dad didn't answer. After five tones the message box kicked in and Dimitri disconnected.

Could there be something wrong? Dad had gone out to do the evening check on the pump system. That was part of his job as maintainer of the desalination plant. He checked all the pumps and the seals first thing every morning and last thing at night. Often Dimitri went with him on the morning run, but not at night.

Not at night, when the great, dark vastness of the ocean could swallow you faster than you could blink. Not at night, when the hunters were out, giant shadows sliding through the water. Dimitri shivered, thinking about his dad out there alone in the dark.

"Stop it," he said aloud. This was no time to be giving himself the willies.

He called up some zaffa music to cheer him up and went over to Dad's monitor station to see if there were any alarms blinking on the diagram of the plant. Nothing.

He checked his message box, but there was nothing from Dad. His friend Collin had left a message about their homework assignment. That was it.

Maybe he should call Collin back and ask if Collin's dad would come over. Except Collin's dad wasn't an outside worker, he was a city administrator. He probably wouldn't know what to do other than call emergency services, and Dimitri could do that himself.

Was it an emergency, though?

It was starting to feel like one, but Dimitri didn't want to make a fool of himself and call out the rescue team when they weren't really needed. Dad always scoffed at people who did that. Usually they were new to Pacific City, recent arrivals who panicked over some simple problem.

Dimitri tried calling his Dad's com again, then looked all over the apartment for a note or a message, then called a third time. He checked the equipment bay by the dive hatch. Dad's wetsuit and tank were gone, so he'd definitely gone out.

His own, smaller wetsuit hung there, gaping at him. Get into it, a whisper in the back of his head urged him. A wave of fear bubbled up through his limbs.

Dimitri frowned and turned away. He hadn't tried everything else yet.

He went back to the monitor station and started cycling through the cameras, looking for his dad at any of the sites they covered. There were lots of cameras—one at every critical junction or piece of equipment in the desalination plant—and none of them showed a diver. A spotted shark glided by on one screen and made Dimitri jump, then the cycle clicked to the next camera.

He could call Dad's boss, maybe. Except Mr. Whitmore lived topside, so all he'd be able to do would be call Pacific City emergency, too. And it was night. Dad might get mad if Dimitri bothered his boss at night.

"Cameras minimize," Dimitri said.

The cycling images retreated to a small window in one corner of the monitor station, and the plant diagram returned to its normal position in the middle of the holotank. Dimitri rotated the diagram, looking for anything that might have caught his dad's attention, but saw nothing. Nothing, nothing, nothing.

He shut off the music and sat down at the monitor station, straining his brain for anything else to check. His gaze drifted over the holographic icons arrayed along the tabletop, and caught on one shaped like a red wrench.

"Maintenance log!"

The wrench turned brighter in response. Dimitri smacked his temple for not thinking of it sooner.

"Dork!"

The station pinged a query.

"Ignore. Maximize maintenance log."

A spreadsheet rose up in front of the plant diagram. Dimitri scrolled it to the most recent entries. There was one from just after 19:00 hours:

PERMEABILITY QUERY ON INTAKE FILTER 27-A.

Dimitri brought up the status screen for intake 27, one of the fifty giant pipes that drew water into the plant. The volume stats were way down. Frowning, Dmitri ran the numbers back and found they were even worse than they'd been at 19:00.

It meant the water coming in that pipe wasn't flowing as fast as it should be. That's all Dimitri knew, but it was enough. Dad would have checked on it while he was making his rounds.

"Cameras maximize."

Dimitri checked the location chart and brought up the camera aimed at intake 27. It was mounted on the screen cage and gave an angled view of the meter-wide pipe.

He sucked a sharp breath. The screen capping pipe 27 had a large hole ripped in it.

"Camera ... fifty-two," he said, glancing at the chart again.

The image switched to the access hatch in the screen cage. It was hanging open. Bad.

"Backpage and zoom."

Back on the pipe, the image moved in closer to the torn screen. Dimitri couldn't see down into the pipe, but he did see something dangling from its rim. Zooming in even closer, he realized it was a grappling harness, the gear that Dad and the other maintenance techs used whenever they needed to do things around the pipes, to keep from getting sucked into them by the draw.

"Shit. Oh, shit!"

Dimitri looked at the chonometer: 21:43. His father would

soon be out of air, if he wasn't already.

Too late to call for help—it would take the rescue team too long to get there. Shut down the plant? He'd watched Dad do it and thought he remembered how, but he wasn't authorized. It wasn't something you just did. It cost thousands of dollars to shut the system down, and thousands more to start it up again.

And he didn't absolutely *know* his dad was down in the pipe. He just thought so.

No time, no time. Dimitri ran for the equipment bay and called rescue while he was struggling into his wetsuit. His explanation was kind of crazy and broken, but he got the idea across.

"OK, stay there," the dispatcher told him. "I'm scrambling a rescue team now."

"I've got to take him some air!"

"It's better if you just stay there. The team will be out there in five minutes."

Screw that. Dad could suffocate in five minutes. He could be suffocating *now*.

"Just stay calm and keep talking to me," the dispatcher said.

"Right."

Dimitri ran through the safety checklist as fast as he dared, and slid his comcard into the headset just before he pulled it on. The headset molded itself to within a centimeter of his face and threw up its array of diagnostic displays. With a flick of his eyes he sent them to the background, then took down a spare grappling harness from the gear bay.

He had to cinch all the straps and buckles down to their tightest, and the harness still fit a little loose on him, but it would have to do. Grabbing a full pony bottle of air, he cycled the dive hatch and went in the water.

Cold and dark. It was always cold, but the dark made him gulp his air faster than he should. His com lost the dispatcher and he kicked up to touch the outside of the structure and reacquire the signal.

"Are you still there?" said the dispatcher. It was a woman. He hadn't even noticed that before.

"Yeah, I'm here."

"You sound like you're breathing hard. Try to calm down, OK?"

"OK."

Keeping contact with the building, he worked his way out from under it and up the side. The plant stretched away into the darkness. Off to the left, the lights of Pacific City glowed hazily through the dome. He'd rather have swum toward the lights, but that wasn't his goal. Turning away from the city, he turned on his lamps and kicked off toward the plant.

He brushed his hands against the uppermost pipes as he crossed the massive assembly of pumps and filters that made up the plant. He felt his tension growing as he approached the edge of the draw field. The light from his lamps picked up the dull red edge of the screen cage, a huge, mesh box that surrounded all the intakes for the plant. He reached the cage and drifted to a stop, one hand against the mesh.

Really a first-level filter, the screen cage kept anything larger than a centimeter away from the intake pipes, keeping out plant matter, fish and other critters, and anything else that could clog or even damage the finer filters down inside the pipes. The reverse osmosis process the plant used to remove salt and other minerals from the water required high-pressure filtering, and what better pressure to use than a hundred feet of ocean?

Every twenty seconds the pipes drew water. When he was a little kid Dimitri's dad used to bring him out here once in a while. Dimitri had loved to get up above the cage and let himself be sucked against it over and over by the draw.

You absolutely could not move when the draw was pulling you against the screen. Even Dad couldn't.

"Are you still there?" asked the dispatcher.

"I'm here."

"The rescue team is leaving now. They'll be there in a few minutes."

"OK."

"Just stay calm."

"OK."

Dimitri worked his way down the cage to the open access hatch he'd seen on the monitor. He went through it and paused, fighting off a fit of shivering.

Nothing between him and the pipes now.

He looked at the hatch, debating whether to close it. Yes, he should—otherwise critters would start drifting in and clogging up the filters. Maybe this precaution would win him some points to counter the chewing out he was going to get for coming in here.

He swallowed, remembering the time Dad had yelled at him for goofing around the screen cage without permission. He and Collin had gone to play in the draw. When they'd come back Dad had met them at the hatch, white-faced and silent, his green eyes glaring. He'd waited for them to get out of their dive gear and marched them into the condo, where he proceeded to chew them a new one in a rage-clipped voice.

"Never, *never* go out in open ocean without an adult and without getting my permission first!"

"But, Dad, we were each other's buddies—"

"I don't care if the whole polo team was out there! You don't go near the screen cage without an adult—namely me—supervising!"

Dimitri closed his eyes, remembering. There'd been no physical punishment, but the memory of Dad's fury had kept him from going near the screen cage again. He hadn't even asked Dad to bring him here to play. Now he was *inside* the cage, without even a buddy, trying to save Dad.

Boy, would he look stupid if Dad was somewhere else altogether. Boy, would he get grounded, probably till he was thirty.

He pulled the hatch shut behind him and took a slow, deliberate breath, then kicked off toward the pipes. He came in a good five meters below their tops, watching the water above them the whole while.

Small specks—anything littler than a centimeter—drifted in the water. Dimitri saw the bulk of the nearest intake pipe looming in his peripheral vision as he neared it.

He felt forward with his hands, still watching the water above. Suddenly the specks all flew downward and the distant thrum of the filters vibrated through the water.

Dimitri winced, imagining he felt the draw even though he knew he was well below it. He scrabbled at the pipe, trying to find a handhold, while his hindbrain counted.

One chimpanzee, two chimpanzee, three chimpanzee ...

After ten seconds the draw stopped. Dimitri gave a small sigh of relief.

"You all right?" asked the dispatcher.

"Yeah."

"I know this is scary."

Yeah. Shut up.

He found a runner rail on the outside of the pipe and clipped an anchor line from his harness to it, then glanced overhead, looking for the number on the pipe. Six. He needed to be one pipe over, and two rows down. Kicking off, he clipped to the next pipe and released the first clip.

The intakes sucked water again, and this time he forced himself to keep moving. He worked his way back to pipe twenty-seven, doubling his clips until the draw stopped. When he reached twenty-seven he clipped *all* of the harness's anchors to the two rails he could reach, and began to spider his way up the pipe.

Two meters from the top the pipe throbbed under him as the draw started again. Unprepared, he let out a small sound.

"You OK?" asked the dispatcher at once.

Dimitri closed his eyes. "Yeah."

"Why don't you drink some water? That might help."

"Um, OK. Maybe you could talk to me?"

"Sure. You know the team will be there in just a couple more minutes. Nothing to worry about."

Dimitri lowered the volume until he could barely hear her in the background, and continued to the top of the pipe where the other grappling harness—or rather, the two frayed straps that were left of it, hung dangling. Seeing them made him start breathing fast again, and he muted his com output so the dispatcher wouldn't hear.

The draw stopped. Dimitri poked his head over the top of the pipe, aiming his lamps down inside.

Torn harness strap drifting from one of the interior runner rails. Dark shape lying against the next screen, ten meters down.

Dad. Not moving.

A lilt of inquiry in the dispatcher's voice caught Dimitri's attention. He pulled his head back from the pipe and took his com output off mute, then raised the input volume.

"Huh?"

"I said where was your dad the last time you saw him?"

"Uh—he went out on his maintenance rounds. They should check the intake pipes at the plant. There was something on the maintenance log."

The draw started, tugging at him hard, this close. He cringed against the pipe and worked his way down it a bit, hand over hand on the runner rail. His heart was thundering.

"OK, they can check that. Don't worry. Just stay calm."

Dimitri swallowed. "Yeah. Thanks."

He muted the output again. When the draw stopped, he would have twenty seconds to get to the inside of the pipe and clip his harness to the rails. He unclipped all but two of them now, and noticed his hands were shaking.

He put a hand to the pony bottle to make sure it was still on his belt. The draw stopped and he worked his way up to the top edge of the pipe again.

He reached one arm over and clipped the first harness anchor to the inner rail. He'd done two when something dark came at him from the side.

Turning his head brought his lamps to bear on the dagger-filled maw of a shark.

"Aahh!"

He yanked the pony bottle from his belt, grazing his hand on the clip, and shoved it with all his might into the shark's nose. The shark swerved away, into the darkness.

Dimitri turned, dangling against the pipe, his lamps sweeping wildly as he tried to see the shark. He glimpsed a dark shape not far off, turning, coming around.

Sobbing, he gripped the slippery sides of the pony bottle, ready to hit the shark again. It came toward him, waggling from side to side, sneering with all those horrible teeth.

The pipe against him thrummed to life. The shark disappeared, sucked down into another pipe, straight through the screen over its top, which wasn't meant to resist anything as massive as a shark.

Or a man.

Dimitri grabbed at the rail as the leads he'd clipped to the inside of the pipe yanked at him. He clung against the rail with one hand and hugged the pony bottle to him with the other, then closed his eyes, gasping as he fought down the panic.

Stupid. He shouldn't have come out. He was just going to get himself killed along with Dad.

How the hell had that shark gotten in here?

Through the open access hatch. Now it was down in another pipe, and another screen had been breached. *That* was going to cost some money to fix.

Never mind. Not his problem. He had to get to Dad.

The draw stopped, and he unclenched his hand from the runner rail. Before he could think about it too much he swung himself over and into the pipe, through the torn screen, and started clipping more of his anchors to the inside rail. He paused to clip the pony bottle to his belt again, then with shaking hands anchored all his leads.

It actually hurt to unclip the last two from the outside of the pipe. He was going to get sucked down, he knew. The harness should keep him from being pulled down too far, but then, Dad's harness should have kept Dad from going into the pipe at all.

The dispatcher's voice was a drone in the back of his head as he worked his way downward, clinging to the rail. She sounded pretty excited, but Dimitri didn't have time to calm her down. He shut off the volume completely so he could concentrate.

Halfway to his dad the draw began. A strap whipped his arm and the suction pulled him from the rail before he could tighten his grip. He dangled in the harness, the straps digging into his back and shoulders, straining against the intense pressure of the intake as he stared at the top of the pipe above him.

It stopped after what seemed like a whole minute. Gasping, Dimitri regained the runner rails and struggled downward again until he reached the next screen, where his father lay unmoving.

Dimitri pulled his father onto his side. A glance at the tank gauge showed him Dad was almost out of air. He swapped in the pony bottle and made sure it was delivering, then shook his father by the shoulders.

"Dad!"

No response. Dimitri checked the vitals readout on the wrist display of his father's wetsuit. Pulse—slow but there. He wasn't dead, but he wasn't conscious either.

Draw.

The pull slammed him into his father, slammed them both into the screen. Dimitri cried out.

His leg, which was against the screen, felt like it was going to get mashed right through it. His brain shut down except for the part that kept crazily counting chimpanzees.

When he got to eleven the draw stopped. There were only supposed to be ten chimpanzees, but probably he wasn't thinking too straight. Maybe adrenaline made you count fast.

Sobbing, he took his dad's face between his hands. Dad's eyes were closed. Dimitri's hand brushed an unfamiliar shape at the back of the wetsuit.

A lump. A lump on dad's skull the size of an oyster.

Dimitri gave a moan, then scrambled to strap Dad into the harness with him, using some of the anchor straps. It would put more strain on the rest of them, but he couldn't think of what else to do.

He started up the runner rails with the five anchors he had left and his father dangling behind him. He was not quite halfway up when the draw started again.

Prepared this time, he managed to cling to the runner rails

at first but the dead weight of his father dragging on him pried his fingers from the rails. The anchor straps snapped taut with a sharp jerk.

Dimitri stared helplessly at the clip ends. The clips would hold, but even the heavy duty straps weren't meant to take the load of two people.

Seven chimpanzee. Eight ...

His teeth were chattering and he clenched them to stop it. When the draw ended he scrambled up the rail as fast as he could, pulling the anchor lines up, clamping them, pull, clamp.

He'd stopped looking up and was surprised when he reached the top of the pipe. Beams of light were dancing in the water overhead. He started to laugh, then remembered he wasn't out yet.

He unclipped an anchor, reached over the edge to clip it to the outside, and the draw took him again.

He tried to keep his arm over the edge but the draw was pulling at him, the edge of the pipe cutting into his arm, he couldn't hold it. He tried to shift and lost his grip.

Down into the pipe again, water pulling at Dad pulling at him pulling at the harness and he could feel it starting to give, then he swung against the side of the pipe, bashing his head.

OK, that's what happened.

His ears were ringing and his head felt like it had been hit with a sledgehammer. He closed his eyes.

Nine chimpanzee. Ten.

He floated, relieved. In a minute the draw would start up again. There was something he ought to be doing, but he couldn't quite remember what. He was just so tired.

And anyway, he was drifting up. The harness was pulling him. Maybe they were going up to heaven.

⚬

Dimitri woke into silence. He didn't recognize where he was at first, but after a minute he started remembering and realized he was in the Pacific City med center.

He sat up. Something beeped. A pretty blonde medic came in the open doorway and smiled.

"Feeling better?"

"I guess."

Actually, now that he thought about it, he was aching all over. He rubbed at one shoulder. The medic checked the array on the wall by the bed, then nodded.

"You're doing fine. Gave us a slight scare there. You got a pretty good clock on the head."

"H-how's my dad?"

She smiled again, softly this time. "Very well, considering. He's right next door. Want to visit him?"

"Yeah."

She reached out to help him from the bed. He let her—it was easier than arguing. His head swam a little and he was glad for her supporting arm as they walked to the next room.

Dad lay unmoving in the darkened room. He hardly looked like he was breathing at all, but the readouts on the array beside him were flickering. The medic leaned over them for a closer look. All Dimitri could look at was Dad.

Why did he look smaller? Was it all the medical stuff around him? Or just the paleness of his skin?

The medic brushed against the bed and Dad's eyes flickered open. They fixed on Dimitri and a slight frown creased Dad's forehead.

Oh, no. He doesn't remember me. He's got a—a concussion or whatever, and he'll never be the same.

Dimitri swallowed and tried to smile. "H-hi, Dad."

His father blinked a couple of times. "I understand you saved my life."

Not knowing what to say, Dimitri gave a half shrug, half nod. "I guess."

"You came into the screen cage."

Here it comes.

Dimitri braced himself and nodded. His father stared flatly at him for an endless minute.

"What took you so long?"

Startled, Dimitri opened his mouth, but before he could say anything he was yanked into his Dad's arms. It hurt his sore shoulders, but he didn't mind.

He didn't mind one bit.

The Cornfield

I was in plenty of fights and shot at plenty of Yankees, but if I ever killed one before Sharpsburg I never really knew it. You can fire at the enemy all day long and some will fall, but when you are in a line of battle it's hard to know if it was your ball that did the job.

Many a time I stood in line with Jim Callaghan and Bill Piper and Bill Lessing and every other Bill in the Tom Green Rifles, and we'd all fire a volley and each of us claim to have dropped a bluecoat. It was a game we played, bragging after the fight who got the most hits, and I guess we believed it but we didn't honestly know, at least Jimmy and Bill and I didn't.

We got a hint of the truth in the bayonet charges we made at

Gaines' Mill and again at South Mountain just two days before Sharpsburg, because then we could see the terrified faces of the Yankee skirmishers as they fled before our steel. But me and Jimmy and Bill never got a poke at them.

We didn't discover then what it was to take a man's life, face to face, gazes locked and the both of you trying in earnest to kill one another. I truly believe none of us knew what it was to kill before we got to the edge of the Cornfield.

It was ripe, that corn, but we never picked it. We'd been eating nothing but green corn and apples for so long we were sick of the stuff—it had literally made every soldier in the Texas Brigade sick—and not a man touched an ear as we passed along the south edge of the field the night of the 16th September, 1862.

We'd arrived at Sharpsburg the day before and all figured we'd be in a fight soon enough. The Yankees had taken exception to Marsh Robert's decision to visit Maryland, and there'd already been the little dust-up around about Harper's Ferry, after which we came north to Boonesboro and on to Sharpsburg.

Our noble General Hood was called upon to take us across Antietam Creek and into position on the left of the line, where there were farms and patches of woods and a plain old house the Dunkers used for a church. None of the residents were in evidence, all having skedaddled when they heard we were coming to town.

We got into line and stayed there while the Yankee artillery flung shells at us all day and night and all the next day. Then the evening of the 16th we were sent forward to support Law's Brigade who'd been jumped on by some Pennsylvania Yankees. That was when we first saw the Cornfield.

It looked like any other cornfield, drying stalks turning golden in the setting sun, smelling of harvest time. We did not know this cornfield's significance to ourselves at the time. Candy, our little white terrier who went with us everywhere, ran into the field and rustled in amongst the stalks, hunting mice.

"Hey, look, there's a little ghost in that corn," Bill said, and we all laughed. Looking back I think maybe it was an omen of what was to come, but of course we didn't know it then.

Now, even going into a fight as we were doing that evening, a Confederate soldier can strip a cornstalk of every ear without missing a step. But we passed it by, because the thought of more corn just about turned our bowels to water.

We had not had a mouthful of bread or meat in weeks, and we'd been promised regular rations that night. We were anxious to finish our work and get on with the truly important business at hand—fixing our first hot meal in three days.

No grim reaper thoughts among us as we passed along south of the corn and into the woods to the east. We were laughing and joking as usual about who would shoot the most Yankees, until musket fire drew our attention to our business.

Our skirmishers had run right into the Yankees and surprised them, and fired point blank into their faces. Right away the screams and yells started.

It was already shadowy under the trees and we fired at the silhouettes of Yankees darting between tree-trunks. This was closer than I had been to an enemy line before, and my heart began pumping pretty fast.

The enemy were shadow-shapes, obscured by the smoke of the first few volleys. They looked like ghosts to me, and I had to shake my head to clear the little frightened thoughts away. I'm a Texan and no coward, but that was the closest I had yet been to a man-to-man fight in a battle.

As we pushed the Yankees back we began walking over the ground where Law's Brigade had been hit. We stepped over men who lay dead and dying, moaning and cursing, some thrashing in pain. This was an ugly sight but not a new one and we pressed on, the sooner to get our work over with.

A little further on we started walking through Yankee dead as well. The Pennsylvanians all wore the tail of a buck deer in their caps. Jimmy stumbled into one and gave a yelp loud enough to be heard over the racket of the rifles. I looked at him and saw he was staring down at the dead Yankee like he'd never seen a body before.

The Yankee's face was pale as ice with awful staring eyes and his mouth hanging open in frozen surprise. His chest was shot three times, the blood from the wounds staining his blue coat black in the dying light.

That is the kind of sight a soldier doesn't like to remember, and I nudged Jimmy away from it, but Bill didn't seem to mind it. He picked up the Yankee's cap and pulled out the bucktail for a trophy, tucking it into the cord that he used to keep some sort of shape to his own limp hat.

"Move on, there!" came a voice I knew and hated.

It was Sergeant R. B. Fletcher, who had taken a personal dislike to me during our discussion of the disposition of my horse when I had first joined Company B, and had generously extended his sentiments to my friends in the months since. Fletcher was a martinet and a bully. He had no sense of humor particularly with ourselves.

Now he pushed Jimmy, who was still shaken, and raised a hand at me but I leaped out of his way and marched on before he could get near me. Bill got between Jim and Fletcher and the sergeant had to find someone else to harass.

We strode on and caught up with our line in the darkening wood. It was harder to see now, with smoke lying thick and the flashes of the rifles dazzling the eye. We had to walk carefully, sometimes only avoiding stepping on a wounded man because of his groans. We would stop when we thought we had a target, fire, load, and move forward again, peering at the ground to see the dim shapes of the fallen.

I caught sight of a bucktail Yankee and I fired and saw him jerk and fall. I was nearly sure it was my shot that hit him, surer than I'd ever been before. The way his head tilted aside as he dropped seemed a sort of personal gesture, as if he was asking why I'd gone and done that.

My brother Jamie is the philosopher, not myself, and he would be able to argue all kinds of lofty ideals about such a situation. I never did have a lofty habit of mind, but as we stumbled over the dead in that wood east of the Cornfield, I found myself thinking of old Pastor Wells back at home, saying, "always remember, Matthew, that God will punish wrong even if no one else catches you." Why I was remembering that I had no idea.

I thought of Momma, also, who hadn't wanted me to join the army. She couldn't bear even thinking of the possibility that she might lose a son.

I remembered how she cried when I said I was going with or without her and Poppa's blessing, and I wondered now at how cruel I had been to say so. I had thought, at the time, that it would all be much easier than it had turned out to be.

We did not push the Yankees all the way out of the woods. Things seemed to grind to a stop there under the trees, and we stood with our backs to a road that ran through the woods and fired round after round until it was so dark that all we could see of the Yankees was the flash of their rifles.

We were almost out of cartridges and had nothing to aim at any more, and the officers finally called it off. We marched back through the woods, where already the evil smell of death was mixing with the choking smoke. When we stepped out of there the sky was a heavy, starless indigo, and every man breathed deep of the clear air and heaved a sigh.

The Cornfield looked ghost-gray now in the evening. Candy scuttled out of it and fell in with us on our way back to where we'd been stationed that morning, in another stretch of woods west of the turnpike.

General Hood spoke to General Jackson and got us relieved for the night so we could cook a hot meal. We settled down behind the lines in the woods by the Dunker church and waited for our supply train to come up with the rations. It had started to rain, and while the trees protected us some it was still a dreary night, but we didn't want to go to sleep and miss our rations.

Bill put together a fire and a dozen of us sat around it. Giles roasted slices of apple on the end of a twig, and tried to feed one to Candy who was having none of it.

Candy was our great friend and loyal companion. He had been named in honor of a candy maker from Austin, the man who'd given him to Isaac Stein of our company.

Candy was up to anything and while he did not take active part in the battles he was never far off. At first he was Isaac's, then B Company's, then the 4th Texas' mascot and finally all of the Texas Brigade claimed him. He was a rare little trooper.

That night Candy curled up around Jimmy's feet by the fire and heaved a big sigh. I felt about the same way myself.

I sat next to Jimmy and inspected the soles of my boots, which were just about worn through. There was a hole starting in the ball of each foot, and I wondered if there was a cobbler in all Maryland who would put new soles to a pair of Rebel boots for Confederate money.

They were good boots, made by a Mexican bootmaker in San Antonio, and they had lasted me more than a year of hard marching. This was better than most of my comrades had fared, many of whom were barefoot.

Our last issue of clothing and shoes had been back in March, and we were looking pretty rag-tag by now. I had drawn neither shoes nor clothing at that time. The uniform my sister made was still holding up, and the boots had been all right then.

The only thing I could have used was socks, and we weren't sent any by the quartermaster. I had taken to wearing both my pairs of socks at once, and when we had a little time to rest, I'd wash the outer pair and switch them with the inner pair. I thought about doing that now, but decided against it. With the rain they might not dry in time for our next march, and there would surely be a march tomorrow, for we knew a big fight was coming.

The Yankees had their lines drawn up in sight of ours. Hood's Division would be called up in relief the minute we were needed.

"Where the hell's Carter with our rations?" Bill grumbled.

"Him and Wade are having a feast of it all to themselves, likely," said Giles, holding out his stick to Bill, who took the apple slice from it and yelped as it sizzled his fingers.

"How many Yankees you boys kill today?" Bill said, tossing the apple from hand to hand.

I looked at Jimmy, who hadn't said a word since we got into camp. "I didn't keep count," I said.

"You didn't? Afraid I'd beat you out, eh?" Bill said.

I didn't bother to reply. I was watching Jimmy, who sat staring into the fire, looking glum as a wet polecat. His thin face was even more pinched than usual, and I knew it wasn't just hunger.

"Hey, Jim?" I said softly, "What was it about that dead Yank that bothered you so?"

Jimmy swallowed, and looked at his knees. "When I first saw him I thought he was—he looked just like my Uncle Tim."

"Oh," I said.

"Stupid," Jimmy muttered.

"No."

There was not much conversation after that. The rain drizzled on and there was no singing, no laughter. Just wet, weary Texans waiting for our rations. Finally the rain stopped and we slept a little, tired and blue as we were.

The supply wagons arrived just before dawn, and we lined up eagerly for our ration. It was only flour, but that was better than anything we'd had for days, so we quick made up loops of dough and twined them on our ramrods to bake over the fire.

By that time it was starting to get light, and the artillery commenced to lobbing shells at the Yankees and theirs lobbed shells back at us. They did not trouble us, however, as we were well behind the front line.

It was foggy and the mist muffled the sounds of fighting, but we could hear the rifles spitting at each other again off to the west. We sat around the fire watching our dough bake with single-minded attention. Candy gave a sharp bark, as if to explain to us as how he'd enjoy sharing our breakfast. He would have had his fill, but just about then a shell burst in the woods about twenty yards from our fire, and more came screaming and roaring overhead.

"God damn you to hell," Bill shouted, shaking his fist toward the Yankee guns to the north.

We had all jumped to our feet, and another shell burst in the air right over our heads, making me drop my ramrod in the fire. I cussed as I fished it out, the dough flattened and covered with ashes, which I tried to brush off.

Bill squatted back down and thrust his dough in the fire, but it was too late. Sergeant Fletcher came stomping through the woods shouting to us to fall in.

"Go to hell," Bill shouted.

In a flash Fletcher grabbed the front of his shirt and screamed into his face. "You send them Yankees to hell, boy, what else are you here for! Get into line!"

Fletcher shoved Bill away and for a second Bill looked ripe to murder him, but Fletcher was already going on, rousing the rest of the company into their ranks. Bill contented himself with cussing and we fell in.

I swallowed the half-baked, ash-covered ruin of my breakfast and wiped the ramrod clean on my pants before loading my rifle with the first round of the day. This has a Yankee's name on it, I thought, and tried to get mad, but the fog and the lump of raw dough in my gut kept me cold.

We advanced out of the woods to find a farmhouse burning east of us, with our artillery on the high ground between it and the Dunker church. We crossed the turnpike and moved north toward the Cornfield, which looked nothing at all like it had the night before.

Half its stalks were broken and battered and a pall of smoke hung over it and the pasture to the south, where Yankees stood with heaps of dead men at their feet, firing at Lawton's command not thirty yards away. What remained of Lawton's men retired through our ranks as we came up, then we raised a yell and fired such a blast into the Yankees that they retreated in a hurry back into the Cornfield.

Yankee guns spat case shot at us from out of the corn, but we fired on their gunners until they were forced to retire. We moved up to the edge of the field, stepping over dead and wounded men of both armies, some lying in ranks as though felled by a scythe.

The 1st and 5th Texas went into the corn while the rest of us faced west across the turnpike. Jimmy and Bill and I were right at the edge of the Cornfield, and we rested our rifles on the top rail of the fence along the turnpike, peering across at the west woods where we'd tried to cook breakfast. Some Yankees had gotten into its north edge and we started firing at each other across the pike, while all hell seemed to be going on around us.

The Cornfield rattled with Yankee canister and shook like it was alive and scared out of its mind. I glanced back and saw Candy dart into it, and I screamed at him to come back but I doubt he heard me, in any case he didn't return. For some reason this made me mad at last, and I loaded and fired, shrieking curses at the Yankees across the pike, aiming at anything that moved.

Bill gave out a broken cry and went to his knees, his face a mass of blood. Jimmy bent down to him but the next second he stood up again, screaming with rage as he loaded and fired, loaded and fired.

The air was still as glass and thick with smoke. A ball zinged by my ear so close it burned me, and icewater poured through my veins, but I only cussed harder. I could see that some kind of commotion was going on across the turnpike, though the smoke was so heavy the Yankees were only vague shapes.

I spotted a flag and aimed below it. My first shot had no effect and I loaded to fire again. Just as I was taking aim, a roar of fire blazed out from a cannon beyond the fence and a sheet of canister flew at us, splintered the fence rails, and felled our whole rank.

Jimmy went down with the others. I could hear the balls thudding into them. I was hit by only one ball which grazed my thigh, and I had a fleeting thought that Momma's prayers must have preserved me, because every other man in the front rank was down.

I was alone with the groaning, writhing heaps of my companions beside me. Without thinking I stepped to my right, into the Cornfield.

Voices jabbered in my head, Momma praying and weeping, Sergeant Fletcher scolding and Bill laughing and saying "How many Yankees? How many, boy?" The most sensible voice, if any could be called sensible, was brother Jamie of all people, telling me in a goddamn practical tone that the corn was no more protection than the rails, less in fact, and that I'd better do something.

I found I was breathing very hard. I started to crouch down but there were dead men at my feet and I didn't want to be close to them.

I heard Fletcher yelling and the second rank moving up to fire at the Yankee gunners. I also heard a high, shrill yapping.

"Candy!" I hollered, and he barked back, and I went deeper into the corn, trying to find him. It made no sense, and I knew it, but I was moving and didn't dare stop.

The Cornfield was a nightmare of smoke, broken stalks, and dead and wounded men. I stepped on something slippery and nearly fell, then hurried on without looking to see what it had been.

"Candy!" I shouted, getting hoarse from the smoke.

Something white moved at my feet and I looked down. It was not Candy. It was part of a flag—the 5th Texas's flag, made from the wedding dress of General Wigfall's wife. Our own flag was identical to it except for the bullet holes, but ours had not been taken into the Cornfield.

What I had seen was the big, white Texas star in the center, and it had moved because a Yankee soldier was trying to pick it up. He was not ten feet away from me, had black hair and a moustache and beard trimmed all tidy.

As we looked at each other he dropped the flagstaff to draw a pistol from his hip. I aimed my rifle and fired at his face, which was a mistake because he dodged enough that the ball only cut him, and I did not have my bayonet fixed.

He aimed his pistol and I swung the muzzle of my piece at his arm, trying to knock the gun out of his hand. He kept hold of it and I kicked him in the chest to knock him over, then dropped on top of him trying to wrestle the gun away. He clubbed me with it before I could get hold of his arm, and for a second I couldn't see straight.

He tried to hit me again but I caught him this time and twisted the gun out of his hand. I put the muzzle against his chest and we sat there, staring murder at each other.

And I thought, this is a man and he has a family and a wife maybe and children. This is a man like myself and why am I about to kill him?

And the voices all burst into argument in my head and the simple answer cut through them: "Because if you don't he will surely kill you."

Right or wrong had no part in this. It was a matter of staying alive, and if killing one Yankee could mean that and moreover mean keeping a man of my company or my brigade from being killed, then by God it was worth doing. I pulled the trigger, and the blast deafened me and blood spattered up in my face.

I got up, shoved the pistol through my belt, picked up my rifle, and dragged the 5th's battle flag free. I did not raise it as that was not my duty or privilege, but I did carry it out of the Cornfield.

When I got back to the pasture I saw our regiment retreating from the turnpike, back south toward the Dunker church and our fires of the morning. I followed, furling the flag as I stepped across the heaps and rows of dead.

Sergeant Fletcher saw me rejoin the line of retreat. His cold eye was on me but he said nothing, nodded once, then looked forward again.

Half our regiment fell in that field on that day, but we were not the hardest hit. That honor went to the 1st Texas, who lost four out of every five men in the Cornfield.

Candy was taken prisoner by the Yankees—one of our wounded men saw him in a band wagon and he never returned to us. At least he made it out of the Cornfield alive.

After that I never thought twice about killing a Yankee. It was part of the war; it was what we were there for. But I never joked about it again.

And I never kept count.

About the Author

Pati Nagle was born and raised in the mountains of northern New Mexico. An avid student of music, history, and humans in general, she loves the outdoors but hides from the sun.

She writes in a variety of genres, but is most often drawn to fantasy or (as P.G. Nagle) historical fiction. Her stories have appeared in *Asimov's Science Fiction*, the *Magazine of Fantasy & Science Fiction*, and in various other magazines and anthologies, including *Elf Magic,* which featured "Kind Hunter," the story that sparked the ælven world now featured in her *Blood of the Kindred* and *Immortal* fantasy series. Her latest novels are a mystery written as Patrice Greenwood, *A Fatal Twist of Lemon*, and a stand-alone contemporary fantasy, *Dead Man's Hand* (Evennight Books/Book View Café).

Pati Nagle lives in the New Mexico mountains with her husband and lots of wildlife. She loves to walk in the woods and look up at the stars.

www.patinagle.com
www.pgnagle.com

Other Books by Pati Nagle

Blood of the Kindred series
The Betrayal
Heart of the Exiled
Swords Over Fireshore

Immortal series
Immortal
Eternal

Many Paths: Stories of the Ælven

Pet Noir

A Fatal Twist of Lemon
(by Patrice Greenwood)

Dead Man's Hand

available at:

Evennight.com
BookViewCafe.com

or your favorite bookseller